GRIM TEMPEST

An Aisling Grimlock Mystery Book 8

AMANDA M. LEE

WinchesterShaw Publications

PROLOGUE

11 YEARS AGO

The minister's words whipped past me faster than the wind. He kept speaking even though I was positive everyone in the crowd had stopped listening minutes before.

He talked about Lily Grimlock's zest for life, her love of children and family. He talked about her giving spirit and how she donated time to charity. He talked about how she had a firm hand with her children, rambunctious monsters who he was convinced would one day grow up to be marvelous members of society.

That was his word, not mine. Marvelous. There was no way I would ever call my four brothers marvelous, and as awesome as I fancied myself I wasn't feeling very marvelous because Lily Grimlock, my mother, was gone long before her time.

The minister didn't care. He kept rambling even though each word was like a dagger through the heart. I thought I might fall over due to the wind and rain. A storm was brewing, had been since the moment we found out Mom died in a fire, and it wouldn't weaken in the foreseeable future. I knew that without hesitation.

He talked about a romance for the ages, which caused a sob to wrench from my father's chest before he regained control of himself and squared his shoulders. My poor father was absolutely wrecked, yet he felt the need to stay strong for his five children, all of whom could barely put one foot in front of the other as we marched through endless days of numbness and tears.

It was weird. We saw death regularly – we were reapers, after all – but the loss of our mother threatened to tear apart everything we knew.

We would no longer return home after school (or whatever it was my older brothers did now that they'd graduated) and find her waiting with healthy snacks and a big smile, eager to hear about our day even if we didn't want to share the information. My father was the one who liked to get us hopped up on sugar and then set us loose on the neighborhood. My mother was more measured in her approach.

Not any longer.

She wouldn't be there when school was out. She wouldn't be there when I was upset with one of my brothers. She most certainly wouldn't be there when Dad blew a gasket because I snuck out of the house or had a date.

It was just us now.

Without thinking, I slipped my hand into my father's, leaning closer to him in an effort to ignore the wind and rain.

He glanced down at me, his purple eyes filled with pain and repressed tears, and took me by surprise when he leaned over and kissed my forehead. "It's okay, kid," he whispered. "We'll be out of here in a few minutes."

"Then where will we go?"

"Home."

Home. Was it still home? I had my doubts. The house was as big as a castle and it never struck me as overwhelming until Mom died. Now I felt as if I could get lost in the numerous rooms and hallways and never be found because people would forget to look for me. I hated that.

Dad squeezed my hand as the minister wrapped things up, keeping me close as he waded through the sea of well-wishers and nodded in turn at co-workers and neighbors as they offered condolences.

He glanced over his shoulder every few seconds to make sure my brothers followed, that they were close. He had no intention of leaving anyone behind, and even though he understood the intricacies of death and how people reacted I could tell he wanted to be away from the crowd. He wanted his family – now and forever one member down – to huddle and regroup. That's all he could see. That was the end of his current road and as far as he was concerned there was nothing past it.

I held it together as we moved between people, allowing Dad to handle most of the talking as I stared into nothing. It wasn't until we were almost through the crowd – I could actually see the limo Dad rented only twenty feet away – when I realized the last people Dad would have to talk to were the worst of all.

Carol Davenport, all sneer and glare, pasted a fake look of sympathy on her face as she rested her hand on Dad's arm. "I'm so sorry for your loss, Cormack."

Dad was no fan of Carol Davenport, but he'd interacted with her more than anyone could possibly want because I was constantly fighting with her daughter Angelina, who was my age but nowhere near as lovely and endearing. Angelina and I had made a habit of going at each other with words – the occasional punches and hair yanks thrown in for good measure – and I realized after a moment that the idea of fighting with her now held some appeal.

I was wiped from mourning and I hadn't slept in what felt like weeks. It was really days, but perception is a funny thing. My mother hadn't been gone for more than eighty-four hours, yet I seemingly couldn't remember a time before we started mourning her. Intellectually I knew it existed. I remembered a life where she wasn't gone, and it wasn't all that long ago. It felt far away and mired in cloudiness. Those memories were hazy.

More than anything I wanted things to return to normal. They never would – I knew that – but I wanted it all the same. I desperately needed to feel like myself again, if only for a moment and even if I regretted it after the fact. What better way to feel like myself again than to fight with Angelina?

I lifted my chin and offered her a haughty look, searching through my weakened mind to get an insult rolling, but she spoke before I could ... and ruined everything.

"I'm sorry about your mom."

Angelina's voice was soft and she almost sounded sincere, which caused me to trip over my tongue as I narrowed my eyes.

"What?"

"I'm sorry about your mom," Angelina repeated, smoothing the front of her black dress as she shifted from one foot to the other. "You must be really sad. I know I would be. It's just so ... terrible. I don't know what to say to you."

I knew what I wanted her to say. I wanted her to insult me, maybe even kick my shin so I could chase her down and justifiably rip out her hair without causing a stir. I most certainly didn't want sympathy from Angelina freaking Davenport. I hated her. That was not going to change. If she felt bad for me – enough to come to my mother's funeral – that meant the world really was changing into something I couldn't recognize.

"Say 'thank you,' Aisling," Dad prompted, squeezing my hand.

He had to be kidding, right? Now, on top of everything else, I was supposed to thank Angelina. I didn't want to thank her. I wanted to punish her. I wanted to rip out her stupid flat-ironed hair and make her eat it.

Dad wouldn't look kindly on that, though. He was barely holding it together. If I melted down I had no doubt he'd do the same.

"Thank you," I murmured, cringing when Carol leaned closer and smiled at me. It was more of a grimace than a smile, but because she'd only ever screamed bloody murder in my direction I wasn't sure what to make of her change in attitude.

"You poor dear." Carol made a clucking sound with her tongue. "This is going to be hardest on you, isn't it?"

"She'll be fine." Dad protectively wrapped his arm around my back. "She has me. She has her brothers."

"Yes, but she no longer has her mother," Carol noted. "She's the only girl. It's like she's an outsider in her own house. Girls her age need a mother and now she doesn't have one."

Dad's cool control snapped. "She's not an outsider. She'll be perfectly fine. Now ... if you'll excuse me." Dad moved to edge his way around Carol, but she remained where she was and cut off his avenue of escape.

"I just want you to know that I'll be around if you need anything," she purred. The way she touched Dad's arm made me realize she was flirting with him – or at least she thought she was – and Dad obviously recognized the effort because he shrank back and pulled me in front of him, as if I were a human shield that could ward off the Devil's finest assassin.

"I have everything under control." Dad was firm as he rested his hands on my shoulders. "Now, if you'll excuse me, I need to get my children home. I think we need a quiet night together."

"Of course." Carol backed away, although she clearly wasn't happy about Dad's brazen rebuff. "Just keep me in mind if you need anything."

"Of course." Dad's tone told me he would rather hire the murderous doll from the Chucky movies to help him instead of spending time with Carol, but he managed to maintain at least a modicum of dignity. "Come along. It's time to go home."

I fell into step with him, stopping long enough to meet Angelina's gaze one last time. The moment Dad moved past Carol her veneer of sympathy slipped. Angelina's remained in place.

"I really am sorry," Angelina said. "I know it doesn't mean anything coming from me – and nothing will change down the line because we hate each other and that will never change – but I'm sorry about your mother. She didn't deserve what happened."

"No, she didn't."

I let Dad pull me away and waited until we were all settled in the back of the limo to speak. "I don't like Angelina being nice to me."

Dad cast me a sidelong look. "I wouldn't worry about that. She'll be back to her horrible self tomorrow. Even the Devil can't be mean at a funeral."

That was an interesting take on the situation. "Does that mean I can punch her tomorrow?"

Dad nodded. "Sure. Try to do it in the yard so we can watch. I think we all need a pick-me-up."

I brightened, although only marginally. "That's something to look forward to, huh?"

Dad leaned his head back against the seat and closed his eyes. "You don't believe it now, but things will get better. You'll be able to look forward to living life again and not feel guilty because you're leaving Mom behind. I promise."

I rested my head against his shoulder. "I'm not sure that's true, but I'll take your word for it."

"Good."

"I'm also going to find a way to beat the crap out of Angelina tomorrow, so if the cops show up don't act surprised."

Dad's lips curved. "We all do what we can for the team."

"Yeah. I think my part is going to be loud."

Dad patted my knee. "I would expect nothing less."

ONE

PRESENT DAY

"It's going to storm. I can feel it."

I peered out the front window of the non-descript Royal Oak bungalow and stared at the darkening sky.

"I like storms ... but only when I'm home," I added. "I like watching horror movies, climbing under a blanket with one of my guys and totally rooting for the blond bimbo to get it. What I don't like is being stuck outside in a storm, because it makes my hair frizz and I don't enjoy walking around in wet jeans. Do you know what I mean?"

I turned to find Harry Turner, the esteemed chief of the Royal Oak Police Department, eyeing me with what could only be described as disdain. Essentially, if I were the ant encroaching on the family picnic, I would be under someone's boot right about now.

"What?"

Harry made a face no one could love. I'm talking deranged clowns, creepy dudes in white vans and those douches who stand on street corners and call out "Hey, baby, do you want to zoom and boom" to multiple women in the hope one of them will respond. Even those guys wouldn't enjoy the look on Harry's face.

"What did you say your name was again?" Harry asked, his tone clipped.

"Aisling Grimlock." I shifted so I could look over the stack of paperwork sitting on the small table near the window. "Do you have anything good in here? I mean ... do you have any reports on window peepers or drunk folk caught urinating on park benches?"

Harry was flummoxed. "Why would you possibly ask that?"

I shrugged, noncommittal. "I don't know. It was just something I was thinking about."

"You were thinking about public urination?" Harry narrowed his eyes to dangerous slits. "I think that says a little something about you."

I was in no position to argue so I decided to change the subject. It wasn't as if I was in a hurry – Harry was dead, after all, and only his spirit remained to judge me – and I wanted to wait out the storm that looked to be brewing. A cheery conversation seemed the way to go. Of course, Harry was anything but cheery.

"Did you ever consider changing your name?" I had no idea what made me ask the question. As a grim reaper, I'd been trained by my family (also grim reapers, for the curious) to suck souls first and ask questions never, but I was looking to kill time. That meant I could ask a series of stupid questions if I felt like it.

Harry planted his hands on his hips, his beer gut protruding at an angle that made him look pregnant rather than manly. "Why would I want to change my name? Harold is a perfectly acceptable name."

"Yeah, but it says here that everyone calls you Harry," I pointed out. "To me that's an unfortunate moniker to have. Don't get me wrong, it would be worse if you were a woman, but didn't people walk around teasing you about your hairy butt and back when you were a kid?"

Harry was clearly affronted. "Excuse me? I don't have a hairy butt or back."

I stared at him for a long beat. I didn't believe that for a second. "Take off your shirt."

Harry's eyes widened even further, even though I wasn't sure that was possible. "What?" He was agog. "You can't be serious."

I could tell the spirit wasn't keen to play the game, so I strolled across the room, stopping close to the couch, and knelt next to the body resting in the middle of the aged rug. Harry had done his best to ignore his own corpse since I showed up to collect his soul – he'd made a few comments about dying too young and called me several names, something I was used to – but he watched me now with overt dislike, and I could tell he was about to blow a gasket.

"Don't touch me!" Harry strode in my direction and lashed out with an ethereal hand that went completely through my arm. "Hey!"

I ignored his outrage and carefully grabbed the collar of his shirt, pulling it so I could expose the upper quadrant of his beefy back. Yup, exactly what I thought. "You have enough back hair to create wigs for a fleet of dolls. Heck, you could make wigs for kids with cancer. Why didn't you ever shave this?"

"I'm Italian." Harry stubbornly folded his arms across his chest. "That's normal when you're Italian."

I took in his pale and waxy features and wrinkled my nose. "You don't look Italian."

"Well, I am."

"Your last name is Turner. That's not an Italian name."

"I'm Italian!" Harry barked the words so loudly most people would've backed down just to shut him up. I'm not most people.

"Really? Let me check your file." I pulled out my iPad and touched the screen, scrolling past the incidentals of Harry's life and focusing on his genealogy. "It says here you're German, Polish, Jewish and Austrian. There's nothing about being Italian here."

"You're making that up." Harry squared his shoulders. "I'm president of the Royal Oak Italian League of Great Americans. You can't be president if you're not Italian."

"Is the Italian League of Great Americans like the League of Extraordinary Gentlemen?" I was quickly losing interest in the Italian debate. Potential superhero shenanigans were much more entertaining. "Can you turn into a literary character at the drop of a hat?"

Harry worked his jaw but no sound came out.

"I guess it doesn't matter." I let go of the shirt and stood. "I'm not going to check for the butt hair, by the way. I'm convinced I'm right, and even I have my limits. I'm pretty sure that checking a corpse's butt for hair is over a line even I won't cross."

"Well, as long as you're going to finally embrace good manners,"

Harry drawled, rolling his eyes. "I can't believe this is happening. I'm too young to die. I keep hoping this is a dream and I'll wake up."

"You wouldn't believe how many times I've heard that." I moved to a bookshelf across the way and studied the antique trinkets and leather tomes littering the shelves. "Hey, what's this?" I pulled a metal item off the shelf and held it up, flipping it from left to right as I tried to make the pieces move. "Is this some sort of medieval torture device? I bet it's a sex toy, huh?"

Harry made a disgusted sound and moved in my direction. He reached up, as if to take the device, but ultimately realized he couldn't make contact with it and stopped before running his hand through me a second time. "That is not a toy, Ms. Grimlock. That's an expensive antique and you're going to break it."

"That's not what I asked. What is it?"

"You wouldn't understand."

I recognized the tone. My brothers used it when we were kids and they thought I was too female to comprehend the game they wanted to play. As if you had to be smart to play tag or blow things up. Those were the only games they ever wanted to play, and no one needed brains to undertake the endeavors.

"Try me," I pressed, holding the metal contraption in front of my face. "Seriously, is this something men used to torture women with back in the Dark Ages? It looks painful."

"Oh, good gravy." Harry mimed rubbing the tender spot between his eyebrows. He looked as if he had a headache, but he no longer had a body, so that wasn't possible. "It's a compass."

I furrowed my brow. "My brothers had compasses when we were kids – although I have no idea why, because it's not as if we spent any time in the woods. We're city folk at heart – and they didn't look anything like this."

"It's not a directional compass." Harry spoke as if he was talking to a small child who just happened to be asking the world's dumbest questions. "It's a geometry compass."

"Oh." Realization dawned. Now that he mentioned it I did vaguely remember a device like this from my high school years. "That's no fun at all." I returned the compass to the shelf and grabbed one of the books. I read the title out loud. "Metaphysical Explanations for Modern Scientific Discoveries."

"That's a first edition," Harry barked. "Put it down!"

"It sounds like a real page-turner." I was blasé as I shook my head. "Don't you have anything good to read around here? How about some J.K. Rowling or Charlaine Harris? I love their stuff."

Harry looked appropriately horrified. "I can't believe you just said that."

"Yes, I'm shocked and appalled, too," I drawled. "The public's need for entertaining drivel is just ... there are no words." I mock fanned my face. "Why do you have all this stuff?" I picked up a crystal and flipped it over. "You seem all straight-laced and everything, but some of this stuff is metaphysical."

Harry was back to being haughty. "And what do you know about the metaphysical?"

"I'm a reaper. I know more than you think. In fact, I probably know more than you by virtue of who I am."

Harry had the grace to look abashed. "Yes, well, I still think all of this is above your pay grade."

I didn't jolt when the bolt of lightning split the sky on the other side of the window, followed immediately by a jarring rumble of thunder, but it took me by surprise all the same. I flicked my eyes to the window and stared. "I hope this is a fast storm."

"So you can absorb my soul and go on with your day?" Harry challenged.

"Pretty much." I saw no reason to lie. "You're my last charge of the day. I don't want to spend too much time with you if I don't have to. I'm ready to go home and be lazy."

"I'll bet that's a common theme for you," Harry deadpanned. "Are you the worst employee at the reaper office?"

"We don't have an office." I thought of Grimlock Manor, my father's manor. "We do have a mansion. It has statues, a back-from-the-dead mother who occasionally drops in when she's not eating people, and even a random gargoyle that comes and goes when things get bad. Oh, it also has snakes in the basement. My father says the stories my brothers told me when I was little aren't true – regarding the snakes, I mean – but I know better. There are snakes down there, and they're not the fun trouser snakes I usually like to play with. Hmm, wait, that totally came out wrong."

"I think it came out right," Harry shot back, his temper beginning to fray. "You're clearly not a person of substance. In fact ... I think I recognize your name. It's very familiar to me."

"I have a common name."

"Right." Harry rolled his eyes. "Aisling Grimlock. I know I recognize that name from somewhere. It was in a set of reports that recently crossed my desk. I'm certain of it."

Oh, well, that was interesting. I considered returning to the desk so I could sort through the stacked reports, but ultimately I knew it didn't matter. Whatever he thought he could pin on me would be hollow.

"You probably remember me because I'm the one who discovered zombies a few weeks ago," I supplied.

"I know it will come to me," Harry muttered, ignoring my statement. "Oh, I know." Harry tried to snap his fingers, but no sound emerged. "You're the idiot who thought she saw zombies on the street."

"I believe that's what I just said." I calmly picked up a brightly-colored disc from the shelf. "What's this?"

"It's a metaphysical power distributor."

"Meaning?"

"Meaning that you're not smart enough to understand what it's for," Harry sniffed. "It's for increasing wisdom – something you're severely lacking – and you're not the sort of person who can channel the appropriate energy to utilize it."

I couldn't be sure, because I knew absolutely nothing about metaphysical stuff, but I was fairly certain that was an insult. "It looks like something a kid made in fifth-grade art class anyway." I returned the disc to the shelf. "As for the zombies, they were totally real."

"Oh, really?" Harry made an exaggerated face. "If the zombies were real, what happened to them?"

"I fought the jerks animating the corpses and killed them."

"You killed people?" Harry's eyes went wide. "Are you admitting you murdered people?"

"Technically I didn't murder anyone. My mother did. It's totally okay, for the record. They were both bad people and were going to cause more harm if we left them to run around and wreak havoc on the community. Nobody wanted that."

"I need to make a call," Harry hedged, keeping his eyes on me as he shifted toward the table in the center of the room. His phone rested on it and I knew what he was thinking. Ultimately it didn't matter, because he couldn't lift the phone to dial it. Even if he could, no one could hear him on the other end of the call.

"Go ahead and make your call," I suggested, grabbing a silver disc with ornate carvings and studying the intricate detail. "I can't wait to hear what you'll say to them. I think whoever answers the phone will get a kick out of a ghost calling to warn about murderers who ended the potential zombie apocalypse, but that's just me."

Harry made a series of distressed sounds as he fruitlessly attempted to grab the phone. "Zombies aren't real," he gritted out, frustration practically filling the room in waves.

"I bet you thought grim reapers didn't exist until twenty minutes ago," I pointed out, never moving my eyes from the silver disc. There was something magical about it, something almost otherworldly. I couldn't put my finger on it. "I'm willing to bet a lot of things exist that you never believed in. If we had time, I'd introduce you to my mother. She was a reaper who almost died and now she's some half-wraith thing. She was kept alive for years by a half-crone who thought she could manipulate magic and live forever. It turns out she couldn't.

"Now my mother is hanging around and has a pet gargoyle named Bub," I continued. "I kind of like the gargoyle, even though he's all kinds of sarcastic and looks like a rubbery owl-dog. As for my mother, I don't really trust her, but I'm in a real pickle because I have four brothers. All of them – whether they want to admit it or not – are desperate to have some sort of relationship with her.

"I don't know if it's because I'm the lone girl or simply the most rational member of my family – don't you dare laugh – but I'm the only one still fighting the issue," I said. "I want to trust her. I mean … she's my mother. That means she's earned a modicum of trust, right? I don't know that I can, though. Even though she's done all the right things and helped us, I can't help feeling something is terribly off."

"Drats!" Harry swore under his breath as he tried to wrap his fingers around the phone. "I can't interact with the physical world."

"No, you can't." I licked my lips as I surveyed him. "What are you even trying to do? Do you think you can call your precinct and have me arrested for what I told you? How do you think that would end?"

"I have no idea how it'll end," Harry replied calmly. "I only know that there were some lingering questions regarding you, specifically what you were doing wandering all over the county once you were a suspect in a murder, and I think my detectives should know that they were wrong to close the case."

"They weren't wrong." I shifted my eyes to the window as the storm lessened. That was good. It would allow me an opening to absorb Harry's soul and escape. I slipped my hand into my back pocket for my scepter. I found it in the other pocket, but thankfully it was there and I hadn't misplaced it (which has happened more times than I can count and absolutely infuriates my father). "There are a lot of things in this world that you can't possibly understand, Harry."

I was mildly sympathetic to his plight, but I was also tired and ready to put this day behind me. There would be no more messing around. Of course, if I told my father the story of this interaction he'd think I'd done nothing but mess around and give me a lecture because ... well, I think he just likes lecturing people. It's what keeps him young. He really didn't get me at all if he thought I did nothing but chat with the dead to amuse myself. I'm a professional, after all.

"I still think you should be investigated for what happened," Harry pressed. "Several bodies were discovered, and I'm guessing you were tied to all of them."

"That's where you're wrong, Harry." I offered my calmest smile. It was the only one that didn't look as if it was straight out of a horror movie. "I wasn't tied to all of them. The bad guys were."

"You're a reaper. You're essentially walking death. Doesn't that mean you're one of the bad guys?"

"No." This time my smile was genuine. "There are things out there much worse than us. Be glad you don't have to face them. You're getting off relatively light." I brandished the silver scepter. "Are you ready to go into the light?"

It was a lame joke, but the best I could do under the circumstances.

"Absolutely not," Harry sputtered. "I'm not ready to die, and the case isn't closed on you."

"Maybe not. You won't be the one conducting the investigation, though. Take heart in the fact that you've done your level best, but it's time to move on."

"I don't want to move on."

I didn't let him muster further argument, instead absorbing his soul and cutting off whatever else he was going to say. I took a moment to study the room once he was gone, glancing around to make sure I'd left nothing out of place.

Then I headed toward the front door to finish my day. What I found on the other side was the last thing I wanted to see, which meant I should've been expecting it.

"Son of a ... !"

2

TWO

The air was musty when I stalked down the front steps and fixed my best friend and mother – who just happened to be standing on the front sidewalk – with the darkest look in my repertoire.

"What do you two think you're doing here?"

Jeremiah "Jerry" Collins, my partner in crime since I was five, offered up an amiable smile. "Hey, Bug. I haven't seen you all day. I wondered where you disappeared to."

I knew him too well to fall for his innocent act. "I got up late and didn't have time for breakfast. I had a container of yogurt, which tasted like crap because it's basically health food, and I headed straight to my first charge because I didn't want to be late and risk Dad's wrath. Griffin was supposed to tell you."

In addition to being my fiancé, Griffin Taylor was also my room-mate. Jerry used to hold that title and still lived next door, so we'd gotten into the habit of heading to Jerry's house – he was a masterful cook, after all – for breakfast almost every day. Griffin and I were lazy on the domestic front, so we were fine with it. Jerry enjoys breakfast guests because he's a doter at heart, and I can avoid work because I'm intrinsically lazy. The only drawback to the situation is that Jerry takes it as a personal affront when I miss breakfast.

"Griffin did tell me," Jerry supplied. "He also split your serving of peach waffles with Aidan so nothing went to waste. I simply wanted to check and make sure you were safe."

I narrowed my eyes, which were a violet color that almost everyone noticed and commented on. They were a family trait I shared with my father and brothers. The only member of the family who didn't boast purple eyes was my mother, who steadfastly studied the landscaping on either side of the walk rather than insert herself in the conversation. It was a strategic move.

"And how did you even know where I was?" I challenged, shoving my scepter in my hoodie pocket and surreptitiously scanning the neighborhood to see if we were drawing a crowd. "I don't believe I shared my itinerary for the day with you, so ... this is quite the coincidence."

"I was out taking a walk with your mother and we happened to stumble across you." Jerry adopted an innocent expression I recognized from childhood. "It was purely coincidental."

"You just said you were checking on me," I reminded him.

"I believe you misheard me."

"Oh, geez." I pinched the bridge of my nose. "I can't even ... I'm going to tell Aidan you looked at his iPad, by the way. The only way you would've known my schedule is to look at his work files. He'll be angry and you'll be punished."

Jerry's smile was serene. "What makes you think I don't like being punished?"

Ugh. He knows exactly how to weird me out. When he first hooked up with my brother – my twin brother, for the record, so that makes it doubly weird – I didn't handle things with grace and acceptance. He was hurt and annoyed at my reaction. I really can't blame him. It wasn't my finest moment. Occasionally he picks the oddest times to set me off. I'm convinced he does it as payback for my memorable meltdown.

"Yeah. We're not going to talk about that." I flicked my eyes to Mom and found her kneeling next to a dark bloom I couldn't identify.

It was spring in Michigan and the flowers were starting their inevitable comeback. Even before Lily Grimlock disappeared for a decade – we thought she was dead and, in truth, she wasn't far from it – she was a horticulture enthusiast. "What are you two doing in this neighborhood if you're not looking for me?"

"We're looking at landscaping," Mom replied, straightening. She flashed a smile that reminded me of the mother I'd lost and smoothed down the front of her black coat. Since returning from the dead she opted for more muted colors. "Jerry wants to plant some flowers around his back patio."

"Yours, too, Bug," Jerry added. "I think your back patio is completely lacking in personality, and I can't have an ugly patch next to my corner of perfection."

"I don't like flowers."

"You like flowers," Jerry countered. "You just don't understand them ... and you hate bees. Maybe we should take a landscaping class or something."

That sounded absolutely horrific. "I'm good."

"I can spend some time with you," Mom offered, taking me by surprise. "I love gardening."

I remembered that well from my youth. "Well ... ." It wasn't that I wanted to dissuade her from offering. In truth, I was on the fence when it came to spending time with the woman. I loved my mother beyond reason and mourned hard when she died. The woman who came back, though, was not my mother. At times she showed hints of the person she used to be, but she was so much more than what she presented to the outside world that I couldn't force myself to look past the oddities.

"You don't have to, of course," Mom said hurriedly, her pale cheeks flushing pink. "I didn't mean to pressure you."

I ignored Jerry's scornful stare and forced a smile. "I guess a few flowers wouldn't hurt."

Jerry clapped his hands, excited. "Yay!"

Despite the overwhelming love I felt for him because he was one of the few constants that didn't share my last name, there were moments I wanted to punch him in the groin. He knows exactly how to manipulate me, which is beyond frustrating. "So, other than landscaping, what are you guys doing out here?" I gestured for them to move along the sidewalk. "This is the police chief's house," I explained. "Someone is bound to come looking for him, and it won't be good if they find us here."

"Good thinking, Bug." Jerry tapped the side of his head and grinned. "As for what we're doing here, I got some samples back and we need to look at them."

Of course. I should've seen that coming. Jerry was more invested in the wedding than I was. I was invested in the marriage – and even though I had a few fears knock me for a loop from time to time, I firmly believed the marriage would be good – but the wedding itself was cause for constant headaches.

"Oh, you're not going to make me look at a bunch of white napkins again and maintain they're different colors, are you?" Memories of Jerry's linen assault from the week before flooded to the forefront of my brain.

"Those were different colors, Bug," Jerry insisted. "One was eggshell, which is my personal favorite. The other two were corn silk and Dutch white."

"They were all the same color."

"They were not," Jerry sputtered, his fury from the original argument returning. "You're color blind if you think those were the same colors." He turned to Mom for help. "Tell her that eggshell is the way to go."

Mom looked caught. "Well, um, I didn't see the samples, Jerry."

"I brought them." Jerry pointed toward the end of the street. "There's a coffee shop. I thought we could go over a few things while we all have an opening in our schedules."

I felt ridiculously ambushed. "Jerry, I'm working."

"I happen to know this is your last charge of the day." Jerry was firm. "You have plenty of time for a wedding strategy mission."

"A wedding strategy mission sounds like something the G.I. Joe characters wouldn't be keen to participate in," I muttered under my breath.

Jerry was attuned to my moods and had very good hearing. "You'll live."

"Whatever." I could've fought the decision, but I knew if I did I'd ultimately lose. Not only that, but Jerry would punish me if I dared walk away from the opportunity to enjoy his vast wedding knowledge. "I could use some coffee."

"Don't sound so excited, Bug," Jerry drawled, falling into step with me as I glanced back at Harry's house. "It's only your wedding. Frowns and dramatic sighs are what every bride should wear for the big day."

"It's not the big day yet." I licked my lips as I forced my eyes back to the front. "As for wedding plans, I don't see why I even have to be involved because you're the one who ultimately gets to make all the decisions, Jerry."

"That's because I have the best taste." As if he didn't want me to challenge him on that fact, Jerry picked up his pace. "Come on. Caffeine is calling."

I shook my head as I watched him, my emotions jumbled.

"He's a lot to deal with, huh?" Mom asked, moving to my side. "You love him, but you want to strangle him. It's written all over your face. That's often how I felt about you lot when you were growing up."

It felt odd to discuss my childhood with a woman I was convinced was sucking souls to survive, but it was a better conversation than the white linens debacle. "He's just excited."

"He seems more excited than you," Mom noted, smiling at the sun as it peeked through the clouds. "I think it's going to turn into a nice day after that storm earlier."

"It feels it," I agreed.

"About the wedding," Mom hedged, turning serious. "If you're having doubts, you have plenty of time to back out."

The statement was innocent enough. She sounded like a concerned mother trying to talk to her daughter about potential problems. The thing is, I knew differently. Ever since she turned back up, she'd had issues with Griffin.

I couldn't put my finger on why. Part of me wondered if it was because she simply didn't want me marrying a police officer. It wouldn't be the easiest life because I would worry if he was late and wonder if something bad happened if he missed a text. Of course, I was a grim reaper and I'd been in ten times the danger that Griffin had since we'd hooked up. There were obstacles in every relationship.

In truth, I fell for Griffin because I couldn't do anything else. From the moment I saw him there was something that drew me to him. He claimed to feel the same, as if destiny was somehow exerting a guiding hand. I wasn't sure I wanted to be that schmaltzy, but I knew I loved him and he was genuinely the only option for me.

"I want to marry Griffin." I kept my tone firm, hoping I didn't sound as if I was spoiling for a fight, even though I was more than willing to engage in one if it came to that. "We belong together and we're happy."

"But you seem to be dragging your feet on the wedding."

"No, I'm dragging my feet on Jerry's vision of the wedding," I corrected. "I don't want some big overblown affair, but that appears to be exactly what I'm getting. I'd be happy getting married barefoot on a beach, quite frankly. Jerry and Dad have vetoed that option."

"Your father simply wants you to have the best."

"I know." This was Dad's lone shot to be the father of the bride. Being the father of the groom wouldn't be nearly as entertaining for him. "The wedding decisions are getting to be a bit much. I'm looking forward to the marriage, though. That's the most important thing."

Mom didn't look convinced. "Aisling, you don't have to say that if you don't mean it."

I bit back an annoyed retort and tugged on my flagging patience. "I mean it. I know you don't like Griffin, but I love him."

Mom balked. "I didn't say that I dislike Griffin."

No, but she'd shown it multiple times. "You might want to let it go," I suggested, reaching for the café's door and holding it open so Mom could enter before me. "If you push too hard on Griffin, he won't be the one removed from the situation." I was deadly serious. "I'm getting sick and tired of hearing your opinion when it comes to him. When you try to be sneaky about it – like you are today – it makes me even angrier."

Mom locked gazes with me, something dark passing through her eyes. I couldn't quite get a handle on the emotion before she spoke. "I'm not trying to undermine Griffin."

I didn't believe it. More importantly, she recognized I didn't believe it. Still, a busy coffee shop was the last place to have this argument. "See that you don't."

I dragged my eyes from Mom's face when a rumble of thunder caught my attention. I shifted my gaze to the busy street in front of the coffee shop and frowned when I realized the sun had completely disappeared.

"I didn't know it was supposed to storm again," Mom supplied, changing course.

"I didn't either. I thought it was just the one storm and then it was supposed to be clear for the rest of the week."

"I guess the weather forecasters were wrong."

"What else is new?" I closed the café door as the first drops of rain hit the pavement. It was soft at first, barely a sprinkle. It turned into a tempest quickly, though, and before I could even move to the counter to place a drink order the fat rain pellets were bouncing off the sidewalk due to the velocity with which they hit.

"It took you long enough to get here," Jerry complained, barely sparing a glance for the storm. "I have linens for you to look at. I have some bouquet ideas, too. I also think that we should discuss what you're going to do with your hair."

I swiveled quickly, my dark hair flying. "What do you mean by that? I'm not getting a haircut."

"I know you're not." Jerry rolled his eyes as if I'd said the silliest thing in the world. "No one expects you to get a haircut, Bug. Your hair is lovely. I even think the white streaks will look divine with your gown. But I do think we need to have a discussion about you wearing it up."

"Oh, I like the sound of that." Mom's smile was quick and easy. "She has a long and graceful neck. She would look beautiful with her hair up."

"I'm not wearing my hair up," I argued. "I don't like wearing my hair up. I prefer it down."

"Yeah. We'll talk." Jerry patted my hand. "I'm going to snag a table with your mom. Order coffee and Danish for everyone and bring it to the table when it's ready."

I made a face. "Since when am I the group waitress?"

"Since we're going out of our way for your wedding," Jerry replied. "Make sure you get my latte with nonfat milk."

"Yeah, yeah." I was annoyed beyond belief with my best friend when I turned toward the barista behind the counter, a trio of orders on my tongue. I stopped before I could issue drink orders when I saw the look on the young woman's face. She was focused on the front of the building rather than me, forcing me to swivel. "What's going on?"

She stared out the front window, her curiosity and worry obvious. "Look at that."

I followed to where she pointed and frowned when I saw the two men on the sidewalk throwing punches. They screamed at one another – words I couldn't quite make out – and pummeled each other with frightening belligerence.

"They were just talking normally right before the rain hit," the barista said. "I don't know what happened. It was like ... a switch flipped or something. They just started beating the crap out of each other."

That was definitely odd. "Maybe we should call the police," I suggested.

"Yeah. I'll do that."

I didn't know what else to do so I watched. The fight was straight out of *Rocky* and neither man looked to be giving up.

"Call for an ambulance, too," I called out. "I think one or both of them will need a trip to the emergency room."

❧ 3 ❧

THREE

"**A**nd then one guy pulled the other guy's hair – which revealed a certain toupee situation – before the other guy popped him in the jaw and knocked him out."

I enthusiastically reenacted the fight outside the coffee shop for Griffin once he got home from work that afternoon, wiggling my hips and hopping back and forth so he could grasp which character I was at any given moment.

"It sounds like quite the fight," Griffin offered, his feet resting on the coffee table as he reclined on the couch. "I'm surprised you didn't go outside and try to stop it."

"It was raining."

Griffin cocked an eyebrow. "I've never known you to be afraid of inclement weather."

"It was raining hard."

Griffin grinned as he made room for me on the couch. He patted the open spot enticingly. "Come sit with me and I'll make sure you don't get stormed on."

"That could go in a dirty direction if you're not careful," I pointed out, sliding into the spot and resting my head against his chest as he slipped an arm around me. "What do you want to do about dinner?"

"I've been fixating on that all day because I missed lunch," Griffin replied. "I was thinking we should have something delivered. We can either do that Takeout Waiter app and get Middle Eastern or do pizza and wings. It's your choice."

"Middle Eastern."

Griffin snorted, his dark hair tickling my cheek as he shifted. "Somehow I knew you were going to say that." He rested his hand on my abdomen as he got comfortable. "How was your day otherwise?"

It was a normal conversation, I realized. I was a reaper and collected souls for a living, yet the easy nature of our relationship and Griffin's accepting attitude made things comfortable despite how different our work worlds were. This was the thing I wanted forever, even if I had to suffer through the world's most overblown wedding to get it.

"Mostly boring," I answered after a beat. "Although, do you know who I absorbed today?"

"I'm almost afraid to hazard a guess."

"Harry Turner."

Griffin stilled. "That name sounds familiar, as if I should know him. Why do I recognize that name?"

"Because he is – or I guess was is more apt now – the Royal Oak police chief."

"Seriously?" Griffin smoothed my hair away from my face so he could see my reaction. "Do you know how he died?"

I shrugged. "I can't really remember. He took a header off the couch, though, so I think it was a heart attack or something. There was no blood or guts, so I'd would rule out murder."

"Unless it was poison."

"Good point, but that's not the vibe I got, and I can't remember caring enough to look. He was a bit crabby when he figured out who I was, by the way."

"So you talked to him?" Griffin's expression shifted to something more serious. "I thought you were told to suck and run and not engage your charges. I believe I've heard more than one family conversation about just that."

I stuck out my tongue to show my maturity. "Thank you, Dad."

"Ha, ha." Griffin poked my side. "I'm not telling you how to do your job. That's your deal. I'm curious why you decided to talk to him, though."

"It was because a storm was coming and I didn't want to be forced out into it. I thought he might be interesting to talk to. It turns out he was more dismissive than anything else."

"Why do you say that?"

I told him about my conversation with Harry, including the part about his back, which sent Griffin into gales of laughter. When I was done, he'd calmed enough to be thoughtful.

"So he basically told you that Mark Green closed the case on you?"

Griffin's keen interest surprised me. "What else was he going to do? I clearly didn't kill the guy on the street ... or the one who ended up in our backyard ... and no one can tie me to the bodies discovered at the cemetery."

After the zombie attack – something I still had trouble wrapping my head around – we'd accidentally left several bodies behind in the cemetery where the final fight occurred. My father's home office employees – just think of them as part of the grim reaper happy cleaning service – thought they'd found every one, but they'd missed a couple of bodies in the bushes. The evening news was spinning it as a local mystery, but the story was quickly losing steam, forgotten in the wake of the next if-it-bleeds-it-leads item.

"I know, but I couldn't help but wonder if Mark was going to keep watching you for a bit," Griffin admitted, referring to the detective who had hounded me for days. "He seemed determined that you had something to do with what happened."

"I technically did have something to do with it, simply not in the manner he thought."

"Either way, I'm glad to know he's stepping back from the investigation." Griffin ran his fingers over mine, absently tracing between them. "So how did Harry take it when he realized he couldn't make a call?"

"He was agitated and annoyed, but ultimately there was nothing he could do."

"Well, I guess what's done is done." Griffin rested his chin on my shoulder. "I don't suppose you could order dinner now, could you? I'm exhausted and starving. It's going to make for a cranky combination in about an hour."

"Sure." I could order dinner without talking to a live person so I was more than willing to order. I grabbed my phone and tapped on the app. "What do you want?"

"A steak kebab dinner with rice and a fattoush salad."

"Sounds good. I'll get the same."

"Order something sweet for dessert, too," Griffin ordered.

"Don't I count?"

"Someone is feeling romantic." Griffin's tone was full of teasing. "I'll romance your sweet socks off later. I want cake or something. I need the sugar rush."

I added the item to the order and sent it before turning my full attention to Griffin. Now that I was done talking about my day – a story that took thirty minutes when it could've been shared in five – I realized he looked exhausted. His day had clearly been worse than mine.

"Tell me about what you did today," I prodded.

Griffin shrugged, noncommittal. "It was the standard stuff. I don't have an open case at the moment so I spent most of the day doing paperwork. I did get called out during the storm because we had a sudden rash of violent incidents. It was a little weird."

That sounded strange. "What kind of incidents?"

"The initial call came in during the first storm. It involved a car accident on Woodward." Griffin didn't appear agitated while sharing the story. "One driver blamed another driver, and then the drivers of two cars involved after the initial crash joined the argument. It was basically everyone screaming, pointing fingers and threatening to sue one another."

"That sounds like a delightful day. Did you get wet?"

"Yes, and I didn't even melt."

"You're a big tub of melting goo," I countered. "I plan to prove that after you've eaten your cake."

"I look forward to you trying. I was only outside for thirty seconds, though. Then the uniforms showed up and I foisted it off on them."

"What about the rest of your day?" Something was bothering him. He didn't often share tidbits about his cases, probably because I had enough doom and gloom in my work that he didn't want to overload me, but I recognized he needed to talk about something.

"The rest of the afternoon was a little odd," Griffin admitted, his expression turning troubled. "I don't know how to explain it. It was as if a toxic gas of irritation fell over the city for twenty minutes. It happened really fast and then was done."

"And it happened to coincide with the storm?"

Griffin nodded. "The second storm, yeah. The first one there were only a few incidents and they were all normal. That second storm, though, that was something else. I think that's what added to the agitation. It was coming down hard."

"Which is why I didn't go outside to break up the fight. It was a safety issue."

"I don't want you breaking up fights between strange men regardless. It definitely is a safety issue, just not how you meant it. As for the rain, though, it seemed to come out of nowhere and it flooded the old streets quickly. Usually we have some notice before that happens."

"Yeah, I thought about that, too." I moved my legs so I could rest them on his lap and turned to face him. "The forecasters mentioned the first storm, but the second seemed to come out of nowhere. That's weird, right?"

Griffin smiled, amusement lighting his handsome features as he moved his hands to my feet and started rubbing. "Now that you were right about the zombies, does this mean you're going to start attaching nefarious motivations to other things?"

"What do you mean?"

"The storm. You're acting as if someone created the storm to cause problems."

Was I? That's not how it felt. "I don't think that's what I was saying," I cautioned. "I just meant that the second storm was weird and I saw a fight during it. You obviously saw something, because you've been going out of your way to not talk about what happened during the second bout."

Griffin swallowed hard. "You noticed that, eh?"

I nodded. "You're not good at hiding your emotions, at least from me. It took me some time to figure you out – I'm sure you remember the meltdown I had when I thought you were having sex with your sister – but I think I know you relatively well now."

"I would really appreciate if you didn't phrase it that way, the part where you thought I was dating Maya," Griffin said, pressing a quick kiss to the tip of my nose. "As for knowing me, you're right. I feel as if you know me better than anyone."

That made me feel proud for some reason. "I think you know me, too."

"Oh, we're turning into the schmaltz twins, huh?" We shared another soft kiss before Griffin sobered. "Something else did happen during the storm. You're right about that. It happened to one of my co-workers."

"What?"

"He punched his wife in front of the station."

I was dumbfounded, uncertain what to say. "He punched her?"

Griffin nodded. "Right in the face. All of us were standing in the lobby watching the storm, not sure what to make of it, when we noticed Peter outside with his wife. They've been married for only a few months so we've made a little game out of betting how long they'll make out for before saying goodbye."

"And he punched her instead?"

Griffin held his hands palms out and shrugged. "I don't know, baby. They were talking and acting normal. There was a lot of touching and a few kisses. We were, of course, being jerks inside while commenting on it. Then the rain started.

"I swear we didn't have any hint that it was coming," he continued. "It started and Peter initially put his arm over Lani's head to cover her from the rain. Everyone was talking about how sweet it was before things turned sour."

"Sour how?"

"They started arguing. They were heading toward the door when they stopped to fight. It was clear that they were arguing, although none of us could make out why. Lani was actually the first one to make contact. She smacked him across the face, which was surprising because she's pretty docile. He laid her out in response."

I had no idea what to make of the story. "What did you do?"

"We ran outside and grabbed him. I was one of the first there. I dragged him through the front door while everyone else helped Lani. They basically picked her up and moved her inside even though it would've been smarter to wait for an ambulance. It was raining something fierce, though, and they weren't far from the door, so we were only outside for a few seconds."

"What did Peter say when you got him inside?" I was genuinely curious.

"He fought hard at first, as if I were some enemy he needed to beat," Griffin replied. "One of the guys came out from behind the desk to help me subdue him. We wrestled him down and another guy cuffed him.

"While we were waiting for emergency personnel to show up, I tried to talk to him. He was spitting mad at first," he continued. "After a few minutes he seemed to come back to reality. He was completely freaked out when he realized what was going on. He fought us that time for a different reason."

"I don't understand. What do you mean?"

"He wanted to know what happened to Lani and why she was unconscious."

"He didn't remember?"

"That's what he said."

"Did you believe him?"

"I ... ." Griffin broke off as he searched his busy brain. "I kind of think I believed him. He seemed so upset, so distraught, that there was no consoling him. Of course, I didn't want to console him after what he'd done.

"Lani regained consciousness in the lobby when the emergency responders arrived," he continued. "She asked questions and remembered everything that happened. She was upset, but she was almost more upset by what Peter was going through."

I rubbed my cheek, uncertain how to respond. "I'm not generally the one to take the side of abusive jackholes, but it sounds to me as if he entered some sort of fugue state."

"I know it's crazy, but that was my initial thought. It was almost as if we were dealing with two different men. One of them was a monster and the other was the nice guy we've all come to know. If he was putting on an act about not remembering it was a heck of a show."

"So how did things work out?"

"Lani went to the hospital and Peter was transported there for observation," Griffin answered. "No decision on charges yet. Lani isn't being cooperative. She's convinced he has a brain tumor or something."

Now that was an idea. "Jerry and I watched a Lifetime movie once that was like that. The guy was the perfect husband and father until one day he turned into Michael Myers. Come to find out he had a brain tumor. He could've survived with the tumor but would always remain a jerk or risk death and have it removed."

"It was a Lifetime movie, so let me guess how he chose," Griffin said dryly.

"It was a lovely funeral."

Griffin snickered as he slipped his arm around my waist and tugged me closer, positioning me so I was essentially on his lap. "That sounds like the worst movie ever."

"It was terrible," I agreed. "Those *Facts of Life* chicks need to work, though. I don't begrudge them a paycheck. Besides, the movie was funnier than any sitcom I've seen in years. Jerry and I had a good time watching it."

"Good to know." Griffin rested his brow against mine. "In all serious-ness, I think it's possible that Peter is suffering from some form of mental problem ... or maybe a physical one that hasn't been diagnosed. If the doctors don't find anything, he's looking at losing his job and going to jail."

"Even if his wife doesn't want to press charges?"

"He did it in front of all of us. We can hardly look the other way."

"Yeah. I guess not." I rubbed the back of his neck as I considered the conundrum. "What would you do in the same situation?"

Griffin was caught off guard by the question. "What do you mean?"

"Would you live with the tumor or risk dying to have it removed?"

"Oh, that." He smirked. "I thought you were asking if I've ever considered belting you."

"I happen to know that everyone who has ever met me has considered that."

"I haven't."

"You lie."

"I haven't." Griffin was firm. "There are times I've felt the need to take a step back from you so I don't yell – and there are other times I've given in to the yelling, although I've almost always regretted it after the fact – but I've never once considered smacking you around. That's not how I was raised."

"My brothers have smacked me around and lived to tell."

"That's different," Griffin said. "I would argue the normal hair pulling and slapping you guys engaged in as kids and teenagers isn't the same thing. If one of your brothers punched you, I can guarantee that your father would've handled that situation with his own fists."

I tilted my head to the side, considering. "I guess. Still, I'm not easy to live with."

"You're not as bad as you make out, which I think is a product of you wanting to be a badass in front of your brothers," Griffin countered. "You're not all that hard to live with."

"So you don't want to knock me around?"

Griffin shook his head. "I might want to wrestle with you a little bit, but I never want to hurt you. I can take a lot in this world – my own pain included – but I can't take hurting you. That's too much for me."

I knew that to be true. I saw his reaction after I was forced to visit the hospital a few days during the Christmas holiday. "So you would choose the operation."

"Over hurting you? Absolutely."

"So you're hoping there's something physically wrong with Peter," I mused. "You would rather him be sick, even so sick he might die, rather than acknowledge he might simply be an abusive jerk."

"I've never seen him act that way. I have to hope something else is going on. Sometimes ... sometimes there are worse things than death. Hurting someone you love is one of those things."

I couldn't help but agree with him. After a few minutes of quiet I shook my head to dislodge the melancholy. "Wow. That got deep."

"Way too deep," Griffin agreed, glancing at the clock on the wall. "Our food should be in here ten minutes. Do you want to make out with me on the couch like teenagers until it gets here?"

"Now that is something I totally want to do."

"Somehow I knew you'd say that."

4

FOUR

Although he tried to hide it, I knew Griffin remained upset about his co-worker when we woke the next morning. He wasn't his normal chatty self, and once I was dressed and ready to leave for breakfast next door, he waved me off and said he would join me in a few minutes, making a lame excuse about having to find a different shirt before leaving.

"I'll be right behind you."

I stared at him for a beat, conflicted. Finally I decided hiding the issue wouldn't be good for either of us. "If you want to call and check on Peter you don't need to make up an excuse. I get it."

Griffin's grin was sheepish. "You read me well, don't you? Sometimes I think it might be too well."

"You just don't like it that I'm so magnificent I can read your mind. That makes me all-powerful and all-knowing, which is enough to cause every man in my orbit to want to crawl in a hole and never escape because he's uncomfortable with my mind-reading abilities."

Griffin snorted, amused. "You're humble, too."

"I'm definitely that." I shrugged into a hoodie and turned serious. "It's okay to want to check on him. I kind of want to know what's going on, too. It's freaky. You don't have to hide it."

"I know." Griffin let loose a sigh. "I just didn't want to ruin your morning with something mildly depressing."

"I think Jerry is making pancakes today. Those will uplift my mood." I took a step toward him and wrapped my hand around his wrist. "It's probably better if we just tell each other what's going on. That was your original suggestion, and it's worked so far ... at least for the most part."

Griffin pursed his lips. "You're right. I shouldn't have hidden it. I don't know why I did."

I knew why, but I didn't think now was the time to drop my unique brand of super intelligence on him. "It's okay. I'll hold Aidan and Jerry off from eating your portion of the pancakes for as long as I can."

Griffin planted a quick kiss on my lips. "I won't be long. I just want a general update."

"It's okay. Take all the time you need."

I left through the front door and hopped over the small island that separated my front walk from the townhouse where I used to reside. Originally I thought moving – even though I'd only shifted my personal belongings fifty feet or so – would be difficult. Griffin and I spent every night together, but I worried we would agitate one another and spend most of our time bickering.

In truth, we'd had only one or two arguments since moving in together, and both of those battles revolved around my job and my penchant for finding trouble. Griffin was ridiculously easygoing – something I wasn't used to because I grew up in a dramatic household – and he really only put his foot down when he thought I was walking into danger.

I accidentally tripped over the small fence Jerry set up as a decorative accent, snagging my toe on the metal and slamming it into the concrete, where it bent in a manner I knew would drive Jerry absolutely nuts. I cringed as I caught myself and bent over, lifting the small piece of fencing so I could attempt to force it back into its original shape. I tried three times before shoving it in the ground. I would simply tell him a kid with an aversion to decorative fences did it if he asked. Otherwise I'd lie and deny.

What? That's my way when it comes to stuff like this. Why own up to something that's going to cause strife? No one wants that.

I rapped my knuckles against the door once before pushing it open and entering. I could hear Jerry rattling around in the kitchen as I kicked off my shoes and headed into the living room. That's where I found Aidan, a grim look on his face as he watched the morning news. He wasn't exactly what I would call a morning person, although he was often cheerier than me, but his morose expression told me that he wasn't going to be a pleasant conversationalist this morning.

"What's up with you?" It wasn't a standard greeting, but I was hardly a standard sister so I figured it was fine. I launched myself onto the couch and rested my feet on the coffee table as I got comfortable next to him. "What are you doing?"

Aidan remained focused on the television and didn't as much as glance in my direction. "What does it look like I'm doing?"

My brother's tone told me now wasn't the time to be sarcastic. I'm a Grimlock, so that's exactly how I opted to approach the problem despite his obvious signs of distress. "I think you look like you're trying to broker world peace."

Aidan scowled. "Do you think that's funny?"

"Most of the time I think I'm downright hilarious. You apparently don't think I'm funny, though."

"No, I don't think you're funny at all," Aidan agreed. "In fact ... why don't you try out your comedy routine on Jerry? I think he could use some company in the kitchen."

"Fine." I raised an eyebrow as I rolled to my feet. If I didn't know better, I'd think my brother was suffering from a raging case of PMS. I headed toward the kitchen, slowing long enough to note the blanket and pillow that were folded and shoved under one of the living room side tables, conveniently located in a place most people wouldn't search.

Hmm. That was interesting. The blanket and pillow would indicate someone had slept on the couch the previous night. I always thought Griffin and I would have relationship growing pains as things moved forward. I never thought it would be Jerry and Aidan.

I plastered a bright smile on my face as I sauntered into the kitchen, determined to get some answers. I knew that I'd have to put up with allowing Jerry to vent long and loud to get those answers, but I was philanthropic enough to take one for the team if it meant hearing some fun gossip.

"Hey, Jerry. How are you this fine and overcast morning?"

Jerry tossed me a weary glance. "I'm fine, Bug. How are you?"

There was absolutely no life to his answer, which threw me for a loop. "I'm delightful. Griffin and I ordered Middle Eastern food and he gave me a foot massage. Then we took a bath together and watched television in bed while listening to that third storm that came out of nowhere. It was pretty much a perfect evening."

Jerry looked dubious. "You know, two years ago we considered a perfect evening a loud and drunken night at the bar. Now we're home-bodies who only care about how comfortable our pajamas are. It's a little distressing."

"I haven't given it much thought," I admitted, surprised by his downer attitude. Usually when Jerry and Aidan fought my best friend couldn't wait to launch into the tale and get me on his side so we could double-team Aidan into submission. "Um ... is something going on?"

Jerry turned swiftly and focused on whisking batter. "Why would something be up?"

"I don't know. I just thought I might've sensed a vibe here this morning."

"Well, everything is fine. I mean ... it's perfect. We had a lovely evening and morning. Up? Nothing is up. That's absolutely absurd."

Jerry always was a terrible liar. When we were kids I had to lie to him so he would think he was telling my parents the truth before we left to do something outlandish. He was far too transparent otherwise.

"Jerry." I gentled my voice, unsure how to proceed. "If something is wrong, you know you can tell me, right?"

Jerry slammed the metal bowl on the counter, the sound echoing throughout the room and causing me to jolt. "Nothing is wrong."

"Okay." I held my hands up in a placating manner and took a step back. "I'll just get out of your way."

"Nothing is wrong," Jerry repeated.

"I get it. Nothing is wrong." I flicked my eyes to the front door when it opened, relieved to find Griffin walking through. I was fairly certain I'd entered a bad episode of *The Twilight Zone* and was happy to have reinforcements. "There you are. I was getting worried."

Griffin offered up a peculiar look. "You were getting worried about what?"

"You." I was a better liar than everyone in the room, but even I couldn't pull off that simple answer.

"What's going on?" Griffin asked, sensing trouble as he glanced between the kitchen and living room. Aidan didn't as much as look in our direction. "Am I missing something?"

That was an interesting question. We were both very clearly missing something, though what was anyone's guess.

"Things seem a little tense in here," I whispered, lowering my voice. "I think Aidan and Jerry aren't talking."

"Really?" Griffin was intrigued rather than worried, which meant he didn't grasp the magnitude of what I'd said. "What do you think they're fighting about? Do you think they played Risk last night without us or something?"

Jerry and Aidan (and, okay, me) were terrible losers, so we had something of a moratorium going on when it came to board games. Every once in a while alcohol fueled us and we forgot that moratorium. If Jerry and Aidan were fighting over a board game that went flying, that would make me feel markedly better because it was something they would only pout over for a few hours.

"Hmm. I hadn't even considered that." I turned my eyes to Aidan. "Did you guys play a game last night?"

"Not unless you consider WWE wrestling a game," Aidan replied. "I'm watching the news, Aisling. There's more going on in this world than your nonstop need to talk. Can you give me a few minutes?"

His tone was biting and caused Griffin and me to offer twin looks of surprise.

"Sure. No problem."

Griffin put his hand to my elbow and prodded me toward the small dining room at the back of the townhouse. It offered us a spot where we could talk privately – as long as we lowered our voices – and watch Aidan and Jerry at the same time.

"I think you were right about them fighting," Griffin started.

"When are you going to realize that I'm always right?"

Griffin ignored the jab. "Maybe we should head out to breakfast, just the two of us? I'm not really keen on sitting through the world's most uncomfortable meal to start my day."

It was a fair point. Still, Aidan was my brother and Jerry was my best friend. I felt the urge to help. "I don't know."

"We can stay." Griffin immediately adjusted his stance. "I'm just saying that we're not a part of this argument. Maybe we'd both be better off leaving them to work things out on their own."

What fun would that be? "I think they need me to act as referee."

Griffin made a tsking sound with his tongue. "You just want to get the dirt about why they're fighting. You're a gossipy little thing."

"You say that like it's a bad thing."

"I'm warning you that this could blow up in your face." Griffin adopted a practical tone. "You don't like it when you're fighting with Jerry. Out of all your brothers, you like it least when you're fighting with Aidan. I think it might be that twin thing, but I'm not sure.

"Just be prepared if they both explode all over you," he continued. "They're clearly on edge. And as much as I love you – and I do – you're not known for being the sort of person who can magically smooth over arguments."

I was pretty sure he meant that as an insult. "It will be fine."

"Okay." Griffin held up his hands in defeat. "When this backfires on you, I don't want to hear a word about it. I'm not going to be sympathetic when you come crying to me ten hours from now and want me to make things better."

That was a pointed warning ... and dig. "It will be fine." I decided to change the subject. "How is Peter?"

"Oh, he's definitely better, but mired in guilt." Griffin brightened considerably, which made me feel better for him even though I remained worried about Jerry and Aidan's relationship. "The doctors found an overabundance of epinephrine in his bloodstream."

Hmm. "I don't know what that means."

"Apparently it's a chemical reaction when people fight, although I haven't gotten all the specifics yet and I'm pretty far from a scientist,"

Griffin explained. "The doctor can't say for certain this is what made Peter act the way he did, but he thinks it's a likely culprit."

"So that leads to the next question," I mused. "How did Peter get so much epinephrine in his brain?"

"They're searching for answers. Lani hasn't left his side. She keeps insisting he would never hurt her – he's never so much as laid a finger on her during a disagreement – and she refuses to press charges."

"So what will you guys do?"

Griffin shrugged. "I'm not sure yet. Right now we're waiting to let the doctor do his magic. If it's a medical condition, Peter can't be blamed."

"Which is what we're all hoping for, oddly enough." I rubbed my hand over my chin and focused on the back of Aidan's head. He seemed ridiculously tense. "I have an idea."

Griffin screwed up his face into a sour expression. "Oh, I hate it when you say things like that."

I ignored his tone. "I want you to talk to Jerry and feel him out. I'm going to do the same with Aidan."

Griffin immediately started shaking his head. "That's a terrible idea."

"And I think it needs to be done, so it's going to be done." I refused to back down. "I don't like it when those around me are fighting."

"Baby, you love it when your brothers are fighting and you started it. I don't know who you're trying to fool, but it's not going to work on me."

"This is different." I meant it. "They're really upset."

Griffin heaved out a sigh. "Fine. I'll talk to Jerry. But if he tells me to mind my own business, I won't push him. I'm only willing to go so far with this."

"Fair enough."

I COULD HEAR Griffin and Jerry talking when I sat next to Aidan on the couch. This time I was quieter when I addressed him. I was also more aware of his mood, so I kept my voice even as I asked the obvious question.

"What happened?"

Aidan opened his mouth to snap out what I'm sure was an insult, but instead he changed course mid-retort and held his hands palms up as he shrugged. "I don't know what happened. Things completely fell apart last night."

"I don't know what that means."

"Jerry turned ... hostile ... out of nowhere. I mean, he didn't just turn mean and angry with his words. He tried to hit me. He actually tried to punch me."

I was dumbfounded. "Jerry tried to hit you? Why? He doesn't believe in punching people. He thinks that's a testosterone-run-amok thing."

"I know. That's why it took me by surprise the way it did."

"Huh." I ran my fingers through my hair as I tried to process Aidan's admission. "Tell me more. When did this happen?"

"We were fine during dinner last night," Aidan replied. "We went to that vegan place he loves and he got that salad he's convinced cleans him out so he will live forever."

"Yes, I've heard about the salad. He even made me eat it once. It tastes like ass."

"It does," Aidan agreed. "I was fine with it because he seemed to be in such a good mood. It was storming when we hit home. We tried to wait it out in the parking lot, but the storm seemed to go forever."

"I know." I thought back to the frequent lightning and never-ending downpour, something occurring to me. "How was he in the car before you got out?"

"He seemed fine. He didn't turn angry until we were running toward the townhouse. Then, out of nowhere, he started yelling at me. And when I told him he was being ridiculous he threw a punch. Luckily for us he's never thrown a punch before and missed my face, but ... I don't know what to make of it. He was absolutely furious. I've never seen him that way."

My stomach did an uncomfortable roll. "What happened when you were back inside?"

"He stormed into the bedroom and took a shower. I could hear him muttering about what a jerk I was before he slammed the door. Then, suddenly, when he got out of the shower he wanted to make up. He pretended he had no idea what had gotten into him and apologized, but I wasn't in the mood to make up."

"So you slept on the couch," I mused.

"Yeah. I'm angry with him. I can't just forget what he did. That's not the sort of relationship I want."

I didn't blame him. The story was eerily similar to that of Griffin's co-worker, and I couldn't shake the niggling worry that they were related. "What if it wasn't his fault?"

"What do you mean?"

I shrugged, noncommittal. "What if something made him act that way?"

"Like what?"

I didn't know how to answer, but the storm seemed the easiest scapegoat. I kept the notion to myself, and merely offered a wan smile. "I don't know. That's not the way Jerry is, though. We both know that. Something must've happened in his head to make him act that way."

"I agree, but that doesn't mean I should put up with being punched for no reason."

"No, but ... it's not as if this is a regular occurrence with Jerry."

"I'm not going to argue that point, but I'm still angry. I don't know what to make about any of it. I need some time to think. He's been pouting in the kitchen all morning, which isn't helping matters."

"He probably feels guilty."

"Well, he should."

I ran my thumb over my bottom lip. "A lot of people fought during the storms yesterday. Griffin and I talked about it. They had a lot of arrests, and almost all of them were due to fighting."

"So you think the storms made people fight?" Aidan didn't look convinced. "How could that possibly be true?"

I had no idea, but I was determined to find out.

5

FIVE

Griffin walked me to my car after our tense breakfast. He linked his fingers with mine, as if it were a normal day, but gave them an extra squeeze before releasing in front of my vehicle.

"Did Jerry say anything useful?" I asked.

"He just said they fought and he threw a punch and he feels guilty."

"That's basically what Aidan told me, too. Aidan is extremely upset, and I'm worried."

"I wouldn't worry too much. I'm sure they'll get over it. Guys throw punches all the time and it doesn't turn into a big deal. In fact, throwing a punch could be a good thing when it comes to men. It gets out latent aggression and things return to normal quickly after that."

Something about his cavalier attitude rubbed me the wrong way. "You didn't say that yesterday when your buddy coldcocked his girlfriend."

Griffin shifted from one foot to the other, uncomfortable. "Because that wasn't the same thing at all."

"Really?" I arched a challenging eyebrow. "Why is that? Because Lani is a woman and Aidan is a man?"

"Well ... um ... ." Griffin didn't answer. Most likely because he knew there was no answer that would appease me.

"It was the same thing," I pressed. "Just because Aidan is a man and can defend himself, that doesn't mean what Jerry did was right."

"Of course it doesn't," Griffin said hurriedly. "I'm not saying it was right. Jerry is beating himself up over it, too. He doesn't understand why he did what he did. He described it as something inside of him snapping."

"Just like what happened with Peter." I irritably rubbed the back of my neck as I leaned my hip against the car. "It happened during the storm last night."

Griffin pursed his lips.

"I can tell what you're thinking," I muttered. "You think I'm making something out of nothing."

"I didn't say that," Griffin shot back. "I've learned that your instincts are generally spot on, but this is different than anything we've dealt with before. Evil people, even wraiths, were at the heart of everything else we've ever faced. I have trouble understanding the concept of evil storms."

He wasn't the only one. That didn't mean my wariness wasn't warranted. "I don't know why it's happening, but it certainly seems to be a thing," I argued. "The exact same thing happened to your co-worker and my best friend. That can't be a coincidence."

"It can't?" Griffin obviously didn't believe that. "Jerry has always been wound a little tight, Aisling. Quite frankly, given all he puts up with and how fussy he is, I'm surprised this didn't happen sooner. I'm sure things will work themselves out."

It was obvious I wasn't going to be able to sway Griffin to my way of thinking so I merely shrugged and forced a smile. "You're probably right."

Griffin scanned my face for a long time, his gaze probing and uncomfortable. "You don't think I'm right, do you?"

Lying would've been the obvious way to go, but I had no intention of doing that. "No. I think you're wrong and I'm right."

"Baby, you always think you're right. I've never once heard you admit to being wrong."

"That's because it's never happened. I keep waiting for it to occur, but I think I'm probably doomed to disappointment."

Griffin ran his tongue over his teeth. I could practically see the war raging in his head. Finally he merely held up his hands and nodded. "You're right. You're always right. I should've realized that months ago. I think it would've saved us a lot of arguing."

Oh, now he was just placating me. "You don't think I'm right."

"I don't," Griffin agreed. "But we're at a stalemate here. I think you've got what happened with Peter caught in your head and you're looking for a paranormal reason for what Jerry did because it seems so out of the ordinary.

"People snap, Aisling," he continued. "People have bad days."

"Punching the person you love isn't a bad day."

"I agree. Still, sometimes things happen. I think Jerry got worked up and lashed out and he regrets it. I think he regrets it so much you'll never have to worry about a repeat performance."

I thought about the look on Aidan's face, the depression weighing down his shoulders, and shook my head. "It's more than that."

"Well, we'll have to agree to disagree. I'm sorry, but I don't think it's more than that, and I'm not going to lie just to make you happy."

"I don't want you to lie." That was true. Mostly. "It's just ... I don't like emotional upheaval in my life. I want everyone to get along."

Instead of reacting with sympathy, as I expected, Griffin barked out a laugh. "Baby, you like it when people are worked up, and you know it. This is a little bit different from the discontent you generally like to sow, but in general you like a good old family brawl.

"It's going to be okay," he continued. "I promise. Things will work out."

I wanted to believe him. I wanted to press him on the issue until he agreed with me. I wanted things back the way they should be so I didn't have to dwell on them all day. I knew none of those things were going to happen, so instead I offered up a smile.

"Everything will work out," I agreed, leaning forward so I could give him a quick kiss. "Everything is going to be absolutely fine. I have faith."

"Good. That makes two of us."

THINGS WERE SO NOT going to work out. I should've realized I was in for a crap factory sort of day the moment I tripped over Jerry's stupid fence. Instead it took running into my nemesis – yes, I have one and she's awful – at my favorite coffee shop to make me realize things were about to worsen.

"Hello, Angelina."

Angelina Davenport, her usually bouncy brown hair tied back in a subdued ponytail, swiveled slowly when she heard my voice. She was ahead of me in line, a woman with a big purse and chipmunk cheeks sandwiched between us, and she didn't look any happier to see me than I was to see her.

"Oh, well, Aisling," Angelina drawled. "Did the herpes convention let out early? I thought they were keeping you guys for three days so they could conduct experiments."

Darn it. That was a pretty good opening shot. The fact that she didn't even need a moment to think was frustrating. She was on top of her game. "They sent me out to find a speaker," I supplied. "The one they had died and you were the next on our list. I was just heading out to find you. Luckily for me you turned out to be easy to find. I didn't even have to head to the nearest street corner to ask your pimp if you could take some time off. You know how I hate hanging with your pimp."

The woman between us widened her eyes to comical proportions when she realized things were about to get loud. "Oh, dear." Angelina and I both ignored the way she fanned her face and looked around for help.

"I'm surprised you'd risk running into my pimp because he wouldn't hire you," Angelina shot back. "He said you were too easy to be a prostitute. I mean ... that's weird, right? Who is too easy to be a prostitute?"

Angelina looked victorious, but I knew I had her beat.

"That doesn't even make sense," I complained. "Prostitutes are paid for sex. Sluts give it away for free. You can't be too easy to be a prostitute because that's part of the gig."

Angelina balked. "That's why it was funny."

"It's not even remotely funny," I countered. "It would've been funny if you said that I was fired for doing too many free promotions. The way you worded it made no sense."

Angelina made a face. "It made perfect sense, you whore!"

"Oh, whatever. By the way, I heard you got ass crabs and you've been spreading them around. You might want to get a tonic or something."

"I can't believe this," the woman between us muttered, her eyes landing on someone behind me in line. She looked almost happy to see whoever it was, but there was no way I would fall for that and allow her to smack me over the head with her huge purse when I wasn't looking. Believe it or not, that's happened multiple times, and I refuse to fall prey to bad acting from the elderly squad ever again. "Thank goodness the police are here," she said. "I'm not going to be killed in a coffee shop after all."

When she mentioned police I couldn't stop myself from glancing over my shoulder. I almost expected to find Griffin standing there. Perhaps he thought better of thinking me an alarmist over the storms. Instead I found someone else entirely. Unfortunately, I recognized the face, and the detective wasn't a member of my fan club.

"Detective Green," I said mildly, forcing a smile. "It's wonderful to see you again. I can't tell you how much this moment brightens my day."

Instead of reacting to the sarcasm with a sneer, which was his way, Mark Green merely rolled his eyes. "Yes. You look thrilled to see me."

"You're a police officer," the woman said, pointing toward the badge affixed to Green's belt. "Did you hear what these women were saying? You need to arrest them for public indecency."

In one of our rare shows of unity, Angelina and I snorted at the exact same moment.

"We're not being indecent," Angelina argued. "We're being rude and mean, but there's nothing indecent going on."

"She's right," I added. "If we were being indecent we would've stripped off our tops and showed you our boobs. Now that would've been indecent."

"Especially on her part." Angelina jerked her thumb in my direction. "Her boobs are infested with scabies and are frightening to even the most hard up individuals on the streets."

Green pursed his lips. "I don't want to be part of this conversation."

I didn't blame him. "Leave him alone, Angelina," I ordered. "He's trying to be nice, but your foul stench is knocking him for a loop. Next time you pick a perfume, try something different from Eau de Crotchrot."

"All right, that will be enough of that." Green, finally at his limit, strode forward until he stood between Angelina and me. He gestured toward the woman and indicated she should step ahead of Angelina in the line. "Ma'am, why don't you go ahead?" He let loose a charming smile. "I'll stay behind and talk to these two ... ladies ... and see if we can't come to a meeting of the minds. How does that sound?"

"I would rather you arrest them," the woman sniffed, giving Angelina a wide berth as she stepped around her. "I guess I'll have to take what I can get. I'll definitely be writing your boss a letter telling him how ineffective you are, so be prepared for that."

Green managed to keep his smile in place, although just barely. "Yes, ma'am."

I eyed Green for a long beat as the line shuffling finished and then exhaled heavily as I searched for something to say. Our relationship was never going to be easy. He thought I was a murderer and that I somehow managed to hide it. I thought he was the world's biggest turd − even larger than Angelina and her fake boobs − but that was neither here nor there. I was in a precarious position because I'd been with his dead boss the day before.

"So, I hear your boss bit the big one yesterday," I offered. As far as openings go, it wasn't going to earn a spot on my greatest hits list.

Green's eyebrows winged up. "How did you hear that?"

"My boyfriend is a cop," I reminded him, briefly worrying that news hadn't broken yet. If the story hadn't reached the newspapers I'd look suspicious if I had too much knowledge. I was lucky to have a boyfriend in law enforcement, so I decided to use it to my advantage. "He told me when word started to spread."

"Oh." Green seemed to swallow my lie, which was a good thing. "I guess that makes sense. I didn't realize the other departments were already hearing word of his passing. It's difficult all around. I guess it's good he's being remembered."

"Yes. It's always good to be remembered." I flicked a dismissive look to Angelina. "You, for example, will be remembered as the woman with the worst case of ass crabs the tri-county area has ever seen." I grinned when she frowned. "Did you see how I carried that thread from one subject to another? That's how you win an insult war."

"Whatever." Angelina didn't bother to hide her eye roll as she focused on Green and extended her hand. "I'm Angelina Davenport. It's nice to meet you."

Green introduced himself, a real smile playing at the corner of his lips as he took in Angelina's pale countenance. He probably thought there was a chance he might get lucky – which was true because Angelina never met a man she didn't want to jump and use for whatever he could give her – but he didn't seem to notice the dark shadows under her eyes or the way her shoulders slumped as she shuffled forward in line.

"I'm sorry you have to put up with Aisling," Angelina offered. "She's the world's worst person, and I pity anyone who feels compelled to talk to her. I'm assuming you're thinking of arresting her for something. That's the only reason someone as smart and charming as you could possibly want to share a discussion with the antichrist."

I mimed puking at Angelina's flirting attempt. "He doesn't want to date you. The Royal Oak Police Department frowns on their officers coming down with a venereal disease and putting the public at risk. That means you're out of the running."

Green slid in smoothly and took over the conversation before Angelina, who looked furious, could respond. That was probably a good thing. "So how do you guys know each other?"

"We went to high school together," Angelina replied, changing course. "It was the worst four years of my life. She was awful."

"Oh, don't try to pretend like you graduated in four years," I chided. "It took her six years, Detective Green. She got held back after giving the principal, gym teacher, band leader and Spanish instructor gonorrhea."

Angelina let loose with a growl. "The gym teacher was a woman."

"See," I said to Green. "She's not denying she's an equal opportunity slut. You should run away as fast as you can."

"I'll keep that in mind," Green said dryly. "I'm guessing the animosity between the two of you is legitimate. At first I thought it was a game, but you clearly seem to hate one another."

"Oh, we definitely hate each other," I intoned. "I could never like a woman who goes years without shaving her armpits. Who knows, though? You might like that."

Angelina glared at me, hostility rolling off her. "I've had about enough of your mouth."

"That's good. I felt the same way about you ten years ago. You're finally catching up."

Green held up his hands to silence us. "Listen, I don't want to get in the middle of ... well, whatever this is," he said. "Chick fights are only hot on television. So, you have two choices: You can keep doing what you're doing and then find someone to pay bail once I arrest you or you can stop and let things go."

"I'm fine with being arrested," I offered. "It would hardly be the first time. My father keeps bail money handy."

"That's because your father is a moron," Angelina said. "He's always spoiled you rotten even though you're the world's worst human being."

"That insult lacked a little zip," I noted. "You might want to load up on caffeine and try again."

"I'd appreciate if you wouldn't do that," Green interrupted. "In fact, I want this conversation to be over with. You're disturbing the clientele. With that in mind, Ms. Davenport, why don't you let me buy you a coffee and we'll take a seat in the corner over there?" He gestured to the dark corner on the far side of the shop. There were no open seats anywhere near it. "Then, Ms. Grimlock, you can buy your own coffee and do ... whatever it is you do."

Angelina beamed at Green, clearly happy to be his chosen coffee date. "That sounds fantastic."

Green returned the smile. "Great." He spared me one last glance. "Try to behave yourself."

That was easier said than done. And, as I watched Angelina and Green chat each other up while waiting for their coffee orders, seemingly in their own little world as they steadfastly tried to ignore me, I couldn't tamp down the worry niggling at the back of my brain.

There was no way this could be construed as good, right? I didn't think so.

6

SIX

I finished with my two charges before lunch. It was a slow day, which was fine with me, and I was considering returning home to catch an episode of *General Hospital* and eat potato chips when my phone dinged with a calendar alert.

I frowned at the readout when I realized exactly why my schedule was so light. It had been planned two weeks before and I'd forgotten about it. Well, to be fair, it was more that I'd purposely willed the appointment out of my mind.

"Oh, well, great." I growled and tapped my foot on the pavement as I internally debated if I could get out of the appointment. As if on cue, my phone rang. "Hello?"

"Good afternoon, love of my life," Griffin said cheerily, setting my teeth on edge. "As per our agreement two weeks ago, it's my job to remind you that you have your dress fitting this afternoon and no matter what, you can't duck out of it."

Most future husbands wouldn't understand my aversion to wedding dress shopping, but Griffin found it funny. When Jerry set the appointment and insisted I would be forced to die if I attempted to wiggle out, it seemed like a good idea to put Griffin on the case. He wouldn't allow me to forget, which was exactly why I was getting this call.

"You put the dress fitting in my calendar, didn't you?"

"I did," Griffin confirmed, seemingly unruffled by my tone. "I put an alert on my phone, too, but I was worried I might be tied up with a case so I programmed your phone first so we were doubly covered. Surprise ... and you're welcome."

"I didn't thank you."

"You will later. I'm thinking you will thank me with kisses and sex."

Even though I was agitated, I couldn't stop myself from laughing at his bravado. "Oh, well, is that what you think?"

"Yup."

"What if I decide to duck out of my appointment?"

"I don't care what you wear to get married," Griffin replied. "You can be naked for all I care. It doesn't matter to me. It does, however, matter to Jerry and your mother. You have to weigh your aversion to seamstresses poking and measuring you against a disappointed mother and best friend."

"I don't really care what my mother thinks," I grumbled.

"You care what Jerry thinks. Also, now that he's had a bit of time to chew on the situation, you might be able to talk to him about his fight with Aidan."

I balked. "I don't want to do that. He'll turn it into a big deal."

"You guys turn everything into a big deal," Griffin pointed out. "I think he needs a friend, and because you're his best friend, I believe it's your duty to listen to him fret."

Sadly, I knew Griffin was right. Jerry never had a problem listening when I complained. He deserved the same from me. I heaved out a resigned sigh. "Fine. I'll go. If the taffeta strangles me, though, and I don't make it to the wedding, I want you to remember this is all your fault."

Griffin chuckled. "I'll take my chances. Did anything else happen today, by the way? Are you still working on your evil storm theory or have you moved on to something else?"

Oddly enough I was so busy during the morning I didn't have time to dwell on the storm hypothesis. "I haven't decided on that yet. I did have another issue arise this morning, though, and I don't think it's a fortuitous turn of events."

I told him about my exchange with Angelina, not leaving anything out because he genuinely enjoyed hearing whatever insults I came up with in the spur of the moment, and I wrapped up with Angelina's coffee tete-a-tete with Mark Green.

"So basically it's as if my worst enemies have joined together to bring me down," I concluded. "I don't think it's going to turn out to be a good thing."

Griffin was so silent on the other end of the call I thought I might've inadvertently dropped it.

"Are you still there?"

Griffin stirred. "I'm here. I'm just thinking about what you said. I'm not sure that Angelina is much of a threat to you, but she does have certain information about your family that makes me uncomfortable. If she shares that with Green ... well ... it might force him to look more closely at you."

I hadn't considered that. "Angelina doesn't know everything," I argued. "She only knows bits and pieces."

"She knows enough that we would have real trouble explaining it. She was there for the whole mirror monster thing. She was also there when a wraith attacked at Grimlock Manor, and she saw you take it out."

Crap. I'd forgotten all about that. "Yeah, but if she tells Green that stuff he'll think she's a loon," I said after a beat. "Even if he's predisposed to think I'm a murderer – which he is – he's not simply going to believe we're reapers because Angelina says it. He's much too practical for that."

"I think you're right, but it's a situation I want to watch all the same."

That made two of us. "Well, there's nothing more we can do about it today. Have you heard anything else on Peter?"

"Not so far, but I'll keep you updated. If the doctor blames it on evil storms, you'll be the first to know."

I didn't find his sarcastic tone attractive in the least. "Great. I can't wait." Two could play the sarcasm game. "I have to go. Jerry will be early, and if I'm late he'll have a meltdown."

"And we don't want that. Try to talk to him while you're there, maybe see if you can calm him down. I'm sure everything will be better by tonight."

"I certainly hope so."

"Me, too. Have fun. I love you."

"I love you, too."

JERRY WAS WAITING FOR me in the dress shop's lobby when I arrived. I was only two minutes late, which is the same as being early in my world, but he didn't look happy when I breezed through the door.

"Where have you been? I was starting to get worried."

I glanced at the clock on the wall and cocked an eyebrow. "I was crossing town. I thought speeding up and getting into an accident was probably the wrong way to go so I followed traffic laws instead. Forgive me for my stupidity."

Jerry ignored the sarcasm and held up a garment bag. "Try this on."

I narrowed my eyes. "What is that?"

"Your dress."

"I haven't picked out a dress," I reminded him. "We agreed on three that were supposed to be sent here in my size so I could try them on and then we were going to go from there."

"Yes, well, this is the one I like."

I was torn. I understood he was upset. He looked it. His big eyes, always so full of life, looked dull, and the misery wafting off him was enough to almost crush me. That didn't mean I had any intention of letting him bully me into a dress I would hate.

"I want to see them for myself." I was firm as I walked forward and snagged the garment bag. I unzipped the top and poked my nose in, fighting the urge to gag the moment I saw the overflow of lace and beadwork. "Absolutely not. This was not on my list of approved dresses."

"I know." Jerry planted his hands on his hips. "I added one. I didn't think you were getting the full picture of how perfect it would be for you so I decided to add it. I didn't tell you because I knew you'd make a fuss."

AMANDA M. LEE

"I'll still make a fuss," I warned, shoving the dress at him. "I'm not wearing that."

"Why not?" Jerry adopted a pitiable tone. "I think it's beautiful and you'll look beautiful in it, Bug. Why won't you just try it on for me?"

"Because I'm going to hate it and it's going to make me want to punch you," I automatically answered, instantly hating myself when I saw the shift on Jerry's features.

"Oh, well, you don't have to try it on," Jerry said primly, setting the dress aside. "I was overreaching. Um ... try on your other dresses." He sat on the couch next to the elevated area with the mirrors. "Pick whichever one you want."

I grabbed the nearest garment bag from the rack and fixed Jerry with a worried look. I knew I should say something – other than the absolutely moronic thing I'd already said – but I was too uncomfortable. I needed to gather my thoughts first. "I'll be right back."

Jerry flashed a smile that didn't make it all the way to his eyes. "I'll be waiting."

I drew the dressing room curtain and kicked off my shoes, silently lambasting myself for saying something so stupid to my best friend. I barely paid any attention to the dress as I tugged it on. By the time I stepped out I was ready to tackle the situation head-on.

"You look fantastic," Jerry gushed, jumping to his feet and directing me toward the mirrors. "Look at you. All you need is a tiara and you'll look like a princess."

I growled. "No tiara."

Jerry pretended he didn't hear me. "You're a vision."

I shifted my eyes to the mirror and took in my reflection. Jerry seemed excited by what he saw, but I was of the opinion that I resembled a large Q-tip more than anything else. "I don't know," I hedged, shifting so I could study the lace overlay at the back of the overblown frock. "I don't like that. It looks weird."

Jerry skewered me with a glare. "How can you possibly not like the back of that dress? It's classic, elegant, and the dress isn't so white that it washes you out. It's absolutely perfect."

The fact that he believed that made me wonder if he knew me at

56

all. "Jerry, there's a big bow on my ass and it makes me look emaciated on the top here because I don't have enough boobs to fill it out."

Jerry rolled his eyes. "It's a sample size, Bug. The dress will be brought in at the top to fit you."

I didn't think that would help. "I don't like it."

"Ugh." Jerry heaved a sigh. "Fine. Put on the next one. Maybe we'll have an easier time with that."

Once I was out of the lace monstrosity I grabbed the second bag and tugged on the dress. It was less garish than the first, but only barely. I wasn't all that concerned with my dress. but I was legitimately worried about Jerry, so I decided to be more forceful the second time I exited the dressing room.

"So, as I was saying, I'm sorry about what I said."

Jerry pressed his hand to his heart and blinked back tears. "You're an absolute vision, Bug." He blew me an exaggerated kiss and dabbed at his eyes. "I mean ... there's never been a prettier bride."

I dubiously stepped in front of the mirrors and almost jolted at my own reflection when I realized the circumference of the skirt was bigger than a circle made up entirely of my brothers. "No way!"

"Yes way." Jerry moved next to me so he could tug on the back of the dress to tighten it around my breasts. "See. It looks absolutely lovely. You need a tiara with this dress. It also needs a veil."

I grimaced at my reflection. "I look like that woman from that scary story we used to tell," I complained. "What was her name again? Bloody Mary. That's it. That's exactly who I look like."

"You don't look like her at all," Jerry countered. "You're an absolute dream."

"No, I'm an absolute nightmare." I swished my hips and groaned when I realized the dress didn't look as if I were moving at all. "Jerry, this skirt is the thing that Godzilla fears. It makes noise when I walk, although it doesn't shift at all."

"It's supposed to look like a bell."

"It looks like the bell that flattened the hunchback."

Jerry furrowed his brow. "What hunchback?"

"The one that played football for that one team."

It took Jerry a moment to wade through the mess that was my mind. "The Hunchback of Notre Dame?"

"That's the one."

"Yeah, you don't look like that, but now all I'll be able to picture is that dress flattening someone," Jerry said. "Go try on the third one."

"Fine. If it's as bad as these other two, though, we'll have to start over. I can't tolerate any of these dresses. They're not what I want."

"I don't even think you know what you want," Jerry muttered behind me.

"I heard that."

"I meant for you to hear it."

I paid absolutely zero attention to the third dress. Other than noting it was much simpler and easy to pull on, I spent my entire tenure in the dressing room debating how I was going to apologize to Jerry and get him to talk about his problems. This time when I walked out of the room I marched straight up to him and slapped my hand over his mouth.

"I know you're upset about what happened last night," I announced, snagging his gaze. "I don't think it was your fault, though, and we're going to figure it out. I didn't mean to say what I did before I started trying on dresses. It was mean. That's not who I want to be today.

"Okay, well, I always kind of want to be mean," I clarified. "I was mean to Angelina this morning at the coffee shop. I got off some real zingers, but they weren't nearly as fun as they should be because she looks worn to the bone. I guess her mother's illness is worse than I originally thought. I suppose it doesn't matter, but it almost makes me feel sorry for her. Almost.

"As for what happened with you and Aidan, I don't for a second believe you did it on purpose or even meant for it to happen," I said, opting not to mention my theory about evil storms until I was sure Jerry was settled. "We'll figure everything out. Aidan loves you. I'm sure it will be okay."

I stared at Jerry for a long time before he finally wrapped his hand around my wrist and removed my hand. "Can I speak now?"

I nodded.

"I know Aidan and I will work things out. I still feel guilty. I'm upset because I remember doing it, but have no idea why. It's disheartening to think I have that level of darkness in my heart."

"You're the best person I know." I opted for sincerity. "I know you didn't mean it. Deep down, Aidan knows it, too."

"I wish he would talk to me."

"I'll make him talk to you. Together, he won't be able to fight us off."

"There's a plan." Jerry smiled and it lit up his entire face. "Now, turn around. I think we found your dress."

"What? Oh." I shifted so I could see myself, fully expecting to hate my reflection. Instead I sucked in a breath when I saw the clean lines and simple skirt. The dress was almost completely without frills and yet it fit my personality to a T. "Huh."

"I thought you were crazy when you picked it out," Jerry admitted. "I thought it was ugly and plain. You make it special, though."

"You know what? I kind of like it." I swished my hips and blew out a relieved breath when the skirt moved. "It's kind of perfect, huh?"

"All it's missing is a tiara."

"Lay off the tiara stuff."

"Not in this lifetime."

"Well, they don't appear to have one here," I noted. "I guess we'll have to push off that argument for another day."

"I have one in my car." Jerry moved to hop off the elevated floor. "I'll be right back."

At the same moment he pulled away, a rumble of thunder caused the floor to shake and I snapped my head to the storefront windows. It was storming again, and it looked like a hurricane was about to hit outside.

"No, don't go to your car." I grabbed Jerry's sleeve as tightly as I could. "We'll play with the tiara later."

"I don't mind getting wet," Jerry said. "I can take a shower as soon as I get home."

I grabbed him tighter. "Don't go outside." I didn't want to explain, but I was desperate to keep him with me. For some reason I felt it was imperative that I didn't lose sight of my friend. "Even though this is the dress I like, I'll try on that ugly one you first showed me so we can laugh if you forget about the tiara for now."

Jerry's eyes sparkled with delight. "Really?"

I nodded. "Yes. I'll try it on and let you take one photograph."

"Oh, yay!" Jerry clapped. "This day is already looking up."

I was glad one of us could say that.

7

SEVEN

Griffin called as I was parking at Grimlock Manor.

"Hi, honey." I adopted a fake and breathy voice I knew would amuse him. "I found a wedding dress today and I'm so looking forward to the big event. I can't wait to reenact my shopping excursion for you. I think we're both going to get a big kick out of it."

"You found a dress?" Griffin didn't bother to hide his surprise.

"I did, but I had to try on three ugly dresses to appease Jerry before he'd let me settle on the one I actually liked. He still insists I need a tiara, but I plan to tackle that argument later."

"Oh, well, that sounds like a good idea." Griffin sounded distracted. "Listen, I called for a reason."

I was instantly alert. "What's wrong? You're not hurt, are you?"

"Why would you think I'm hurt?"

"Well ... it stormed."

Griffin's sigh was long and drawn out. "Aisling, you need to let that go. I know you believe you've got it all figured out, but I can't believe in magical storms. That's where I draw the line."

That made one of us. Still, I didn't want to engage in an argument over the phone. I would save that delightful occurrence for when we were together. "I'm not asking you to believe in magical storms," I lied. "I'm fine if you think I'm a whackadoodle."

"I think you're all kinds of doodles." I could practically see Griffin smiling. "I'm calling to tell you that I'm probably going to miss dinner."

That threw me. "I ... oh ... okay. Why?" It wasn't that I blamed him for missing family dinner. There were times I wanted to miss it, too. He was usually fine with mandatory attendance, though, and I wanted to make sure nothing was wrong.

"I'm just really busy," Griffin replied. "I have a murder-suicide I'm working on. It's fairly straightforward, but I want to wrap everything tonight, which means working late."

"Murder-suicide?"

"Yeah, some guy lost his temper on I-94 while changing a flat during the storm and when his girlfriend rolled down the window to ask him what was taking so long he beat her to death with the tire iron. Then, when he realized what he'd done, he walked into oncoming traffic and killed himself. I'm surprised you haven't heard about it. It's been all over the news."

"I've been in a bridal shop," I reminded him, my mind busy. "That sounds awful."

"It is awful," Griffin agreed. "The guy who hit our murderer is extremely shaken up. We had to transport him to the hospital. I guess they sedated him because he wouldn't stop shaking. People tried talking to him, but he wouldn't listen.

"Even before we realized he'd killed his girlfriend and heard witness reports of him walking into traffic we told the guy behind the wheel it wasn't his fault because he probably couldn't see due to the fog," he continued. "I don't think this is something he's going to get over. He's taking it really hard."

My heart rolled. "It happened during the storm?"

Griffin's tone turned chilly. "Aisling, don't start."

"I'm not going to start." At least not with Griffin and not when he sounded so weary. My father and brothers were another story. "If you can stop by toward the end of dinner, I'll make sure Dad keeps something warm for you. Text me when you know what time you'll be heading home. I can bring leftovers back to the townhouse for you. I think it's prime rib night."

Griffin brightened considerably. "And people say you're not domestic."

"Ha, ha." I poked a finger into my right eye and gave it a good wiggle. I was starting to get a headache. "I think my mother is coming for dinner anyway, so you're probably not missing anything." I wanted to end the conversation on a light note. "I believe there was talk of flower selections yesterday, although I tried to tune it out."

"Have fun with the flower selections," Griffin said. "I'd like to be involved in the final decision on the flowers if that's okay."

I was surprised. "You would? I don't even want to be in on the decision and I'm the bride."

"I guess I'm turning into a groomzilla."

I laughed. "We should play a game where you get to be groomzilla. It might be fun."

"All our games are fun. I ... wait. Hold on." Griffin pulled away from the phone and said something to a man talking in the background. When he came back on he was all business. "I have to go. I'll text you when I know more. Enjoy dinner with your family."

"That sounds oddly like a threat."

Griffin chuckled. "I love you. I'll be in touch."

"Okay. Be safe."

MY MIND WAS STILL on Griffin's story when I let myself into Grimlock Manor. I heard at least two of my brothers – Redmond and Braden, I was almost positive – screwing around in the main parlor to my left. That was only one of the reasons I headed to the right.

I found Dad sitting in his office, his gaze intent on his computer screen. He obviously hadn't heard me enter because he didn't as much as lift his eyes.

I took a moment to study him. He was tall and strong ... and he spoiled me rotten, so he was one of my favorite people in the world. He was also a pragmatic thinker. That's why I wanted to float my storm theory to him in private.

"I can hear you breathing, Aisling." Dad remained focused on his work. "If you're thinking of hitting me up for something big, just be forewarned, I'm in the middle of our yearly budget and I'm in no mood to fund your extravagances."

"Since when do I ask you to fund my extravagances?" I groused, strolling into the room and heading toward the scepter hub in the back area. I shoved my silver stick of death into the opening and watched as the orb absorbed my collected souls. When the process finished, I shoved the scepter back in my pocket and turned to find my father staring at me.

Cormack Grimlock may be a soft touch when it comes to certain things, but he is shrewd. The look he graced me with now told me he realized I was about to broach a serious subject.

"What's on your mind, kid?" Dad leaned back in his chair and sipped his cognac. "You look as if you've had a long day. You only worked half of it, so I'm not sure why that would be."

I shuffled closer to his desk, opting to plant myself in one of the large wingback chairs across the way. I tucked my legs under me and got comfortable. "Something weird is going on. I think it might be something ... supernatural."

Dad didn't look especially impressed with my announcement. "Is this like when you told me that you were pretty sure aliens were invading your high school and it would probably be best if you didn't have to go any longer?"

"I still maintain that was a real thing," I shot back. "I could've had my brain sucked by aliens, and you didn't care."

"Yes, if I remember correctly, you believed Angelina was the first victim," Dad said dryly.

"I haven't been proven wrong on that."

"Yes."

"Speaking of Angelina, I saw her today," I said, briefly shifting course. "She looks rough. I don't think she's sleeping."

"I'm surprised you care. A year ago you would've thrown a party."

"Yeah, well, maybe I'm maturing." I didn't believe that, but there was a small chance Dad might. "Have you heard anything about her mother?"

Angelina's mother was reportedly very ill. Terminally so. How long she had left was cause for gossip and speculation in the neighborhood. I had no love for Carol Davenport – just as I had no love for Angelina – but I wasn't the sort of person who could exalt in someone's death. No, really.

"I haven't, but I'm not close with the woman so it's not as if I ask about her, even in social circles. Why?"

I shrugged. "I don't know. It doesn't matter." I turned serious. "As for what's bothering me, I honestly think something odd is going on and I need someone to talk to."

Dad arched an eyebrow. "And you think that someone should be me?"

"I think that you're one of those people who can easily sort through a problem and make me see my own idiocy. Granted, it's rare that I'm an idiot, but Griffin is convinced I'm turning this into some sort of ridiculous thing that it's not so I want your take on it."

Dad didn't bother to hide his surprise. "I think that might be one of the nicest compliments you've ever paid me, kid. Lay it on me."

That's exactly what I did. I very calmly, very rationally, told him everything I knew. I related the fight I'd witnessed. I explained about Griffin's rough two days at work. I even told him about Jerry's fight with Aidan. That was the only moment he reacted, and he didn't look happy.

"Wait, wait, wait." Dad held up a hand to silence me. "Jerry punched Aidan?"

I nodded. "Jerry says he remembers doing it but still can't figure out why he did it. He says it was as if he was overtaken by rage and had no choice but to lash out."

"And you think these things are related," Dad mused, rubbing his hand over his forehead. "You think the storm is somehow causing people to fight. That's what you're saying?"

His tone told me how he was going to rule. "You don't have to make fun of me. I get it. You think I'm crazy, too."

"I didn't say that," Dad countered. "I'm simply trying to wrap my head around all of this. It seems a bit ... far-fetched."

"I know, but it's too coincidental to ignore," I argued. "Everything odd that's been happening, every fight and out-of-character reaction has occurred during a storm. I think I'm onto something."

Dad sipped his drink, I'm sure to buy time, and stared at me long and hard. Finally he decided to speak. Unfortunately he adopted a tone I remembered well from childhood.

"Are you sure you're not letting your imagination run wild?"

He sounded so reasonable that most people would've fallen for his act. I wasn't most people. "I don't believe so. I feel there's something odd going on with the storms and I'm determined to find out what that is."

"And how will you do that?"

That was an interesting question. "I'm going to ... look in books and stuff."

Dad chuckled. "So you're going with the scientific approach?"

"Oh, don't laugh at me." I made a face. "I'm serious about this. Given the fact that I was the only one convinced zombies were attacking a few weeks ago – and I turned out to be right – I'd think you'd give me more leeway on this. Instead you're calling me a liar and laughing at me."

"I've done neither of those things," Dad shot back, waving a finger. "I'm simply trying to understand why you feel the way that you do."

"You sound like the world's worst shrink."

"And you sound like an eight-year-old with a fantastic imagination," Dad said, causing me to scowl. When he realized I was about to hop out of my chair and storm out of the room, Dad adjusted his tone. "Aisling, I believe you want a supernatural explanation to this partic- ular event because of Jerry's involvement. I think that's a natural reaction."

"Jerry isn't the violent sort," I supplied. "He doesn't hit people. Heck, he was the one constantly telling me to stop picking fights with Angelina in high school. That's not how he is."

"I happen to agree with you."

"You do?"

Dad nodded without hesitation. "I've never seen Jerry act in such a manner, which could be exactly why he was due. When you were chil- dren, Jerry was the one standing at the sidelines watching the rest of you wrestle and smack each other around. I often wondered why he didn't jump in. In fact, I asked him one day. Do you know what he told me?"

I shook my head. "No, but it probably had something to do with getting his clothes dirty or risking a scab on his face. He mentioned something like that to me at a certain point. He has a reoccurring nightmare about getting a scab on his face that gets infected and leaves him looking like a circus freak."

Dad chuckled, genuinely amused. "No. He said that he didn't see the point of solving problems with fists rather than words. I remember being surprised by his answer because it was rather profound for a child."

"He probably saw it on *Oprah*."

"Probably." Dad's lips curved. "Just because Jerry didn't engage in shenanigans when he was younger doesn't mean he didn't have the occasional inclination. I think that inclination finally caught up with him."

"And you think that's it?"

Dad nodded. "I do."

I tilted my head to the side, considering. "Well, I don't. I think we have evil storms and we should research them. I don't care what you say, Jerry is convinced something bad happened in his brain. He doesn't understand why he flipped out."

"Great." Dad was back to rubbing his forehead. "Are you going to conduct your research here or at the library?"

"I haven't decided yet." I shifted on the chair. "I know you think I'm being ridiculous, but I'm not. There's something going on. It started out of nowhere. I don't think we can wait for it to end on its own. We don't have that luxury."

"And what do you suggest we do?" Dad challenged. "Are you going to have an anti-rain dance on the back lawn?"

"You jest, but I just might do that. I haven't ruled out anything yet."

"I can tell it's going to be a lovely couple of days," Dad muttered, shifting his eyes to the open doorway at the sound of voices in the hallway. "Your brothers are coming. I suggest you keep your theory to yourself for the time being. We don't want to add to this madness by getting them involved."

I wasn't sure I agreed with that, but for the time being I could get behind the sentiment. "Fine. If you make fun of me, though, all bets are off."

"I would expect nothing less." Dad plastered a smile on his face as Cillian and Braden walked through the door. The smile slipped when he realized Mom trailed behind them, her arm linked through Redmond's as they shared an animated conversation.

"Lily," Dad said quietly, forcing a welcoming smile. "I didn't realize you were coming for dinner tonight."

"Oh, I thought Aisling would've told you." Mom's face remained placid. "I'm here to talk about flower selections for the wedding. Jerry invited me, although Aisling was there and didn't object."

Dad shifted a pointed look in my direction. "Really?"

"Hey, don't give me grief," I warned. "I've had a busy couple of days. Between fighting with Angelina and picking a wedding dress I can only keep so many details in my brain at any one time."

"You found a wedding dress?" Mom was clearly surprised. "I thought that would take you months."

"We plan to get married in June, so there's no way it could've taken me months."

"You're getting married in June?" Mom didn't look happy with the development. She turned her cold eyes to Dad. "Did you know about this, Cormack?"

"Yes." Dad pursed his lips as he regarded Mom. "I don't see what the big deal is. June is a fine month for a wedding."

"Yes, but it's so soon."

I knew what she was really saying. If Griffin and I married in June that meant she was running out of time to change my mind about marrying him. She hadn't given up, no matter how she pretended otherwise, and I could practically see the gears in her mind turning.

"It's not soon enough for me," Braden announced. "I'm sick of talking about it. I want it to be over."

"Uh-huh." Mom's expression was distant. Then, as if she sensed me watching her, she shook her head and offered up a bright smile. I knew it was fake, but couldn't help but marvel at the faux emotion she managed to muster. "Well, the wedding is right around the corner. That means we have a lot of decisions to make. I suggest we start with the flowers."

"I'm fine with that." I remained calm despite my irritation. "We need Jerry first. I promised I wouldn't make any decisions without him."

"Of course we need Jerry." Mom was matter-of-fact. "I saw him in the front with Aidan when I came in. They looked to be deep in conversation, but I'm sure whatever it is won't take long."

I cocked my head, intrigued. "They're out front?"

Mom nodded.

I hopped to my feet. "I'll be right back."

"Aisling, where are you going?" Dad called after me.

"I just want to check on them," I lied.

"You want to eavesdrop," Dad countered.

"You say that like it's a bad thing."

"Oh, geez," Dad muttered. "I would've been better off hoarding cats rather than kids."

"It's too late now."

"I'm well aware. Hey! Leave your brother and Jerry alone. It's none of your business what they're talking about."

That's not exactly how I saw it.

"Come back here, you busybody!"

Dad made a grab for my shoulder as he followed me through the house, but I easily evaded him, increasing my pace until I reached the front foyer. I stopped next to the window on the right side of the door and peered out, my eyes landing on Aidan and Jerry almost immediately.

Mom was right. They looked to be deep in conversation.

"What's going on?" Redmond asked, curiosity getting the better of him as he watched Dad attempt to force me away from the window. "What are we missing out on?"

"Nothing," Dad answered automatically.

"Aidan and Jerry had a fight last night," I answered, slapping at Dad's hands. "I want to make sure they're playing nice."

"What did they fight about?" Braden asked. "They hardly ever fight. They're almost annoyingly in love."

"They just had a misunderstanding," I lied, glaring at Dad as he tried to tug on the back of my shirt. "Don't make me wrestle you to the floor," I warned.

Braden, Cillian and Redmond laughed at the threat.

"Yes, I'm terrified you'll embarrass me and do just that," Dad drawled. "I live in fear of it every day of my life. Get away from that window." Dad was firm as he grabbed my arm and gave a good tug. "That's Aidan's business. If he wants us to talk about it, he'll share the story with us when he's ready."

Cillian narrowed his eyes as he glanced between Dad and me. He was the shrewdest of my brothers – at least when it came to books and reading people – and he clearly understood something else was going on. "Did something happen?"

"What could've possibly happened?" Mom challenged. "Aidan and Jerry are perfect for each other. I'm sure it was just a misunderstanding."

"Oh, it was more than a misunderstanding," I said, doing my level best to stomp on Dad's instep. He steadfastly avoided my attempts, which further infuriated me. "They had a fight while under the influence of the magic thunderstorms."

Dad stilled, his grip on my shirt tightening. "Why did you have to say that?"

I shrugged. "It just slipped out."

"We had a talk about this not five minutes ago," Dad snapped. "We agreed you were going to keep your hypothesis to yourself."

"Wait ... what hypothesis?" Cillian challenged. "I think we're out of the loop here."

"You're not missing anything," Dad argued. "In fact, I wish I weren't in the loop, because the loop is full of a bunch of ridiculous nonsense."

"It's not nonsense. It's true." I pushed against Dad's chest as hard as I could, but couldn't dislodge him. "The storms are making people angry. It's like there are Hulk particles in the raindrops or something."

"What makes you say that?" Mom asked, her gaze pointed.

"That's your question?" Braden deadpanned. "The first thing that popped into my head was asking when Aisling stopped taking her meds."

"That's not funny, Braden," Dad snapped. "Your sister is not impaired. She's simply ... spirited."

"I'm usually the first one to stand up for Aisling, but I think, at least this time, she might be crazy, too," Redmond noted. "I mean ... I love her and everything, so if she really is going to turn into one of those chicks who sits in a corner and tries to eat her own nose I'll take care of her and all. I simply need to know what I'm up against."

"Ha, ha." I used my free hand to cuff Redmond while diligently working to shove Dad away with the other. "I'm not crazy. I know what I'm talking about. The storms are evil and they make evil things happen. I'm not making it up."

"I don't think anyone believes you're making it up, Ais," Cillian offered, adopting a calm and even tone that set my teeth on edge. "That's not the way you do things, and we know you're not a liar."

"Wait a second." Braden waved his hand to interrupt the conversation. "Since when isn't she a liar? This is the girl who told Dad that she ticked off a gang of ghosts and they scratched his Mustang. Do you remember that, Dad?"

"Of course I do," Dad gritted out. "I had to drop five-thousand dollars on a security system for the garage because of it."

"I still maintain that ghosts were responsible," I snapped. "I haven't been proven wrong on that."

"You were on camera bringing the car back in the middle of the night," Braden reminded me. "Dad found a new ding the very next day."

I stopped grappling with Dad long enough to glare at Braden. "You know an awful lot about what happened to a car that was retired from the fleet a decade ago, Braden. Perhaps you were the one controlling the ghosts to mess with me."

"Or maybe he was stealing the car, too, and simply wanted you to be the one blamed," Redmond supplied.

The look Braden scorched Redmond with was right out of a bad Lifetime movie about brothers turning on one another.

"I can't believe you'd narc on me like that," Braden muttered.

"Hey, you were going after Aisling," Redmond pointed out. "She has enough strikes against her, what with believing in evil storms and all. She needs allies."

"I don't need allies." I tried a quick move to escape Dad's grip, but he was prepared for it and all I managed to do was mess up my hair. "I know I'm right about the storms. We've had two days full of them, and the city is coming apart under the weight of the violence."

"What city?" Cillian asked. "If you're talking about Detroit, the city has been crumbling under the weight of violence since long before we were born."

"Your brother has a point," Dad said. "Aisling, if you bite my fingers I'll lock you in the basement overnight! What was I saying again? Oh, right. Cillian makes sense. Detroit is always violent. You have no proof to back up your claims about these evil storms."

"I hate to gang up on you with everyone else, but ... ." Mom held up her hands as if to say, "You're a loon and you know it."

"I don't care what any of you say." I tried one final move to escape Dad ... and almost fell on my face in the process. Dad caught me by the back of my shirt before I could topple over and hit the ceramic tile. "I know what's going on, and you can't convince me differently."

"And this has something to do with why you're so desperate to spy on Aidan and Jerry?" Redmond queried.

"You mind your own business, too," Dad ordered. "Aidan and Jerry are allowed to have some privacy no matter what the other members of this family think. What they're doing outside – or not doing, for that matter – is completely up to them."

"I can't quite keep up with the conversation," Braden admitted. "Are we fighting about privacy issues or Aisling's mental health problems? I can get behind either one, but I need to know where to focus my energy."

"We're not talking about either of them." Dad lost his grip just as the front door opened to allow Aidan and Jerry entrance. I was fighting his efforts, so I pitched forward and landed on my knees in front of them.

"What's going on?" Aidan asked, grabbing me under the armpits to help me stand. "Why are you guys all out here?"

"We were coming to get you," Dad said, quickly smoothing his dark hair as he flashed a broad smile. "We're about to head in for drinks. We didn't want you to miss them."

"Okay." Aidan didn't look convinced as he snagged my gaze. "What were you doing?"

"Dad and I were having a difference of opinion of sorts." I sniffed as I rubbed my sore knees. "I'm pretty sure I won."

"Aisling." Dad's voice was low and full of warning.

"It's nothing serious," I lied, ignoring the head bob Dad gave to show he agreed with my tack. "I could definitely use a drink."

"We could all use drinks," Redmond said. "I'll lead the way ... and pour. How does everyone feel about rum runners?"

IT SEEMED AIDAN AND Jerry made up outside because they were happy and smiling throughout dinner, their eyes constantly trained on one another as they lent only half an ear to the conversations going on around them.

That was probably for the best ... although I was dying for details. I was resigned to waiting for private time with my best friend to hear them.

Griffin appeared before we finished dessert, and one of the servers immediately slid a plate heaping with food in front of him. Griffin thanked her profusely before digging in. He ate with enough gusto to make me believe he'd skipped lunch and was running on fumes.

"Take a breath, son," Dad chided, watching him with equal fascination. "The food isn't going anywhere."

Griffin sipped his wine before responding. "Sorry. I'm starving. Once Aisling mentioned it was prime rib night that's all I could think about."

"You finished your case?" I asked.

Griffin nodded. "As much as can be done. We need to talk to the family tomorrow – they were wrecked today – and make sure we didn't miss anything. It seems open and shut."

"This is this thing I heard on the news, right?" Mom inquired. "The man who killed his girlfriend and then walked into traffic to kill himself?"

"I heard about that," Redmond said. "I didn't realize that was your case."

"I wish it weren't," Griffin explained. "We're overloaded with cases the past few days and down a man so it's just a lot to deal with. I'm sure it will work itself out." Griffin offered up a wan smile. "So what have you guys been doing while waiting for me?"

"Well, Dad and Aisling had a wrestling match because she was trying to eavesdrop on Aidan and Jerry," Braden answered. "Then she told us about some crazy theory she has about evil storms. We're thinking about having her committed. I think that about covers it."

I glared holes in the side of his head. "You just couldn't let it go, could you?"

Braden ignored my irritation. "You wouldn't mind if we locked her up, would you, Griffin?"

"As a matter of fact, I would." Griffin slid me an unreadable look. "You brought up the storms to your family?"

"You knew what she was thinking about the storms?" Dad asked. "How could you let her leave the house when she believes stuff like that?"

Griffin shrugged. "She was right about the zombies, but we all thought she was crazy then."

"Yes, but this is entirely different," Dad sputtered. "Storms are not evil."

"And zombies weren't real until they came after us," Griffin pointed out. "I'm not going to dissuade her from thinking outside the box. She's allowed to believe what she wants to believe."

"But this is ludicrous," Dad persisted, refusing to back down. "Storms don't cause people to go crazy."

Intrigued, Aidan leaned forward. He missed most of the conversation in the foyer and was unaware of my storm rant. "You think the storms are making people act out of sorts?" He risked a quick look at Jerry before focusing on me. "Tell me why."

I licked my lips as I debated how best to respond. "Well ... ." Ultimately I launched into the whole tale a second time, conveniently leaving out Aidan and Jerry's part in the story while carefully watching those sitting around the table for reactions. When I was done, Aidan appeared thoughtful but the rest of my brothers couldn't stop laughing.

"That is the stupidest thing I've ever heard," Braden stuttered. "I mean ... how can you possibly believe that?"

I folded my arms over my chest. "I think it makes sense."

"Aisling, I know that you've always had a fertile imagination, but that's kind of going overboard." Cillian adopted a gentle but pragmatic tone. "Isn't it possible that nerves were simply frayed because of the storm and people exploded?"

"Not like that. Irritation doesn't make non-violent people suddenly violent."

"You don't know Griffin's co-worker," Dad pointed out. "He might be violent and simply good at hiding it."

"I don't believe that's true," Griffin hedged. "Lani, his wife, is adamant that nothing of the sort has ever happened, and I believe her. The doctor did note an increase of epinephrine in his system. They're looking for causes."

"Does that mean you believe the evil storm idea?" Dad asked pointedly.

"I'm not sure what I believe. I know that I believe in Aisling, and I'm not going to make fun of her because she voiced an idea. That doesn't seem fair."

"But she thinks storms are evil," Braden pressed. "Storms aren't evil. They're just wet ... and sometimes cold."

"Well, with reasoning like that, I can't believe I ever thought otherwise," I drawled. "I've seen the light. Braden is right and I'm clearly a moron."

"Well, at least you admit it," Braden supplied.

"Knock it off, you two," Mom interjected. "Now isn't the time to bicker. I don't believe there's good reason to believe the storm theory either, but Aisling clearly isn't crazy. Stop treating her as if she is."

I considered thanking my mother for standing up for me, but thought better of it. She hadn't put much effort into the argument, so I didn't need to go out of my way for a thank-you.

"Aisling is leaving something out of her story," Jerry volunteered, taking everyone by surprise when he inserted himself into the conversation. "One other thing happened, and that's why she's so vehement about it."

"You don't have to," Aidan said, keeping his voice low. "We talked about it. It's fine."

"It's not fine," Jerry countered, meeting my gaze. "It's okay, Bug. They can know."

"Is this why Aisling was eavesdropping in the first place?" Cillian asked.

Jerry nodded. "I turned a bit violent myself last night." He told the story, pausing for the appropriate gasps, and when he was done he looked mortified. "I've never been more disappointed in myself. I still don't know how it happened."

"Did you know this?" Cillian asked Dad.

Dad nodded. "Aisling told me right before she decided to eavesdrop. I thought it would be prudent to keep it quiet, at least for the time being."

"Well, as much as I think Jerry acted out of sorts, I don't think the storm made him do it," Braden argued. "It was a fluke thing. We all know Jerry isn't like that."

"I agree it was a fluke," Aidan said. "But I'm not sure I'm willing to simply toss out Aisling's storm theory. It seems a lot of weird things are going on."

"Oh, not you, too." Dad pinched the bridge of his nose. "I think you're searching for answers that might not exist. Storms aren't evil. I can guarantee it."

"How?" I challenged. "How can you be absolutely certain that storms aren't evil? After everything we've seen the past year – including a mother who came back from the dead and eats people to stay alive – how can you be so sure I'm not right about the storms?"

"Thanks for that, Aisling," Mom growled.

I ignored her. "I'm not saying I'm right. You're saying I'm wrong without any research at all. I don't think that's fair."

Dad heaved out a sigh, clearly resigned. "Fine." He held up his hands in defeat. "How do you intend to prove this notion beyond a shadow of a doubt?"

I shrugged. "I don't know. We have books and stuff."

"And you're going to search all the books looking for mention of evil storms?"

"Maybe. I'm not going to do nothing, though. I will do something … I just haven't decided what."

"If that's your position on the matter, then I'll back you up." Dad didn't look thrilled at the prospect. "If you want to research it, then do it. I don't want to hear another thing about evil storms until you have proof. Do you understand?"

I narrowed my eyes. "Fine. You won't hear a word out of me until I prove that I'm right and you're wrong."

"Oh, if only she'd stopped after, 'You won't hear a word out of me,'" Braden lamented.

"Shut up and eat your cake, Braden," Dad ordered. "I've had enough of your mouth for one night."

"Thanks, Dad," I offered.

"That goes double for you, Aisling. It's time for a quiet dessert. That's my only wish for the rest of the night."

We lapsed into silence for a moment, and then my siblings and I spoke at the exact same time, mimicking the father we remembered from our childhood road trips.

"Not one more word," we growled in unison.

Dad made a clucking sound with his tongue. "Yes. I definitely would've been better off with cats."

✻ 9 ✻

NINE

My brothers refused to stop teasing me even after my father threatened to remove them from his will. In an effort to get away from them, I planted myself in the second-floor library with Jerry and Aidan. In addition to refuge (my brothers – other than Cillian – never met a book they wanted to read unless it had photographs of naked people), I also wanted to check in with them to make sure they were okay.

"You look beat," Aidan said, patting the open spot at his side as he relaxed on one of the couches. "Join us. We've taken to calling ourselves the weary bunch."

"I should get Griffin to make our foursome complete," I grumbled. "I'm not sure where he went. Last time I saw him he was shoveling in cake, but then he disappeared."

"I'm sure he's around," Aidan said, resting his hand on Jerry's knee as he gave me a long look. "Do you really believe what you're saying about the storms?"

I nodded without hesitation. If Aidan wanted to join in the teasing it would hardly be the worst thing that ever happened to me. "Yes. I think there are way too many coincidences piling up in a short amount of time. The only thing tying all the outbursts together is the fact that they happened during the storms."

"Let's say I believe you – and I'm not sure I do, so don't get ahead of yourself – but why would it only affect some people?"

"What do you mean?"

"It didn't affect me," Aidan pointed out. "Only Jerry was affected."

"Oh." That actually hadn't occurred to me. "I don't know. Maybe we're immune because we're reapers."

"That seems a bit of a reach."

"I guess it does." I couldn't help being disappointed. "It still feels off to me, Aidan."

"Well, I'm taking your warning to heart. We're going to do our best to avoid storms as much as possible for the foreseeable future," Aidan volunteered. "But I still don't think I believe your evil storm theory."

"The rest of the non-believers are cackling on the first floor," I noted. "You can join them." I moved to slide off the couch, but Aidan stopped me. "What?"

"I don't think you're crazy." Aidan's gaze was even and clear. "You do tend to let your imagination run wild, though. Maybe that's all this is."

"Maybe," I conceded, "but I don't think so."

"I'm with Bug on this," Jerry announced. "I would rather believe in an evil storm than an evil me."

"You're not evil," Aidan countered. "You just had a bad night. We've talked it out. It's over and done with."

"I still don't like it." Jerry sounded petulant. "I like Bug's theory better. I'm all in with you on this." He held out his knuckles so I could bump them. "We'll stick together like we always do. It doesn't matter who makes fun of us."

"I'm totally with you." As if on cue, the sky through the window illuminated with a flash of lightning. It was quickly followed by a rumble of thunder. "Another storm."

Aidan glanced over his shoulder and followed my gaze. "What are you going to do?"

I shrugged. "There's nothing I really can do. For now I'm going to find Griffin. We're not leaving until the storm is over. I want to make sure he doesn't wander outside."

"I'm actually thinking we're going to stay here tonight," Aidan admitted. "Just to be on the safe side, I mean."

"But you don't believe in evil storms," I teased.

"Why tempt fate?"

He had a point.

I WAS HALFWAY DOWN the hallway and almost to the stairs when I caught sight of something through the open doorway that led to my old bedroom. I paused long enough to push open the door and widened my eyes when I realized what I thought was a pile of unfolded laundry was actually a sleeping Griffin.

He lay on his back, his eyes closed, and his breathing was deep and even. He was completely out of it.

"I guess he was more tired than we realized," Dad whispered, appearing in the hallway behind me. "I half thought the two of you left because I hadn't seen you in a bit. It looks like he needed some rest."

I nodded, my shoulders jolting at another thunder boom. "I'm going to let him sleep. We'll stay here tonight."

Dad cocked his head. "Because you don't want him going out in the storm?"

It seemed a simple question, but I knew it was loaded. "Because I don't want to risk it. It's pretty simple."

"You're welcome to stay here whenever you want. You know that."

I did know that. "I know you think I'm crazy ... ."

"I never used that word and I don't think it," Dad argued. "I simply believe you're misguided on this particular subject."

"Aidan brought up a good point. He was outside during the storm with Jerry. He didn't get angry and throw a punch. It was Jerry. That kind of blows a hole in my theory."

Dad took pity on me and argued my side even though he didn't agree with it. "Unless reapers are somehow immune."

I chuckled. "That's what I said."

"Great minds ... ."

"I don't know what to believe, but I don't think I'm quite ready to give up the idea just yet," I said. "I'm going to research it further. If I don't find what I'm looking for, then I'll let it go."

"That sounds like a solid plan to me." Dad patted my shoulder. "I'll leave you to take care of Griffin. The one thing I think I have going for me tonight is that he's clearly too tired to play the wandering hands game."

"Oh, he can play that in his sleep." It took everything I had not to crack a smile and ruin the moment. "He's gifted."

"Don't make things worse, Aisling."

"I'll try to remember that for next time."

I COULDN'T SLEEP.

Even though I thought I was exhausted and I climbed into bed early with Griffin, after twenty minutes of tossing and turning I knew it wasn't going to happen. I left him to his deep slumber. He very obviously needed his rest.

I paused in the hallway to listen for sounds in the house, but all was silent. That didn't necessarily mean anything. The game room was soundproofed, and my brothers could've congregated there to entertain themselves for the rest of the night. Of course, they also could've headed to a bar or holed up in their rooms.

With little else to do, I headed to the library. I thought I might be able to get a head start on my storm research if nothing else. I looked out the hallway window as I walked. The rain had diminished, but the storm continued, regular lightning flashes casting an eerie glow in the hallway. If my brothers were out in this, I hoped they wouldn't find too much trouble.

I pulled up short when I entered the library, surprised to find Cillian sitting on the floor with a book perched on his lap and a glass of what looked to be brandy on the floor next to him.

"What are you doing here?"

Cillian shifted his eyes to me and smiled. "A bit of light reading."

"On what?"

"Magical storms."

I stilled. "Seriously?"

Cillian shrugged and patted the empty spot next to him. "I figured it was worth a shot. I'm not doing anything else."

"No Maya tonight?" I asked, grabbing the blanket from the back of the couch before sitting. I situated it over my lap before focusing on Cillian's book. It looked to be big, boring and almost completely lacking in photographs – my absolute least favorite type of book.

"Maya had to stay at the hospital," Cillian said, flipping a page. In addition to being Cillian's very-serious girlfriend, Maya was Griffin's sister. The relationship dynamics took a bit for everyone to get used to at the onset, but we'd settled in quite nicely ever since. I had a feeling Griffin would've had more of a problem if Redmond or Braden were romancing his sister. Because it was Cillian, and he was the sweetest Grimlock in the land, Griffin didn't put up much of a defense.

"Is that normal?"

"Her staying at the hospital for an extra shift?" Cillian shrugged. "She's dedicated and wants to help others. She sounded frazzled when she called and didn't have much time, but something she said stuck with me."

"And what's that?"

"That things were slow until the storm started."

I pursed my lips. "You're starting to think I'm right, aren't you?"

"I don't know," Cillian cautioned. "I think it's fair to say that I'm not entirely convinced you're wrong and leave it at that for now."

"I would rather be right."

Cillian grinned as he tucked a strand of his shoulder-length black hair behind his ear. "Oh, I know that very well. I'm trying to see if I can find anything that leads me to believe a poisoned storm is even possible."

"We've seen odd things before," I pointed out.

"We have."

"You just don't think it's possible for something this odd, this surreal?"

"I didn't say that, Ais." Cillian flipped another page, his eyes busy as they scanned the thick wall of text. "I don't know what to think.

Part of me is certain that something really odd is going on. Your idea holds enough weight for me that I'm willing to check it out."

That would have to be enough. I knew Cillian couldn't give more. "What did Maya say about the people coming into the hospital?" I opted to change the subject. "Were they involved in a lot of fights?"

"Like I said, she didn't have much time to talk, but she did say that if she didn't know better she'd have thought someone overloaded the water system with too much testosterone."

Hmm. "Because only men were coming in?"

Cillian tore his gaze from the page and looked at me. "She didn't really say, but that's what I figured. Why? What are you thinking?"

"I don't know." I rubbed the back of my neck as I flexed my ankles and stared at a pair of feet desperately in need of a pedicure. "Most everything I've heard about – the fights I mean – has involved men. The lone exception is that Lani woman."

"She was the one hit."

"Yeah, but Griffin said she slapped Peter across the face first. He made it sound as if it was out of character for her. In fact, he made it sound as if they were so flabbergasted by what she did they didn't see what Peter was about to do until it was too late to stop it."

"So you think Lani was affected, too," Cillian mused. "That would blow our theory that only men are affected."

"I don't know that I ever had that theory. It seems to me we might only be hearing about men because they're stronger and can do more damage. A lot of the female fights might involve hair pulling and biting, but nothing else."

"So basically you're saying all the women are turning into you and Angelina, huh?" Cillian's eyes twinkled.

"That's a terrifying thought. About Angelina, I mean. Not me. People should consider themselves lucky to act like me."

"I believe that's the word making it around the street."

We lapsed into amiable silence and Cillian returned to his book while I snagged another about magical weather anomalies off a nearby shelf. I was just about to lose myself in the text when Cillian spoke again.

"I'm going to ask Maya to marry me."

The statement knocked me for a loop. I almost fell over I was so surprised. "Seriously?"

Cillian nodded, keeping his face impassive as he stared at the book rather than me. "I'm waiting until after your wedding. I don't want to steal your thunder."

That sounded as if it should almost be insulting. "I hardly think you'd be stealing my thunder." I said the words before I thought better of them, but even after I spent more than a few seconds considering them I was fine with the statement. "Ask her whenever you want. Don't let me be your guiding force."

"I want to wait." Cillian kept his voice low. "I need to find a ring first. I need to do something else, too, and that might take more time."

That sounded almost ominous. "What else do you need to do? You're not planning to do something weird like learning how to skydive so you can have a unique proposal? That's an accident waiting to happen."

Cillian barked out a laugh. "Not that." He flicked my ear as he caught his breath. "You're freaking hilarious when you want to be. You know that, right?"

"I am a joy to be around," I agreed.

"That's not exactly what I said."

"That's what I heard."

"I'm almost sorry we got off on this tangent," Cillian lamented. "What was I saying again?"

"You were explaining that you have something to do before you can propose," I supplied. "I turned the conversation weird, and now we're back at the start. What do you have to do before you can propose?"

"Move out of this house."

I wasn't expecting such a simple answer. "Oh." I didn't know what to make of his statement. I was the first and only Grimlock child to even want to leave the relative safety and comfort of Grimlock Manor until Aidan decided to move in with Jerry a few months ago. Before then, all four of my brothers were perfectly fine living with Dad, even though some of them had not only hit the age of thirty but cruised past it. "Do you think Dad will put up a fight if Maya moves in or something?"

Cillian let loose with a dry laugh. "No, but I think that moving your new wife in with your father and brothers is probably a no-no. I'm going to guess that Maya wants a home of her own."

"I don't know. Dad likes her. He might hand over a wing."

"He probably would," Cillian conceded. "I don't think that's what she needs, though. The truth is, I've been considering moving out for more than a year. I've always talked myself out of it because Dad seemed to want us to stay, but I honestly think it's time to go."

"Dad doesn't have a problem with you staying here," I said. "He made all those jokes about how he couldn't wait until we moved out when we were kids, but after Mom died ... ." I broke off, what I left unsaid hanging like an impenetrable curtain of fog.

"I think that's one of the reasons we stayed," Cillian admitted. "Sure, it was nice to have the cooks and maids around. It was nice not to have to do our own laundry or clean. Part of it was on us for being lazy. The other part, that was entirely Dad's doing. He didn't want us to leave."

"I can believe that. He completely melted down when I moved out. Even though I was moving in with Jerry he had a fit."

"He would've kept you forever," Cillian agreed. "He still has trouble with the fact that you're living with your boyfriend and getting married. He's handling it much better than I thought he would, of course, but every once in a while I catch him looking misty-eyed and sad when he's watching you."

That was news to me. "Really?"

Cillian nodded. "You're the only girl and you're the baby. What's really funny is that we all accuse you of being the most immature, yet the three of us – the three oldest – have yet to leave the nest."

I'd never really considered that. "So you're going to find a place to live and then propose?"

Cillian nodded. "Yeah. I think that's probably the mature way to handle things."

"And lord knows we Grimlocks are always mature," I teased, resting my head on his shoulder as I opened my book. "I'm happy for you."

"I'm happy for you, too, Ais." Cillian pressed a quick kiss to my forehead before turning back to his work. "This evil storm stuff is probably crazy, though. I'm just warning you that we most likely won't come up with anything."

"In this particular case, I'm fine being wrong."

"Really?" Cillian's voice was laced with doubt.

"No, I'd much rather be right."

"That's what I thought."

10

TEN

I'm not sure when I fell asleep. Cillian's presence always calmed me, but I was intent on research. And yet somehow I drifted off. When I woke, I found I was half propped against the couch, my head still resting on Cillian's shoulder. He snored lightly as he dozed.

I rolled my neck to assuage the stiffness and when I turned I found Griffin sitting in the chair across from us. He was staring.

"Hey." My voice was a bit raspy so I cleared my throat, making sure to keep my tone low so as not to wake Cillian. "Um ... what time is it?"

"Early." Griffin's expression was hard to read. "You know, most men would be annoyed to find their fiancée sleeping with another man."

I'm always slow in the morning, so it took me a moment to realize what he was insinuating. "What?" I slid my eyes to Cillian. "He's my brother. Don't get gross."

Griffin cracked a smile. He enjoyed messing with me when the opportunity arose. "I didn't know what to think when I woke up in your bed. I was especially confused when I realized I was alone."

"I'm sorry about that." I meant it. "I didn't mean to get so distracted." I dragged a hand through my hair as I shifted, my back protesting the movement. "Ow."

"What's wrong?" Griffin furrowed his brow as he got up and moved to crouch next to me. "Are you in pain?"

I nodded. "I've grown too old to sleep on the floor. When did that happen?"

Griffin chuckled as he sat next to me and dug his fingers into my lower back. "Let me see if I can loosen you up."

"You always know the way to my heart."

Griffin pressed a quick kiss to my forehead before focusing on my back. "What are you doing in here with Cillian?"

I thought about what Cillian told me, about his plans to propose and how he intended to move out. I knew that was a secret even though Cillian didn't admonish me not to spread the word. In this house, gossip would fly fast and furious, and Maya would know about Cillian's plans before he could put anything in place. That wasn't fair to either of them.

That meant I had to keep things to myself, which I wasn't especially comfortable with. I have a big mouth and bad impulse control. I could potentially ruin everything for Cillian and Maya. Crap! Why did he have to tell me? Keeping my mouth shut for weeks – probably months – wasn't in my wheelhouse and we both knew it. I blame him.

Wait ... what were Griffin and I talking about?

"Were you researching something?" Griffin asked, inclining his chin toward the book on the floor.

"Oh, yeah." Now I remembered. "We were trying to look up magical storms to see if we could find anything."

"And how did that go?"

That was a good question. "I don't know." I rubbed my cheek. "I fell asleep."

"That sounds about right." Griffin grinned as he watched me grab the book. "You didn't find anything, so does that mean you're going to let it go?"

"Who says we didn't find anything?" Cillian asked, stirring. He rubbed his eyes as he sucked in a breath to wake himself. "I'm the king of research. I always find something."

"Being the king of research isn't nearly as much fun as being the queen of the universe," I pointed out.

Cillian was grouchy in the mornings, too, so he merely rolled his eyes as he grabbed the book from my lap. "Don't lose my place."

"Did you really find something?"

Cillian nodded. "I did, but you were asleep. I didn't want to wake you. I told myself I was simply going to rest my eyes, but I'm pretty sure that was about six hours ago." He looked to the clock on the wall for confirmation. "Yup. I spent the night on the floor with my sister. That shouldn't result in any teasing from the rest of our pack."

"Ignore them. That's what I do." I tapped the book for emphasis, groaning when Griffin's fingers found a particularly tender spot on my back. "Right there. Oh, baby." I wiggled my hips. "Don't stop doing that."

Cillian let loose a disgusted sigh. "This is so not how I planned to spend my morning." He dragged a hand through his hair. "Stop making those noises, Aisling. They make me uncomfortable."

"That's because you're a big baby," I shot back. It took everything I had not to purr when Griffin found a second spot. "What did you find, Cillian?"

"Oh, right." Cillian flipped back a page and tapped on an article. "I found this. It mentions magic storms being used by mages and warlocks in the 1800s. The text treats the subject as if it's common."

"What does that mean?" Griffin asked, his fingers busy as I shifted so I could lean closer to him. "Do you think Aisling is right about the storms?"

"Let's just say that I'm not as keen to completely disregard the possibility as I was," Cillian said. "I'm still trying to track a few things down, but I want to scan this symbol in and see if I can find some information on it."

"What symbol?" I asked.

Cillian gestured toward the bottom corner of the page. "This one. There're very few illustrations in this book, so I figure this one must be important. It's in the section about magic storms."

My heart skipped a beat when I saw the symbol. I narrowed my eyes and leaned closer. "Huh." That was the only reaction I could muster.

"Do you recognize that?" Cillian asked.

I nodded. "I've seen it before."

"Do you remember where?" Griffin prodded.

"I do. It was the day before yesterday. I was at Harry Turner's house."

"Who is Harry Turner?" Cillian asked. "Is that name supposed to mean something to me?"

"He was the chief of the Royal Oak Police Department," Griffin supplied, his eyes moving to my face. "Aisling absorbed him the day before yesterday. Why would you have seen that symbol at his house, baby?"

"He had a bunch of metaphysical stuff there," I supplied. "He had these disc things." I held up my hands to indicate the size. "They had designs on them. Most of them were glass. I thought they were more decorations than anything else, but one was made of silver and stood out."

"And that disc had this symbol on it?" Cillian pressed.

I nodded. "I remember because Harry yelled at me to put it down."

"Do you think it's still in his house?"

I shrugged. "I guess it would have to be. I kind of lost track of it when Harry distracted me. It's probably there."

"So let me get this straight, Ais." Cillian leaned forward and pinned me with a harsh look. "You saw this symbol on a weird silver disc, and two minutes later we started having violent storms. Is that what you're telling me?"

Oh, well, when he put it like that. "You'd better not be blaming me."

"I'm not blaming you, but that's a hell of a coincidence."

He was right. "You don't think I could have triggered it, do you?"

Cillian opened his mouth to answer and then snapped it shut. I wasn't thrilled with his reaction.

"You do." I tilted my head and scratched the back of my neck. "You think I did this."

"He's not saying that," Griffin said hurriedly before lowering his voice and focusing on Cillian. "You'd better not say that to her," he warned. "She's not to blame for this."

"I'm not saying she's to blame," Cillian said cautiously. "I don't know what to make of the situation. There's no way she could've set off something like this without a magical intervention. At least, I can't think of any way. I don't blame her ... so chill out."

Griffin was mollified, but only marginally. "So what do we do now?"

Cillian shrugged. "More research, I guess. We're going to need help if we want answers quickly."

"Oh, we'll get to the answers." I groaned as I rolled to my feet. "But first I need to find Dad and the others. I think we need to have a little talk."

Cillian didn't understand my shift in attitude. "About what?"

"It's time for my 'I was right' dance," I supplied. "Twice in one month. You guys better start taking notes because I'm on a roll."

Cillian heaved out a sigh as he met Griffin's amused gaze. "I should've seen that coming."

"You really should have," Griffin agreed. "She can't help herself."

"That's because she's annoying."

"I find her cute." Griffin affectionately patted my rear end. "Wait for me. I love it when you do the dance. I don't want to miss it."

"Don't encourage her," Cillian whined. "She'll never stop if you allow her to think it's funny."

"That's fine." Griffin was blasé as he fell into step with me. "I find the dance sexy. I can live with it."

"You might change your mind fifty years from now."

Griffin pursed his lips. "Even then I'll bet I find it sexy."

I beamed at him. "That was a really nice thing to say."

"I have my moments."

"I'm going to share one with you after the dance."

"Knock that off!" Cillian snapped. "I don't want to hear this part of the conversation."

"Yeah, yeah."

DAD WASN'T NEARLY as impressed as I expected him to be when I launched myself into his office and started dancing.

"I was right! I was right! I was right!" It wasn't exactly singing as much as chanting. I swung my hips and tossed my hair to add some oomph to the routine, so that made up for the fact that I was essentially tone deaf. "I was right!" I stomped my foot for emphasis as I struck a pose in front of Dad's desk.

Dad, almost always calm, lowered the newspaper enough that he could peer over the top. "Did you say something?"

"Ha, ha." There was no way I would allow him to get away with that. "I was right about the evil storms. I knew I was, so ... ha!" I extended a finger and made it dance.

Dad reached out to snag the finger to stop it from moving, but I quickly evaded him.

"I was right," I repeated, more emphatic this time. "Bow down and grovel before your queen, because I was totally right."

Griffin cleared his throat from the chair he settled in when I wasn't looking. "That's taking it a bit too far, Aisling."

Hmm. Was he right? More importantly, did I care? "I'm good," I said after a beat. "I think I took it just far enough."

"You would," Cillian complained as he sat in another chair. "As much as I hate to encourage her – and you have no idea how loath I am to do that – I think she might have been right."

Dad was more willing to believe Cillian, so he turned an interested set of purple eyes to my academically-minded brother. "What do you mean?"

"Aisling and I had a meeting of the minds in the library last night," Cillian explained. He looked wearier than I felt. Of course, I got more sleep than him, and he was forced to serve as my pillow, so that was to be expected. "I decided to do some research and she came along and helped for a bit."

"You decided to do some research before Aisling bugged you to do it?" Dad challenged. "Why?"

"Because Maya called from the hospital to say they were making her work a double shift and some of the things she said to me didn't sound right," Cillian admitted. "She said a lot of people got into fights during the storm. The emergency room was overrun. She made an offhand comment about the storm causing it, saying something like they were all joking because they noticed it was always storming when the fights started. That was at least enough to have me looking."

"And you found something?"

"Yup. There were beings called storm wielders hundreds of years ago. Apparently they could create storms to do a multitude of different things, including influence emotions. It wasn't looked at as out of the ordinary back then, but the practice has obviously been forgotten over the years."

"It would seem someone remembered it," Griffin said, snagging me around the waist and pulling me to his lap.

"I'm not done dancing," I complained.

"You're done for now."

"You're done for the foreseeable future," Dad corrected, his tone fierce. "As for the storms ... just because people could do it centuries ago doesn't mean that's what's happening here. How can you be sure?"

"I guess we can't be a hundred percent clear," Cillian conceded. "I think Aisling was on the right track from the start. I know that will inflate her ego, but it makes sense. As far as we can tell, the acts of violence have only happened during the storms."

"But you said it yourself yesterday, Aisling, not everyone has been affected," Dad persisted. "Aidan wasn't affected."

"No, but that could be because he's a reaper," Cillian pointed out. "For all intents and purposes, we're the same as normal humans. We have a slight difference in our blood chemistry, which sets us apart. Perhaps the storms were created to affect only humans."

"But who would do that?" Dad pressed. "Why would someone do that?"

"I have no idea," Cillian admitted. "There is slightly more to the story, though, and it's something I didn't know until this morning. I might've woken you last night if I knew the second part of it."

"Oh, geez." Dad slapped his hand to his forehead. "Do I even want to know?"

"Probably not, but you need to know," Cillian replied. "There was a symbol in the book. I left it upstairs, but I took a screenshot." He held up his phone so Dad could see it. "The book didn't have many illustrations so I thought this might be important."

"What is it?"

"I have no idea, but Aisling saw it two days ago."

Dad turned very slowly, very deliberately, in my direction. "Where did you see it?"

I told him about Harry Turner, leaving out the part where I talked to him for almost an hour. "I didn't think much about it at the time – other than that he was weird – but I remember the symbol from one of the discs on the shelf."

"And why were you poking around Mr. Turner's personal items?" Dad challenged.

"Um ... I'd rather not say." I averted my gaze.

"I think it's good she was poking around the shelf," Griffin offered, keeping a firm grip on me as I squirmed. "That's how we know where to look for the symbol."

"You're only saying that because you're a big marshmallow where she's concerned," Dad groused.

"Because you're the Marshmallow in Chief, I'll take that as a compliment," Griffin said dryly. "Either way, it doesn't matter why she did it. It only matters that she did and we know where to start looking."

"I guess." Dad wrinkled his nose as he leaned back in his chair. "I don't know what to make about any of this. I don't even know where to start."

"I figured we could talk about that over breakfast," Cillian said, sobering. "I might go into the main office and use their library. I have some suggestions for a few stops for Redmond and Aisling today, too."

I perked up. "You have a suggestion for me?"

Cillian bobbed his head. "I do indeed. Madame Maxine."

My smile slipped. "I don't want to go to her. She always gives me crap when she sees me. She makes me uncomfortable."

"You're going, and that's a fabulous idea," Dad said. "I'll pull you three out of the rotation and give Aidan and Braden most of the work for the day. I'll call for two subs so we don't have to listen to them whine."

"What am I supposed to do?" Griffin asked. "I can't very well avoid the rain if something happens. I also can't ask my co-workers not to go out during a rain squall because my girlfriend believes the storms are evil. They'll laugh me off the premises."

"I don't know," Dad said, turning serious. "You need to be careful. If Aisling is right you're susceptible. Not only could you hurt an innocent person, you could hurt your entire future if you react the wrong way while under the influence. I'd say that you need to avoid the storms at all costs until we know more."

Griffin didn't look thrilled with the suggestion. "I'll do my best." He gave me a reassuring squeeze when he saw I was frowning. "I promise I'll be okay."

I wasn't convinced that was true, but there was very little I could do to change the situation. "Hopefully Madame Maxine will have some of the answers we need," I griped. "If I have to put up with her mouth, I'd better get something out of the deal."

Griffin poked my side to ease my bad mood. "I think that's what most people say about you."

I rolled my eyes. "Ha, ha. I ... ." The sound of footsteps in the hallway outside Dad's office tipped me off that my brothers were up and moving through the house. I scrambled to climb off Griffin's lap, completely forgetting what I was about to say.

"Where are you going?" Griffin called after me.

"Don't worry. I'm just going to do the dance for Redmond, Braden and Aidan. They haven't seen it yet. I don't want them to miss out."

"Have fun," Griffin said, not bothering to hide his chuckle as Dad scowled and made a disgusted sound in the back of his throat.

"I definitely intend to."

⚜ 11 ⚜

ELEVEN

"I will punch you if you don't stop doing that."

Redmond, his arms folded over his chest, glared at Griffin as he kissed me before leaving for his shift.

I ignored Redmond, but Griffin offered a wry smile.

"If you don't like it, don't look," Griffin suggested, giving me another kiss before taking a step back and focusing on me. "I know we're working under the assumption that you're immune from whatever this is, but do me a favor and stay out of the rain today, okay?"

I shifted my eyes to the clear sky. "I don't think it's going to rain today."

"It wasn't supposed to rain yesterday either," Griffin pointed out. "I'm not sure how I feel about this storm theory, but I promised to do my best to stay out of the rain. I want you to do the same."

"That shouldn't be hard. You know how I feel about getting my hair wet. Unless it's for a sexy bath, I'm just not into it."

"Oh, merciful Zeus, someone come and save me," Redmond complained.

I grinned as I smacked his arm. "Stop being a baby. I'm ready to go."

"What do you think Madame Maxine will tell you?" Griffin was curious. "Do you think this is a topic she might actually know something about?"

"She knows a lot about everything," Redmond replied. "It can't hurt to ask. The worst we'll have to put up with is Aisling's whining when Madame Maxine insists on getting a gander at her future."

"Why is that a problem?"

"Because Madame Maxine likes to mess with me," I answered. "I'm convinced that's how she stays young. Seriously, the woman never ages. She uses my pain and suffering to smooth her wrinkles. She probably makes a lotion out of it or something as soon as I leave."

Griffin stared at me for a long beat, his face unreadable. "Well, have fun." Griffin yanked open his door. "Text me a couple times today so I know you're okay. I'll do the same."

"Dirty texts?"

"I will kill you if you don't stop saying things like that, Aisling," Redmond threatened. "I'm already at my limit and it's barely eight."

"Yeah, yeah." I waved off his complaints and held Griffin's gaze for a lingering moment. "Be careful."

"Right back at you."

MADAME MAXINE'S SHOP was straight out of a movie. Most people would describe it as cozy, but I wasn't most people. I found the shop uncomfortable and I hated the overwhelming scent of lavender and lemons.

"Well, well, well. Look who it is. What did I do to get so lucky as to deserve a visit from you two on this fine spring day?" Madame Maxine, her ankle-length skirt glittering under the pink gel lights, smiled as she approached. "It's good to see you, Redmond."

My brother, always the people pleaser – especially when it came to women – stepped forward and engulfed Maxine in a bear hug. "It's good to see you, too. I meant to stop by after the whole zombie fiasco, but I hadn't a chance. How are you doing?"

Maxine shrugged. "I've been better. I was sorry to hear what happened with that whole deal. I want you to know that I had no idea what was going down when it happened. I knew something was going on – I've always known that woman was evil – but I had no idea what."

"That's convenient," I muttered under my breath as I feigned interest in an odd-looking hat on a nearby shelf.

"I see you're still full of sunshine and light, littlest Grimlock," Maxine said, offering up a pointed stare when I risked looking in her direction. "How are things for you?"

"They're super," I said with a bit too much enthusiasm. "Thanks for asking."

"They're not actually super," Redmond corrected. "We have a ... um, situation ... to discuss with you. We're kind of at a loss."

"I see." Maxine's eyes never left my face. "Well, I would be happy to share information with you."

Redmond beamed. "Great."

"For a price," Maxine added, causing my skin to crawl. "I believe you know my price, little pouter." She held out her hand for me to take.

I heaved out a sigh, resigned. "I knew it would come to this." Instead of taking her hand right away, I grabbed the flamboyant hat – which featured a feather and small fake skulls as accents – and plopped it on my head. "Why am I always the one who has to pay the price?"

"Because you're the one with the intriguing future," Maxine replied without hesitation. "Don't get me wrong, Redmond will have a lot of fun, but you will lead the rest of your family forward."

I didn't like the sound of that. "Why do you think that? If your answer is that it's because I'm the only girl, I'll be incredibly disappointed. That's very sexist and narrow-minded."

Rather than be offended, Maxine merely snickered. "You'll say anything to distract people, won't you?"

"It's not limited to words," Redmond offered. "She did a dance earlier. It was annoying, and I kind of want to strangle her for it."

"Oh, big words from a big brother." Maxine made a tsking sound as she shook her head. "You don't mean them. You secretly liked the dance."

"I really didn't."

"You did ... other than the fact that it apparently turned on this one's boyfriend." Maxine gestured toward me. "You didn't like that part."

Redmond didn't bother to bank his amazement. "How did you know that?"

"I know many things." Maxine patted his arms. "Your emotions are always right on the surface. They're easy to pick through. Now your sister, on the other hand, she does a better job of hiding her feelings and innermost thoughts."

"I don't believe that. Her emotions always seem easy to read to me."

"Because you see what she wants you to see." Maxine held my gaze and flicked her fingers. "You know the price for information."

"Ugh." I wrinkled my nose but held out my hand all the same. "I freaking hate it when you do this. It gives me stomach issues and gas. It also gives me a headache and premature PMS. It might also give me the vapors, even though I've only read about that in books. Have I mentioned that I hate doing this? It's so stupid."

"Shh." Maxine pressed her eyes shut as she tightly gripped my hand. For lack of anywhere else to look, I studied her face and found that I profoundly disliked the way her eyes seemed to careen from side to side under her lids. It was disconcerting and kind of creepy. "Hmm."

Maxine was thoughtful when she finally released my hand.

"Well, what did you see?" I asked after a beat. I didn't really want to know, but not knowing somehow felt like torture. "Am I going to be swallowed by a giant turtle and disappear into another realm?"

Maxine chuckled as she shuffled toward a table in the corner of the room. She took the time to pour three cups of tea before gesturing for us to sit.

"I saw what I always see when I consider your future," she replied after a moment. "I guess that's not exactly true. I used to see darker things. I still see a few darker things, but they're disappearing rapidly. Your future looks much brighter than it used to."

I didn't know what to make of that. "So I'm going to move to Disney World and reside in the princess castle? That's what you're saying, right?"

"I would've thought you'd be happier moving into Hogwarts at Harry Potter world," Redmond noted.

Hmm. He had a point. "Okay, I switch my vote. I want to move to Hogwarts."

Maxine didn't bother to hide her eye roll. "You won't live in either spot, but I don't think you really care about that. As for your future, it makes for an intriguing sight. I'm kind of curious to see how things will play out."

"You're a seer," I reminded her. "Don't you already know how things are going to play out? Isn't that your entire shtick?"

"No one's future is set in stone, little Grimlock. Every change involves a choice. Your future could go one way with a certain choice or completely the opposite with another. It used to be that when I looked at your future I only saw the potential for dark choices. Somehow you've managed to turn that around, although you haven't done it by yourself. I believe the man who gave you that ring is partially responsible."

I glanced at my engagement ring and frowned. "Are you saying I needed a man to be happy? If so, I disagree. I love Griffin, but I don't need him to be happy." Even as I said the words I wasn't sure they were true. I needed him now to be happy – "now" being the operative word. Before, though, I certainly didn't need him to be happy. It was a convoluted thought process to undertake.

"You don't need a man to be happy," Maxine clarified. "I would never say that. I don't have a man and I'm perfectly happy."

"I'll be your man," Redmond offered, his eyes glowed with teasing. "I've always wanted that job."

Maxine chuckled as she patted his hand. "You will be the man of many women before you find one who can handle your personality. You still have time. Your sister is different. She found her match relatively early, and he's certainly shifted things for her. I can't help but be impressed."

"I don't really want to talk about Griffin," I argued. "We're here to talk about something else. Griffin isn't a part of that. Er, well, he's not a big part." Technically Griffin was the reason I was so worried about the storms, but now wasn't the time to take the conversation in that direction. "We need to know what you know about the magical storms."

I decided that asking if she believed the storms were real and capable of affecting moods was the wrong way to go. I wanted her to understand that I already believed in the storms and lying about what they could do would only irritate me.

"I wondered if anyone would pick up what was happening." Maxine remained calm and cool as she lifted her teacup and sipped. The floral mix she served us smelled like Easter and tasted like grass, so I did my best to avoid it even though I knew I might appear rude. "I shouldn't be surprised that you were the first to figure things out."

"I don't know that we've figured things out," Redmond countered. "Aisling was the first one to float the idea last night and we all thought she was crazy."

Maxine smiled. "Did that drive you crazy, little Grimlock?"

She had no idea. "I was fine with it," I lied. "I'm used to being underestimated."

"That's an interesting way to look at it." Maxine sipped again before returning her cup to its saucer with a loud clink. "I'm not sure what to make of the storms. I've heard of people possessing the power to control the weather before, but I've never seen it. Even so, what's happening now is somehow different."

"Different how?" Redmond prodded.

"Well, for starters, controlling the weather and influencing moods through storms are not the same. In truth, I thought the power to influence moods through storms was long lost to this world ... and that was for the better."

"Who developed the power?" I asked.

"It depends on who you ask." Maxine shifted on her chair. "Some believe the voodoo practitioners in the south somehow managed to harness the weather and used the storm power for rituals."

"But you don't believe that."

Maxine shook her head. "It doesn't feel like them, if you catch my drift."

"Not really."

"The power to control moods is dangerous. It was abandoned by all those who embraced the light centuries ago," Maxine explained. "At first it was used merely at parties and gatherings to make people have a good time. It was started for good reasons, but like anything else, it was co-opted by those who wanted to use magic for more nefarious reasons."

"You're basically saying the spell was taken by the dark side of the Force so the Sith could use it to defeat their enemies," I noted.

Maxine chuckled. "I'm pretty sure that's not what I said, but you're not wrong. Evil people saw they could use the power and decided to experiment in multiple ways. That included causing soldiers to turn on each other rather than the enemy during battle. It also turned into a way to distract adults so children could be taken for other rituals."

My stomach flipped at that. "I would say that's using the storms for evil means."

"Definitely," Redmond agreed. "Why do you think someone would pick this area to unleash the storms now?"

"I don't know, and I'm troubled by it," Maxine answered. "I'm sure there's something bigger at work here, although I have no idea what. Causing humans to fight for no reason other than entertainment seems off unless I'm reading the signs incorrectly. It's far more likely that whoever is doing this is trying to distract people so he or she can either steal something big or take down someone even bigger."

In a weird way, that made sense. "So who would have the power to do this?" I asked. "Someone couldn't simply read a book and make it happen, right? He or she would've needed training?"

"A novice couldn't stumble across an old spell and make this happen," Maxine agreed. "That means we're dealing with someone powerful. Our biggest problem is that we need a motive to track a culprit, and I can't come up with an acceptable motive other than outright mayhem. Nothing in the storm trails makes sense."

"So what do you suggest we do?" Redmond asked. "We need information. Cillian found a symbol in a book and Aisling claims she saw the symbol the other day at a police officer's house when she was there to do a job. Do you know anything about this?" Redmond held up his phone so Maxine could study the screenshot.

Maxine stared for a long time before shaking her head. "I don't recognize that. I wish I did because that would give me somewhere to look, but that's not familiar to me." She swiveled in my direction. "You saw it in a police officer's house? On what?"

"It was on a silver disc. He had a bunch of metaphysical stuff on a shelf and that was one of the items."

"But you didn't see anything else?"

"No. I didn't think anything about it until I saw the symbol again this morning."

"Hmm." Maxine tapped her bottom lip. "That doesn't exactly clear anything up, but I think I can track down a book of ancient symbols and learn more. That will be my top priority this afternoon.

"As for you two, I think you should go to a local shaman I know," she continued, grabbing a sheet of paper from a notebook on the corner of a table and scrawling an address. "His name is Zake Zezo. He's very knowledgeable about long-forgotten spells. If anyone can give you direction, it's him."

"Zake Zezo, huh?" I stared at the address, which was in the heart of Detroit. "What kind of shaman is he?"

"The kind who doesn't suffer fools but enjoys a good conversation," Maxine replied. "He will be intrigued by both of you. Be careful not to share too much of yourselves. He will read surface emotions, so do your best to shield."

"Oh, well, I'm so good at shielding my emotions," I muttered.

Maxine snickered. "Yes, well, you might fascinate him for other reasons. He can't delve deep, so you should be safe."

"Okay. At least we have a place to start." I moved to pluck the hat off my head as I stood. "This is pretty cool. I might come back and get it for Halloween."

Maxine's smile was enigmatic as she pushed back my hand. "Keep the hat."

I balked. "It looks expensive."

"I don't care about price. I am intrigued as to why you gravitated toward it when there were so many others to choose from. That is a conversation for another time. For now, I believe you were meant to have that hat. Take it."

I remained dubious. "Are you sure?" I glanced to Redmond for help but he merely shrugged. I felt caught in that cloudy space where it might be considered rude to turn down a gift but tacky to accept it. "I don't want to take advantage of you."

This time the laugh Maxine let loose was high-pitched and full of mirth. "Oh, I wouldn't worry about that, little Grimlock. No one takes advantage of me, just like very few people can manage the same with you. Keep the hat. Before everything is said and done I think the hat will serve you well. It belongs with you."

"Well ... okay." I returned the hat to my head and beamed at Redmond. "Do I look like a cowboy?"

"You look like a moron," Redmond replied without hesitation. "But if you wear that for dinner I bet Dad and Griffin will think you're cute enough to spoil you rotten. I, however, am immune to your cute factor."

"Since when?"

"Since you learned how to talk."

I knew better, but we had bigger things to worry about. "Come on. We need to track down a shaman. The quicker we get answers the better off it will be for everyone."

"You and I finally agree on something, little Grimlock," Maxine said. "We definitely need answers. We should all keep in touch with one another. Pooling information at this time can only help."

"We'll be in touch," Redmond promised. "Come on, Aisling. Let's see if the shaman wants to see you dance."

TWELVE

Zake Zezo was not what I expected. He was a tiny little guy, bald, draped in loose-fitting robes. His shop was essentially the size of a closet, wedged between a Chicken Shack and a Middle Eastern restaurant on Woodward in the heart of Detroit.

Redmond put a hand to my back, his stance protective. He looked Zake Zezo up and down with something akin to dislike before speaking. "Madame Maxine sent us."

Zake Zezo was blasé. "I know."

"How do you know that?" I asked, sitting in one of the chairs across from him. The small table he sat behind featured a pile of items I didn't recognize – potions, powders and oddly enough, mirrors of varying sizes – and it squeaked when I accidentally bumped my hip into it.

"I know everything," he said, his tone low and ominous.

"Oh, geez." I didn't bother to hide my eye roll. "This guy is all pomp and circumstance and no substance. We should look elsewhere."

"I'm open to suggestions." Redmond took the seat next to me, shooting Zake Zezo a look that warned, "If you touch my sister I'll strangle you with you with your own robes" before continuing.

"Madame Maxine said he might have answers for us. We have nowhere else to look."

Sadly, I knew he was right. "Fine." I licked my lips. "What can you tell us about the evil storms?"

"What can you tell us about the evil storms?" Zake Zezo mimicked my voice to perfection. It was both annoying and eerie.

"I believe that's the question I want answered," I pressed. "We need to know about them. If you have information, we would greatly appreciate you sharing it with us."

"I have information. But I'm not in the habit of sharing."

Redmond and I exchanged weighted looks. Ultimately my brother sighed and dug in his wallet, coming back with a hundred-dollar bill and dropping it on the middle of the table. "What do you know?"

Zake Zezo ignored the bill and instead grabbed a vial of purple powder. "I know a great many things about a great many people. I know all and see all."

"I think this is like when I dressed up as a fortune teller for Halloween that year and offered to tell fortunes for twenty bucks," I whispered to Redmond. "I used that line then."

Redmond snickered as Zake Zezo scowled.

"What?" Redmond challenged. "We're here for answers and you're spouting lines from fortune cookies. I don't know how this is supposed to go down, but we're genuinely at a loss."

"I believe that's your normal mental state, isn't it?"

Under normal circumstances I would've been fine with a random shaman insulting my brother. These were not normal circumstances. "Hey, Mr. Oblivious, we're not here to fool around." I smacked the table for emphasis. "We have questions and we were led to believe you have answers. You need to talk."

Zake Zezo's eyes – an odd shade of gray that I'd never seen outside of a Crayola box – glittered with amusement. "And what happens if I don't? Will you have your brother harm me?"

"No. I'll start singing."

He cocked an eyebrow. "Is that a threat?"

"You have no idea," Redmond muttered. "She's completely tone deaf and prefers eighties head-banging songs when she's worked herself up to start torturing people."

"Do you want me to talk dirty to you?" I challenged.

"I have no idea what that means, but I find you absolutely delightful." Zake Zezo clapped his hands, which were covered in the purple powder, and when he lowered them I realized the dust left behind was magically forming a shape in the gloom.

"What is that?" I asked, confused.

Redmond put his arm around my back, his fierce protective manner on full display. I felt his muscles coil in case we needed to flee. "That looks like ... ."

"A storm," Zake Zezo finished. "It is a storm. It's the storm that's been raging in this area for months."

"We think the storms have only been a factor for the past three days or so," I argued.

"You're being too literal," Zake Zezo chided. "I'm talking about the storm that has been raging in the mind of a single person. That person is responsible for everything that has been happening here for almost a year now."

I had trouble wrapping my head around what he was saying. "What do you mean? I ... what other things?"

"The dead rose from their graves, did they not?"

I balked. "That was Madame Dauphine. She did the voodoo thing because she was crazy and wanted to distract us. She was going after reapers specifically."

"Yes, you're the one who caught and ended her, if I'm not mistaken," he said. "Once you had your answers you didn't look further to see if there were more questions to tackle."

Zake Zezo's roundabout way of talking was beginning to grate ... and fast. "So you're saying someone else was behind the zombies."

"I'm saying someone has had a hand in everything that has touched your life for almost a year." Zake Zezo poured water into an ornate bowl at the center of the table and lowered the tip of his index finger into it, causing a series of ripples to disturb the calm water. "Even little things can cause big disturbances."

"So you're saying that someone else was involved with the zombies," Redmond surmised. "Why, though? To what end?"

"I can't see the thoughts of this individual. I cannot see a face or even thoughts. I can see the ripples, though, and the ripples all originate from the same place. The ripples have been caused by someone – or some thing – that wants to upend your lives."

Redmond furrowed his brow. "Us specifically?"

"Your family. You're at the center of it all."

"All of what?" I asked. "You mentioned the zombies and said there were other things, but what other things?"

"Wraiths. Gargoyles. Zombies. Mirror monsters. Someone alive who should be dead. They're not all separate from one another. They're connected."

"By one person?"

Zake Zezo nodded, the muted light gleaming off the top of his bald head. "Who do you know who has been involved in all these things, even if only tangentially?"

There was one easy answer, but I was uncomfortable giving it voice. Thankfully Redmond, much like the rest of the family, often spoke before thinking.

"Mom."

I pressed my lips together and studied Redmond's face for hints to what he was feeling.

"He has to be talking about Mom," Redmond supplied. "There's no other explanation. Mom is alive but should be dead."

I had trouble arguing with the sentiment, but I didn't want to send Redmond off on a tangent so I remained calm. "Or maybe someone above Mom who brought her back," I suggested.

"Do you think?" Redmond looked so hopeful it almost crushed my heart.

"Mom didn't have the power to save herself," I reminded him, licking my lips. "Genevieve Toth saved her. She was the one with the power. Maybe there's someone else from that little coven pulling the strings. We can't possibly know everyone who is involved because we stopped looking once Genevieve died."

"Killed," Zake Zezo corrected. "She was killed, and I believe you did the deed." His eyes were like lasers when they grabbed my gaze. "Did you feel a shift when she died?"

"I ... what?"

"A shift," he repeated. "No one enters or leaves this plane of existence without disturbing the atmosphere. Given who she was, the nature of her power, Genevieve would've left a very obvious wake when she was ripped from this plane. What did you feel?"

I had no idea how to answer the question. "Nothing. I didn't feel anything."

"Nothing?" Zake Zezo cocked a dubious sparkplug eyebrow. "You must have felt something?"

I searched my memory of the event but it felt as if it happened so long ago that it was more an echo than a firm vision. "I didn't really think about it at the time. She was evil and trying to kill me so that was it. Everyone rolled in at the same time to fight. I've never given it much thought."

"Is that important?" Redmond asked. "Could it be possible that Genevieve didn't really die that night? I mean ... maybe she faked her death or something. Maybe she's been laying low. If you believe Aisling should've felt something, but she didn't, maybe the obvious answer is because Genevieve didn't die."

"I can't rule that out, of course, but I'm not sure that's what I'm feeling," Zake Zezo said. "In truth, the energy I feel is decidedly female. I have no idea who it belongs to. That is the person you're looking for. She's responsible for everything ... including the storms you worry so much about."

"Will the storms keep rolling?" Redmond asked. "Are they done?"

"They won't be done until you stop them." Zake Zezo pinned me with a pointed look. "You have to stop them."

I balked. "Me personally?"

"Your family."

"Why us?" Redmond challenged. "Why does it always have to be us?"

"Because the person doing all of this is fixated on your family, and most especially your sister," Zake Zezo replied. "This woman believes your sister is the key to getting whatever she wants. Now, whether that's true or simply an errant belief really doesn't matter.

"You've been marked by this woman as important, and that means you'll have to be the one to end things when it's time," he continued, adopting a gentle expression as he looked at me with something that could only be described as pity. "You're at the center of all of this, for better or for worse. Only one of you can survive the ultimate battle."

"Oh, geez." I dropped my forehead into my hands. "He just gave me the Harry Potter prophecy. I'm totally going to die now."

"Don't even joke about that," Redmond warned, extending a finger. "You're not going to die." He shifted a dark glare to Zake Zezo. "Don't tell her things like that. She takes things to heart and is a born exaggerator. She'll make a mess of things if you tell her stuff like that."

Zake Zezo was quiet for a full ten seconds before speaking again, his gaze like an anvil on my chest as he looked me up and down. "She will be fine." He smacked the table with his hands and stood, grabbing his money from the center before making small shooing motions with his hands. "It is time for you to go."

"Are the spirits telling you that?" I asked dryly. "Do you have a life to save?"

"No. *The Talk* starts in ten minutes and I don't want to miss it. They're talking about the mystique of the female orgasm, and that is definitely must-see viewing."

"Oh, well, whatever floats your boat."

REDMOND AND I didn't speak again until we were in his truck and headed down the freeway exit ramp toward Royal Oak. The fifteen-minute drive served as something of a catharsis for both of us, although I could tell what was bothering him before he even opened his mouth.

"It's probably not Mom," I offered automatically, the need to soothe him coming out of nowhere. "She wouldn't be able to pull it off, especially because she's been with us during some of the attacks."

"You're right." Redmond let loose a shaky breath. "You're absolutely right. She helped us fight off the zombies."

"And the mirror man," I reminded him. "It's probably not her."

"What about Genevieve?" Redmond asked, navigating his truck toward Royal Oak's busy main drag. "Do you think she could've survived?"

"I don't see how. She looked deader than dead to me at the end."

"That's true. If not her, who?"

"I've been giving it some thought." I tapped my fingers on my knee as Redmond stopped at an intersection. Traffic was practically murder this time of day and it would take us three changes to get through one light. It was ridiculous. "I think we have to be missing a player."

"Meaning?"

"Meaning that I think Genevieve was working with someone else from the beginning and we simply didn't realize it. Believing Genevieve somehow staved off death and managed to recover is a stretch. Mom has been helping us, so believing it's her is also a stretch.

"While I'm not willing to rule either of them out because that would be stupid and I'm far from stupid, I think that we should follow that adage Dad always used to throw at us," I continued. "The simplest answer, however ridiculous, is almost always the correct answer. That means there's another person involved we somehow missed."

"But who?" Redmond edged forward in the traffic and sighed when the light turned red again. "I hate this light."

"Join the club. As for who might be involved, I don't know. Maybe we should have Cillian pull Genevieve's records again. We could've easily missed something because we were fixated on her."

"That's a really good idea. In fact ... ." Redmond trailed off and when I shifted my eyes to see what he was looking at I found Angelina in the crosswalk in front of us. She had her mother with her. The woman was so frail and bent I almost didn't recognize her. "Is that ... ?"

"Carol Davenport," I answered automatically. "I heard she was sick, but I hadn't seen her in a long time."

"She looks as if she's already dead."

That was a sobering thought. "Yeah. I hate Angelina, but I can't help but feel a little sorry for her."

Redmond's eyes lit with mirth. "And why is that?"

"Because she's alone and dealing with the pending death of her only remaining parent. I can't imagine going through something like that without someone to prop me up."

"You won't have to." Redmond patted my hand, cringing when Angelina tried to get her mother to pick up the pace. "I think she's having issues."

"I know. I ... ." The first drop of rain splattering against the windshield caused my heart to constrict. "Oh, no."

"Crap!" Redmond glanced over his shoulder, perhaps looking to see if he could find a parking spot. A rumble of thunder followed the first splash of rain, and I knew things were about to get bad. "What do we do?"

I didn't have an answer so I went with my instincts. "Park," I ordered, opening the door. "I'll help Angelina get her mother inside. We'll carry her if we have to."

Redmond was dumbfounded. "You can't go out in this. What if you're not immune?"

"I have to try." I was firm. "If something happens, tell Griffin I'm sorry."

"Aisling, I can't be the only one who thinks it's a bad idea for you and Angelina to be stuck in the murder-inducing rain together, can I?"

It was a fair question. "I can take her."

"Son of a ... !" Redmond swore under his breath. "Let me help you. You can't do it alone."

"I don't have a choice. We have to get Carol inside or she could be really hurt. As for Angelina ... I've taken her before. It will be okay."

"I wish I could believe you," Redmond growled.

I didn't give him a chance to continue, instead slamming the door and jogging across the pavement. "Angelina?" So far the rain was only coming down in tiny intermittent droplets.

Angelina looked stunned by my arrival. "What do you want? We're doing the best that we can," she snarled. "Don't you say one word to me."

I held up my hands in a placating manner. "I'm not trying to pick a fight. It's going to storm." I pointed at the black clouds for emphasis. "I'm going to help you get your mother inside."

"I don't want your help," Carol barked. "I know who you are. I'd recognize those demon eyes of yours anywhere."

I ignored the insult. "Let's get her inside," I suggested. "The faster we get her out of the rain, the better." I grabbed Carol's arm to offer her support. "In fact, if you want to lift your legs I think we can carry you faster."

Carol shot me a "not in this lifetime" expression that would've made me laugh under different circumstances. "I don't want to be carried. I can walk."

"She wants to keep her independence," Angelina explained. "I never would've taken her out today if I thought it was going to storm. It wasn't supposed to storm."

"Yeah, well, the weather has been ridiculously unpredictable. "Come on, Mrs. Davenport." I tried to force the older woman to walk faster, something she didn't take well.

"Stop rushing me," she snapped. "A little rain never hurt anyone."

Unfortunately that wasn't the case right now. "There's a coffee shop right there." I pointed. "I'll buy you whatever you want if you let us carry you."

"So you can poison me?" She rolled her eyes. "I can't believe you're not in prison yet."

"Yeah. Yeah. I ... ." The words died on my lips when the rain picked up and started coming down in a steady sheet. Panic licked at my innards, and I flicked a gaze to Angelina, my heart twisting when I saw her lips curve down. "Oh, crap! This is about to get bad."

❧ 13 ❧

THIRTEEN

"Y ou're making her move too fast," Angelina complained.

"You're not moving fast enough," I shot back.

"I will rip your hair out if you don't get your hands off me, Aisling Grimlock," Carol barked.

"Yeah, yeah." I shook my head as I grabbed Carol around the waist and tried to lift her. She was tiny, sickness eating away at her, but the position was awkward and I had trouble hurrying her toward the curb. "Just think of me as your taxi."

The rain intensified as a bolt of lightning flashed. It was almost immediately followed by a terrifying rumble of thunder. I was almost out of time. That is, if it wasn't too late already.

"Angelina, I know this is going to sound weird, but I need you to go inside the coffee shop and leave your mother to me." The words sounded ridiculous, but I didn't know what else to do.

Angelina lifted her eyebrows. "Excuse me? You expect me to leave my mother with you. Why would I possibly do that?"

"Because I need it to happen," I gritted out. "The rain is ... dangerous."

"Dangerous? Is it going to cause you to melt or something? I can see that happening because you're a total witch."

"Just ... go inside!" I practically exploded.

"You go inside," Angelina snapped. "She's my mother. She doesn't even like you."

"I really don't," Carol agreed. "You've been an intolerable snipe since you were five years old. Your father spoiled you to the point where absolutely no one could stand you, which allowed you to be a bully. You absolutely terrorized my poor Angelina."

I thought I might tilt to the side I rolled my eyes so hard. "What have you been telling her, Angelina?" We reached the curb, where it took me two tries to lift Carol to the sidewalk. "You were the bully, and you know it. I was a freaking angel compared to you."

Carol and Angelina snorted in unison.

"Angel? You cut the back of my dress at prom so my ass hung out and everyone laughed at me for a full five minutes before I realized what was going on," Angelina groused.

"That was a designer dress," Carol added.

"Hey, I only did that because you were mean to Jerry."

"You mean the fairy?" Carol asked.

"Don't make me smack you around before I save you, Mrs. Davenport," I warned, doing my best to ignore the rain rolling into my eyes. "Everything I ever did to Angelina was because she had it coming. She went after Jerry."

"That's because he's an abomination," Carol sniffed.

"I will kill your mother if she doesn't knock that off, Angelina," I warned.

"She's right." Angelina refused to take my side no matter the argument. "You're the one who has been an absolute monster since we were kids."

"That's not how I remember it."

"That dress cost two grand," Angelina hissed, her eyes flashing. "I loved that dress and I only got to wear it for an hour before you destroyed it."

I remembered that prom with a certain bit of nostalgia that probably wasn't warranted given the circumstances. "Hey, you were very popular that night," I offered, our predicament momentarily fleeing my mind. "Your reputation was never the same after that. You should be thanking me."

"People called me the Grosse Pointe Flasher!"

"Yes, but that's better than what they were calling you before. In fact ... ." I broke off when I saw Angelina wipe a bit of water from her eyes. This couldn't go on. As much as I enjoyed messing with Angelina, if she turned on me while I was trying to control her mother I could lose an eye ... or worse. "Go inside."

"What? Why are you back to that? I'm not going inside."

"You have to."

"I don't have to do anything you say."

"You do today."

"Not ever."

"Ugh!" I looked to the sky, silently admonishing whatever force I believed was working against us to hold off until I could get Carol inside the building. Redmond suddenly joined us. The look on his face reflected worry.

"Why are you still out here?" Redmond moved to grab Carol, perhaps actually lift her in his arms, but I cut him off with a firm headshake.

"Take Angelina," I ordered, worry overtaking me. "I'll handle Mrs. Davenport. You worry about Angelina."

"I think I should help you," Redmond argued.

"And I think Angelina is more of a threat."

"More of a threat to what?" Angelina asked, confused.

Redmond stared at me for a long moment, something unsaid passing between us, and then acquiesced. "Fine." He grabbed Angelina by the waist, ignoring the way she struck out at him, and strode toward the coffee shop. "Pick up the pace, Aisling. I can't believe we're not already out of time."

That made both of us. I watched him with Angelina long enough to realize she was slapping at his hand and screeching, but then I focused my full attention on Carol. "So ... are you ready for some coffee?" I returned to my attempt to herd her toward the coffee shop. "If you would actually try to pick up your feet this would be easier. You know that, right?"

"Why would I possibly want to help you?" Carol snarled.

I recognized something in her voice that wasn't there before and leaned closer so I could study her eyes. Her pupils were suddenly dilated and the way she curved her lips made me believe something bad was about to happen. Of course, I'd conditioned myself to believe that about Angelina's family before the threat of evil storms became real so I knew it was possible that I was imagining things.

Then Carol opened her mouth.

"I told Angelina she should've killed you when you were in high school," Carol hissed in a voice that made my blood run cold. "I told her exactly how to do it and get away with it, but she was such a baby she refused to even try."

"It was probably smart she didn't try," I said, pushing Carol a bit as I tried to direct her toward the door. "Come on. I'll buy you some coffee so you can spew your horrible opinion on others inside."

Carol fought my efforts. "You've always been trash. Your whole family is trash. You have money, but no class."

"Yes, we're thinking of having that put on our business cards," I drawled. "The Grimlocks, where class and money don't meet."

"Do you think you're funny?" Carol's eyes practically glowed with contempt.

"I have it on good authority I'm hilarious."

"Your father ruined you," Carol hissed. "He spoiled you rather than punishing you when you misbehaved. I told him he was making a mistake, but he told me to mind my own business. Who was right?"

"I'm guessing he was." I was quickly running out of patience. "Now get inside."

"You're not the boss of me." Carol jerked away. For some reason, the anger lighting her features made her appear less ravaged by illness. "I'm the boss of me. I'm still in charge ... at least for now. In a few weeks that won't be true, but for now I still say how things are done in my life."

"Well, I would really appreciate it if you would decide to go inside. If you could choose that route, things would be great."

Carol pretended I wasn't speaking. "You ruined my daughter's life. You're the reason she never lived up to her potential."

Oh, crap! Things were about to get worse. I could feel it. "I'm pretty sure that Angelina had a hand in everything that happened. Still, if you want me to apologize, you have to go inside. If you walk through that door I swear I will at least pretend to be sorry about something."

Carol didn't respond other than to narrow her eyes and clench her hands into fists at her sides.

"Son of a ... !" I briefly pressed my eyes shut as I gathered my strength. "You don't want to do this, Mrs. Davenport. It won't end well. I promise you that."

Carol didn't seem bothered by my warning. "Let's see, shall we?"

"No, let's not. I ... crud!"

Carol launched herself at me, her hands flying toward my face.

"You're going to rue the day you messed with my daughter!"

I believed that already and the fight hadn't even started.

"AISLING!"

Griffin entered the Royal Oak Police Department at a run, not stopping until he was at my side.

Detective Green, who was busy asking me questions about my public tussle with a sick senior citizen, pinned Griffin with a dark look when he pulled me in for a hug. "Detective Taylor, I'm in the middle of an interview. If you don't mind ... ."

Griffin cut him off. "I do mind." His eyes flashed. "I just got a call that my fiancée was attacked on a city street, so I dropped everything to get to her. If you don't like it, well, I don't really care." He flicked his eyes to me as he pushed my messy hair away from my face. "Are you okay?"

He looked so concerned I took pity on him. "I'm fine. I have a few bruises on my elbows and butt from the fall, but otherwise I'm perfectly fine."

"What about these?" Griffin tipped up my chin so he could study the claw marks on my neck. "How did this happen?"

I pressed my fingers to the long – and surprisingly deep – scratches. "Would you believe me if I told you a wild jackal attacked?"

"No."

"Well, it was something like a wild jackal." I darted a look to Green before continuing. "I'll fill you in at home."

Griffin looked as if he wanted to press the issue, but he wisely let it go. "Okay." He kissed my forehead before standing. "Is she free to go, Detective Green?"

Green arched an eyebrow. "Not quite yet. I'm still not happy with her responses to my questions. You see, I have no idea what type of detective you are, but when I have a violent altercation in my city I like answers before I close the case."

Griffin ran his tongue over his teeth as he gazed into my eyes. I couldn't read his expression, which was worrisome. Ultimately he moved around my chair and planted himself in the open seat to my right, sighing as he offered a faux smile. "Fine. Ask your questions."

"If you would like to wait over there, that would be preferred." Green pointed toward the lobby.

Griffin shook his head. "I'm Ms. Grimlock's representative. I will be staying throughout the questioning."

"You're not an attorney."

"I don't have to be by law. If you don't believe me, look it up."

It was a challenge. That much was obvious. Apparently the testosterone was about to fly fast and furious. That was the last thing I wanted ... unless Griffin somehow ended up shirtless. What? He's freaking hot. I lucked out in that department.

"Just ask me your questions," I barked, resting my hand on Griffin's wrist to keep him calm. "I want to get this over. It's already dragged on far too long."

Griffin turned his hand over so he could link his fingers with mine but otherwise remained in exactly the same position, his eyes burning holes into Green's smug smile. "If you wish to stay, I have no problem with it."

"That's good," Griffin shot back. "Otherwise I'd have to file a grievance with the state about you trampling Aisling's rights, and you know how messy those can get."

Green's smile slipped. "Yes, well, right. Where was I again, Ms. Grimlock?"

"I believe you were getting ready to cut me loose." I offered up a pretty smile that had gotten me out of more than one ticket. Green clearly wasn't impressed.

"That's not it." He shuffled his papers, as if looking for a reminder to what we'd been talking about even though we both knew he couldn't possibly forget. "Right. So, can you tell me exactly how you ended up in a fight with Ms. Davenport in the middle of the street?"

Griffin let loose a relieved sigh. "Is that it?" He turned to me for confirmation. "You got in a fight with Angelina? I thought it was going to be so much worse."

Green narrowed his eyes at the admission. "Actually, Ms. Grimlock got in a fight with Carol Davenport. She's Angelina Davenport's mother. She's also in ill health and extremely frail."

"I ... huh." Griffin slid a sidelong look to me. "Do I even want to know?"

I answered instinctively. "It wasn't my fault."

"According to witnesses, Ms. Grimlock insisted on helping Mrs. Davenport cross the road even though no one asked for her help," Green supplied.

"It was about to storm," I muttered, jutting out my lower lip as I rubbed my cheek.

Understanding dawned on Griffin's face. "I think Aisling was trying to help."

"I would have no trouble believing that if Ms. Grimlock's brother hadn't forcibly removed Angelina Davenport from the scene, thus separating her from her mother."

Griffin opened his mouth but didn't immediately respond, instead focusing his eyes on me. It was clear he was confused and unsure how to proceed.

"The storm was bad," I said. "Angelina was putting up a fight and I was trying to get her mother inside. Redmond and I thought forcing her into the building was the best way to get Mrs. Davenport moving."

"One of the witnesses on the street said you ordered your brother to move her because, and I quote, 'Angelina is more of a threat.'" Green read from a witness statement. "Would you like to explain what you meant by that?"

"Not really." This wasn't my first time being shaken down by the cops. I refused to break simply because Green thought he was the smartest man in the world. "I was trying to help Mrs. Davenport cross the street. The storm had already hit and I was aware that she'd been ill. I wanted to help her. That's it. There was nothing nefarious going on."

"And yet you decided to engage in a fight with her," Green prodded.

"I didn't engage in a fight." I kept my voice clipped and even. "She said some things to me that were ... unpleasant, but I refrained from fighting even though I'm convinced she and her evil daughter were kicked out of Hell because they're so unpleasant. I mean ... Satan took one look at them and said, 'They're too mean for my hood,' and gave them the heave-ho."

Green arched an eyebrow but otherwise remained silent. I'd gotten off course and I realized it. I needed to correct things.

"She said some things, but I was more intent on getting her inside," I offered. "I think perhaps her medication is influencing her mind, because she turned violent out of nowhere. I'm sure if you talk to everyone inside the coffee shop they will tell you that I didn't attack Mrs. Davenport. She attacked me."

"Is that true?" Griffin asked pointedly. "Did you bother to interview the other witnesses?"

"Of course I did. I'm not new. I'm just trying to understand the nuances of the situation."

"Why not ask Mrs. Davenport?" I challenged. "She was there, too."

"She seems somehow ... confused," Green hedged. "I don't want to make things worse for her. She's been through enough, as has her daughter."

Something occurred to me and I opened my mouth to put Green on the defensive. Griffin beat me to it.

"Given the fact that you've become involved – at least on a superficial level – with Angelina Davenport, don't you think it's a conflict of interest for you to handle this investigation?" Griffin challenged.

Green balked. "We're not involved."

"You had coffee with her yesterday," Griffin argued.

"And you have a date scheduled with her," I added, playing a hunch.

Green was flabbergasted. "Who told you about that?"

"You just did," I fired back.

"We're done here," Griffin announced, getting to his feet. He grabbed my hand and dragged me with him. "If one of the other detectives in your division has legitimate questions about the incident, you know where to find us. Until then, you have Aisling's attorney's name. You're not to contact her without going through him first. Are we clear?"

Green worked his jaw and nodded, clearly unhappy.

"Great." Griffin kept a firm grip on my hand as he led me toward the front door of the precinct. He waited until we were outside to speak. "Are you okay?" He tipped my chin so he could study the scratches. "Those look like they hurt."

"They don't feel great. But I'm okay." I wrapped my hands around his wrists as he cupped my face. "I swear I'm fine. You don't need to panic or anything. The storm didn't affect me."

"I take it the storm affected Mrs. Davenport."

"Big time."

"So both sides of your theory have been proven," Griffin mused. "Did you find out anything else?"

"We got information, but I'm not sure how to use it. Do you want to buy me a late lunch so we can talk it through?"

"I would love to buy you a late lunch." Griffin gave me a quick kiss. "I'm pretty sure you've earned whatever you want today, so you make the choice."

That was a dangerous proposition. "Middle Eastern."

"We just had Middle Eastern for dinner a couple of nights ago."

"You said it was my choice."

"So I did." Griffin offered up a rueful smile. "You're a creature of habit. I find it cute and annoying at the same time."

"Welcome to my very messed-up world."

"Oh, don't worry, I plan to stay here forever."

14

FOURTEEN

Redmond met us for lunch, appearing out of nowhere to follow us to the restaurant. He seemed lost in thought and didn't speak until we were situated in a cozy booth and had placed our orders.

"What's wrong with you?" Griffin asked, picking up on Redmond's mood right away. "You weren't affected by the storm, were you?"

Redmond shook his head. "No, and I don't think Angelina was either. That probably has something to do with the fact that I physically carried her into the coffee shop even though she put up a fight. She wasn't outside long enough to really test our theory."

"So what's wrong?" Griffin pressed.

"I don't know. I simply can't wrap my head around this." Redmond ran his hand over his jaw. "Right up until the moment Aisling insisted on taking Angelina away from the situation I thought that perhaps we were wrong. I saw it, though. I saw it from inside. I saw the shift on Carol's face. She would've killed Aisling if she had the strength."

"I think that's because she was already predisposed to dislike me," I offered. "She said some whacked-out things to me, but I'm pretty sure she believed them before the storm took her over. That's what makes it all the more creepy."

"What did she say to you?" Griffin asked.

"She painted me as the bad guy in my feud with Angelina. I guess I should've expected that. I take very little of the blame on myself when it comes to my relationship with Angelina, even though I clearly didn't make things better. They look at things differently."

"From the stories I've heard, she got what was coming to her," Griffin noted. "You weren't exactly an angel ... ."

Redmond snorted. "More like a devil."

"You weren't an angel," Griffin repeated, "but I don't think you're to blame for this." He leaned back in his seat, his thigh pressed against mine, and gave me a serious look. "May I ask what possessed you to jump out of the truck and insert yourself into that situation?"

The tone of the question made me instantly alert. "It was about to storm."

"So you decided to put yourself in danger to help a woman you hate?"

"I ... wasn't in any danger." The response was lame, but I had nothing else to offer. "I'm immune. We proved that today."

"You didn't know that for sure before you did it."

"We had a feeling."

Griffin narrowed his eyes. "Are you arguing just to argue? You know I hate that."

"I'm not arguing just to argue. I don't do that." I averted my eyes because even I didn't believe the lie. "I'm simply stating a fact."

"Whatever." Griffin played with his empty straw wrapper as he stared into nothing.

As if sensing a brewing argument, Redmond smoothly stepped in to defuse the tension. "It was a spur-of-the-moment thing," he offered. "You have to understand, Carol was always a robust woman. She's dropped sixty pounds and looks as if she's one step from the grave. It was shocking to both of us.

"Aisling didn't jump out to help Angelina," he continued. "She jumped out to help an older woman who was clearly in duress. We knew her from when we were kids — even though she was a mean wench even then — so we couldn't very well just leave them there like that."

Griffin tapped his fingers on top of the table as he glanced between us. "Your poor father must've had his hands full with you guys when you decided to take up for one another as kids. I mean, it's one thing when the kids are tattling on each other. It's quite another when they're holding together as a united front."

"That's not what we're doing," Redmond argued.

"That's totally what you're doing." Griffin cracked a smile. "You can't stop yourself from trying to protect your sister. It's cute sometimes ... although it's totally annoying a lot of the time, too."

I marginally relaxed. "I didn't even realize I was doing it as it happened," I admitted. "I just couldn't ignore them. Even though I hate them, the idea of leaving them in the storm like that was too much. What would've happened if Angelina turned on her mother?"

"I don't know." Griffin grabbed my fingers and gave them a squeeze under the table. "We had another round of violent altercations during the storm this afternoon. Thankfully that storm lasted only about twenty minutes or things could've been a heckuva lot worse."

"You didn't go out in it, did you?"

Griffin cast me a derisive look. "I don't think you're in the position to give me crap for what I did or did not do given how your day ended."

He had a point, but still ... . "It's different. I'm a reaper."

"I don't want to state the obvious because we've already been down this road, but you didn't know that," Griffin argued. "You didn't know anything of the sort, in fact, so I wouldn't push me too far on this one."

I could tell from the tone of his voice that he meant business. "Fine. I'm sorry." I held up my hands in defeat. "I don't want to argue."

"That's good, because I don't want to either." Griffin studied me for a long moment before leaning forward and giving me a quick kiss on the cheek. "Don't pout. I think it was very magnanimous of me to let you off without yelling at you."

"Oh, whatever." I rolled my eyes. "Tell me about the rest of your day."

Griffin's grin was impish. He enjoyed messing with me as much as my brothers did at times. "There's not much to tell. Other than the storm, very little happened. The doctor has confirmed an extra burst of epinephrine to Peter's brain, but he has to see a specialist to determine why, so that case is at a standstill."

"If the cause is rooted in magic, I doubt very much they'll ever get the answers they want," Redmond pointed out. "It's not as if a doctor will blame a storm."

"No," Griffin agreed. "They seem to be moving past it, though. Lani is better than Peter. She's fine with the explanation, which makes me a bit nervous."

"Why does that make you nervous?" I asked.

"Because I've always been taught that women shouldn't forgive men who smack them around," Griffin replied. "My mother was always firm on that. She was very clear when I was growing up that wrestling with Maya was okay. Occasionally smacking and pinching her when I was little was okay, too.

"All right, it wasn't okay, but it wasn't grounds for the firing squad," he continued. "I knew better than to hit Maya when I got older. And, as rough and tumble as you guys are, I've yet to see one of your brothers strike you, Aisling."

I tilted my head to the side, considering. "We smacked each other around quite a bit when we were younger."

"I think that's normal kid stuff," Griffin noted. "At a certain point, that changes."

I flicked my eyes to Redmond. "In truth, I don't really remember you ever smacking me around. Aidan and Braden did quite a bit, but you and Cillian didn't."

"I was older than you," Redmond reminded me. "You were much smaller than me for a long time. When you were old enough to hold your own it simply wasn't right. I could've done real damage to you."

"You pulled my hair and dumped water on me plenty of times."

"Yes, but you weren't hurt by that."

It was an interesting paradigm. I couldn't help being intrigued. "So you're upset that Lani is willing to forgive Peter even though you know the storm made him do what he did," I mused. "That's kind of weird, huh?"

Griffin shrugged. "I don't know that I'm upset that Lani is willing to forgive him so easily," he clarified. "It's more that if I had a daughter

– and because I'm marrying you, Aisling, I'm pretty sure I'll get the mouthiest daughter in the world someday – I wouldn't be okay with her ever forgiving a guy who knocked her around."

"I get that." I did. "I mean, I don't get the part where you think our daughter would be mouthy or anything, but I get the rest of it. For the record, our daughter will be an angel, just like me.

"As for the violence, I don't know what to tell you," I continued. "It's not as if Peter was violent before. Sure, they don't know about the storms, but I think Lani can search her heart and know that Peter would never purposely hurt her. It's easy to grasp those things when you're a woman."

Griffin smiled. "You're very cute."

"Because I have faith?"

"Because you've convinced yourself that any child of ours will be an angel," Griffin replied, shifting when I playfully smacked his arm. "As for everything else, I don't think dwelling on it is a good idea. We need to look forward. We can't change the past."

"Good point." I sipped my iced tea. "With that in mind, we got a bit of a runaround this afternoon. Madame Maxine sent us to a shaman, and the shaman played word games."

"He was a total tool," Redmond agreed. "He did suggest we're dealing with a woman, though. He also said that this woman might've had something to do with the things that we've been dealing with the past year."

Griffin rubbed his forehead. "I don't understand what you're saying."

"I'm not sure it's important," I said. "I think we need to focus on the obvious right now. That means we need to start with the symbol. I mean ... why would a police chief have that specific symbol in his home?"

"I might have an answer for you there." Griffin slid his arm around my shoulders. "I asked around about Turner at work today. I did it under the guise of expressing my surprise at his death and then saying I'd heard mostly good things about him over the years. It turns out there are a few rumors about the guy I've never heard."

"Really?" Redmond leaned forward, intrigued. "What kind of

rumors? Did he wear women's underwear and strip at a transvestite club on the weekends?"

Griffin's mouth dropped open. "Why would you even ask that?"

"He asks that all the time," I answered, shooting my brother a dirty look. "He just likes getting a rise out of people."

"One of these days I'm going to nail that and everyone will be amazed," Redmond countered.

"Whatever. What did you learn about Harry?"

"Well, depending on who you believe, apparently he had a witch for a mother." Griffin was clearly enjoying himself, because he didn't bother to disguise his smile when Redmond and I openly stared at him. "Apparently his mother – one Annemarie Turner – used to threaten to cast spells on people and actually participated in outdoor Wicca festivals in the city."

I had no idea what to make of that. "Wicca is a peaceful religion," I said after a beat. "I can't think of any Wicca enthusiasts who would create a storm of fury and unleash it on everyone. The basic tenet of Wicca is essentially whatever you do to others will come back on you threefold."

"That's what you chose to focus on?" Redmond looked disap-pointed. "I want to know what kind of spells she supposedly cast on people."

"I had no idea any of this was actually a thing until it came up this afternoon, so take these stories with a grain of salt," Griffin warned. "Everyone talked about them for a good hour during our downtime. I was amazed by the entire thing."

"Oh, I'm practically salivating here," Redmond groused. "What spells did she cast?"

"Okay, but I don't like to gossip. Try to remember that." Griffin looked as if the opposite was true as he clearly warmed to his subject. "According to Timothy Dalton, Annemarie hated Harry's first wife despite the fact that everyone thought she was sweet and an absolute delight to be around.

"Apparently Annemarie was jealous because her son spent more time with his wife than her, so she cast a spell and made her constantly sick," he continued. "If Annemarie started feeling better and spent time with Harry, then she would get sick. If they stayed apart, she would get better. This went on for months."

"Did Annemarie own up to it?" I asked.

Griffin nodded. "That's how they knew to look for the pattern. She told them what she did. They didn't believe her and went against her wishes. Until the pattern kept repeating ... and repeating ... and repeating.

"It got bad enough both of them started to believe, and when that happened, well, the marriage essentially imploded," he continued. "They broke up, and the wife was never sick again after the divorce."

It was an intriguing story, but it wasn't exactly proof. "That could've been a coincidence."

"It could have," Griffin agreed. "There's more. Apparently she cursed a neighbor and he died in his sleep. She cursed some kid on her street and he came down with measles so bad he almost died ... even though he'd been vaccinated. Some of the guys swear that others told them bats swirled around her house at night."

"That all seems a bit ridiculous," Redmond sneered. "I mean ... that's like an urban legend that took on a life of its own."

"I don't disagree with you. I'm simply telling you what I heard."

I looked to Redmond to gauge his opinion. He looked as conflicted as I felt. "Well, it sounds a bit crazy to me, but I guess we can do some research."

"I don't know what else to do," Redmond said. "We've already dealt with a seer and a shaman today. We're fighting magical storms. Why not add a witch to the mix?"

Griffin beamed. "This is why I love hanging out with you guys. You're open for anything."

I RODE WITH Redmond to Royal Oak, so Griffin offered to take custody of me after lunch. He didn't have to return to work because he took half a personal day, offering to help me research the witch angle for the rest of the afternoon.

"We can do it in bed," Griffin suggested, wiggling his eyebrows.

"I really hate you sometimes," Redmond grumbled.

Griffin's truck was behind the police station, so we had to walk three blocks to retrieve it. That gave us plenty of time to talk.

"That's a plan," I said. "My car is still at Grimlock Manor. Do you want to pick it up or leave it until tomorrow?"

"Leave it," Griffin answered automatically. "I have plans for you this afternoon."

"I will thump you," Redmond warned. "That's my baby sister."

"She's going to be my wife in a few months."

"I don't care. She was my sister first."

"I think wife trumps sister."

"I think you're on crack," Redmond muttered, shaking his head while I giggled. "Don't encourage him, Ais. It gives me indigestion."

"I think you have indigestion because you ate enough for three people," I shot back, stepping into the crosswalk. "I enjoy it when he's perverted, and it's only partially because I know it bothers you."

"You're a sick woman." Redmond tugged on the ends of my hair. "I can still wrestle you down and put your face in my armpit like I did when we were kids. You know that, right?"

"Oh, I'm shaking in my shoes. In fact ... ." The words died on my lips, the jocularity evaporating in an instant as the sky opened up to a deluge of rain. There was no warning. There was no darkening of the clouds. There was only a huge zap of lightning, which appeared to strike in a tiny park across the way, and a rumble of thunder that caused the earth under my feet to shake.

"Holy crap!" I exhaled heavily, the hair on my arms standing on end. "That was close."

"Yeah." Redmond stared at the sky, wrinkling his nose. "These storms are freaking wonky. There's no rhyme or reason to them. I can't understand why they keep showing up."

"At least we're the only ones out right now," I noted. "We'll be okay. We're immune." The words were out of my mouth before I understood what I was saying.

I swiveled quickly when reality set in, to find Griffin standing in the middle of the crosswalk staring at his fingers. He looked ... lost. I could think of no other word. He seemed to have stopped listening to us and instead focused on something only he could see and hear.

I took a tentative step toward him, my heart twisting. "Griffin?"

He snapped his head up, snarling when he caught my gaze.

"Oh, crap." I felt sick to my stomach. "Oh, crap. Oh, crap."

"That's not helping," Redmond snapped, grabbing my arm and tugging me away from Griffin. "You have to get out of here."

"I can't leave him," I protested. "I won't do it."

Redmond gave me absolutely no wiggle room. "I don't see where you have another choice. Run!"

🦋 15 🦋

FIFTEEN

"**G**riffin?"

I was about to be torn in two. Redmond's hands on my arm would leave bruises because he struggled so hard to pull me away. My heart wouldn't allow me to leave Griffin.

"You have to fight it," I said. "Just ... whatever is going through your head, you have to know it's wrong."

Griffin's eyes were so dark when they locked with mine I thought I'd somehow crawled into a hole and had no way of escaping. Creatures from another world were surely locked in there, and escape was impossible.

"Griffin ... ."

Griffin lifted his hands and squeezed his fingers together, giving the universal "shut up" gesture. "Stop talking."

"Griffin ... ."

"Stop talking!" His voice was like ice. "I am so sick to death of listening to you talk. Do you ever shut up? Do you ever just ... shut your stupid mouth?"

I swallowed hard and fought back tears, rain pelting the side of my face as the thunder continued to roll.

"You need to calm down," Redmond warned, extending a warning finger as he positioned himself so he was between Griffin and me. "I know your brain probably isn't working and this isn't your fault, but if you think I'm going to sit back and let you talk to her like that you've got another think coming."

Griffin snorted, the sound completely without mirth. "She's not the only one with a big mouth. Everyone in your family has a big mouth. I'm pretty sure it's genetic."

"Fine. We have big mouths." Redmond tightened his grip on my arm. "We're going home. When you're feeling more yourself, you're welcome to join us. I'd bring flowers, though." He tugged me with everything he had. "We're going, Aisling."

I slapped at his hand to get him to release me. "We can't leave him!" I grunted as I tried to escape. "He could hurt someone else. He would never be able to live with himself if he hurt someone else."

"I don't want to hurt anyone else." Griffin's eyes landed on me and his lips curved into an evil grin. "I only want to hurt you."

"Aisling, run!" Redmond used all his strength to propel me in the opposite direction, and then positioned himself so Griffin would have no choice but to go through him to get to me.

Griffin didn't seem to care that my brother was tall, strong and built like a running back. He tried to barrel over Redmond, but my brother was ready for him. Redmond had wrestled with Braden, Cillian and Aidan enough as a teenager to read through body language how an attack would come. He swayed to the left slightly as Griffin closed the distance and then slammed his fist into Griffin's jaw, knocking him for a loop with a sucker punch and grabbing him around the waist before his unconscious body crumpled to the ground.

"Help me, Ais," Redmond ordered, groaning as he swung Griffin's body so he could throw him over his shoulder. "We need to get out of here before the cops question us."

I remained rooted to my spot. "Is he okay?"

Redmond took pity on me as he moved toward the sidewalk. "He'll be okay. We need to get him out of the storm. You're going to drive his vehicle and he's going to ride with me in mine."

Tears slid down my cheeks as I struggled to keep up with his long strides. "But ... he'll go back to the way he was, right?"

"I'm sure he will. Jerry did."

"Yeah, but ... ."

"Aisling, I don't have any answers for you." Redmond did his best to keep from exploding, but his agitation was obvious. "We need to get him to Grimlock Manor. After that, we'll decide what to do. For now, that's the only thing we can focus on. Do you understand me?"

I nodded, swiping away the tears as I squared my shoulders. "Yeah. Let's go home."

"Good girl. We'll take this one step at a time."

"I'M GOING TO KILL HIM."

Braden raged as he paced the hallway outside my childhood bedroom. I wanted to punch him – or at least trip him so he careened into the wall – but I could do nothing but watch Dad as he leaned over Griffin's prone form and talked in low voices with Redmond.

"What happened, Ais?" Cillian rested a soothing hand on my shoulder, his voice calm. "Describe what happened for me."

That was the last thing I wanted to do, but I knew Cillian was mostly interested in the scientific aspect. "It happened fast, much faster than it did with Carol Davenport."

"That could be because the second storm was stronger and arrived much quicker," Cillian noted. "It came out of nowhere and was an instant deluge. Griffin didn't even have a chance to take cover."

"He didn't have a chance," I agreed, dragging a hand through my bedraggled hair. "He was angry right away. It was as if something came over him. There was a shift in his eyes and ... he was mean."

"Mean how?" Braden asked, catching me off guard with his vehemence. "What did he say to you?"

"It doesn't matter. He didn't mean it." Of course, I was the one who said that Carol Davenport meant everything she said to me earlier in the day. The anger was doubled, maybe even tripled or quadrupled, but the feelings were already there. Could that be true with Griffin, too?

"Of course he didn't mean it," Cillian said without hesitation. "He loves you. No one can argue with that."

"I still want to kill him," Braden said. "He could've hurt her."

"He didn't, though." I didn't miss the warning look Cillian shot Braden as he rubbed his hand over my shoulder. "Aisling is fine. Redmond was there. We simply need to figure this out and move forward."

"We definitely need to figure this out," I agreed, moving toward the bed and leaving Cillian and Braden to discuss the finer points of research. "Is he okay?"

"He's going to have a bruise on the side of his face as big as your brother's fist," Dad answered, shifting his eyes to me. "I'll bet he'll have a headache the size of your ego." It was a lame joke and I didn't bother to smile. "He should be okay, kid."

"I want to sit with him."

Redmond opened his mouth to argue, but Dad immediately got up and made room for me to settle at Griffin's side.

"I think that's a good idea," Dad said, opting to take a chair at the side of the bed as I sat next to Griffin. "We'll all sit with him."

Redmond glanced between us, his jaw set. "I don't want her sitting by him when he wakes up. He could attack her again."

"He didn't attack me before," I shot back. "He didn't even get near me."

"Not for lack of trying."

"He was just ... confused." I looked to Dad for help. "He didn't know what he was doing."

"I know, kid." Dad jerked his chair closer to the bed and picked a spot near me to sit. "I know he wouldn't purposely hurt you. Even when I didn't trust him at the beginning I knew he would never physically hurt you. He's not that kind of man."

"He was that kind of man this afternoon," Redmond persisted, crossing his arms over his chest. "I don't want her to be the one closest to him when he wakes. We might not be able to get to her if he attacks."

"He won't attack." I was firm. "He won't. It was the storm."

"You don't know that," Redmond fired back. "Maybe the storm got inside and corrupted his blood. Maybe he'll never be the same again."

Griffin wasn't the only one feeling violent. I wanted to launch myself off the bed and wring Redmond's neck.

"Redmond," Dad said mildly, holding up a hand. "I'll sit with Aisling and make sure she's all right. I think you should go into the hallway and talk strategy with your brothers."

"What if he attacks?"

"Then I will be here ... or are you insinuating I can't handle Griffin and protect your sister should the need arise?"

Redmond blanched. "Of course not."

"I don't need protection," I grumbled, tucking the covers tighter at Griffin's side. "He'll be fine."

"Of course he will." Dad's tone was soothing. "Jerry suffered no lingering effects from his episode. I'm sure it will be the same with Griffin." Dad looked back to Redmond. "I told you to go. I'll stay with your sister until Griffin wakes."

Redmond didn't look convinced. "What if you need me?"

"I'm sure we'll manage to muddle through."

Redmond stared at me for a long beat and then nodded, his shoulders stiff. "Fine. I won't be far."

"I'll alert the authorities." Dad leaned back in his chair, comfortable to sit in silence with me for as long as it took for my vocal cords to loosen up. He did the same thing when I was a teenager, and often I ended up owning up to whatever I did wrong simply to avoid the silence. This situation was no different.

"He's going to feel awful."

Dad made a clucking sound with his tongue. "He will. I know him well enough to believe he'll be swimming in guilt when he surfaces. That will be a whole other problem we'll have to deal with. I'm not looking forward to it.

"Right now, though, I want to deal with you," he continued. "What is it exactly that you're feeling?"

"I'm fine." The words were out before I even took a moment to think about them.

"You're very far from fine." Dad leaned forward and took my hand. "You're pale. Your hands are shaking. You're very obviously close to tears and I can tell you've already done some crying. I'll wager that your stomach is upset and even an ice cream bar won't make you feel better. That's on top of the general ache that's probably building in your heart."

"How did you know that?"

"I know you. It's okay." Dad squeezed my hand. "This situation is a nightmare. I won't pretend otherwise. What happened today is not Griffin's fault. It's not your fault either."

"I'm not blaming myself."

"Aren't you?" Dad cocked a challenging eyebrow. "He might be the one you're going to marry, but I'm still the one who knows you best, kid. I know that you're beating yourself up inside.

"You think if you hadn't gotten out of Redmond's truck and helped Carol you wouldn't have been taken to the precinct for questioning," he continued. "If that didn't happen, Griffin wouldn't have left early. He wouldn't have been out in the storm. In your head, this is all on you."

Crap. He did know me. I didn't like that one bit. "I maintain Jerry knows me best." I sounded petulant, but I didn't care. "There are loads of things you don't know."

"Name one."

"I once stole your razor and shaved my legs."

"I know. You dulled the blades so badly I had to wear toilet paper on my face for twenty minutes to staunch the bleeding. Everyone at work asked me if I was having an allergic reaction to my new aftershave."

I couldn't stop myself from laughing. "Fine. Maybe you know me."

"Maybe I do." Dad leaned back and folded his hands across his stomach. "You can't blame yourself. It's a waste of time. Griffin will carry enough blame for both of you as it is. You've got to pull yourself together."

"I am together." I mostly meant it. "You have to make sure my brothers behave themselves. They're the ones who will make this worse."

"I will do my best with your brothers, but I'm not going to admonish them for protecting you. Redmond did the right thing today. He made sure Griffin didn't put his hands on you and he essentially saved Griffin in the process. Now, Griffin might have a whopper of a headache and be in the mood to pout when he wakes, but Redmond is not to blame for that."

"Griffin isn't either." I refused to let that go. "He would never hurt me."

"Who are you trying to convince?" Dad challenged. "I've already said I know that. If I thought he was capable of that he would've been dead long ago. I wasn't joking when I told him that I know how to hide a body."

I pressed my lips together, uncertain.

"Are you saying that you think he really meant what he said?" Dad prodded.

I shook my head, tears threatening to flood forward. "No, but the things Carol Davenport said to me ... I think she really believed them, so ... ." I left the rest hanging, hating the way Dad chuckled as realization dawned.

"So you think Griffin meant it when he said he couldn't stand the sound of your voice."

"He said he wanted me to shut up. That's different."

"That's a semantics argument, and it's hardly important," Dad said. "Do you honestly think Griffin is the sort of man who would stay with you if he didn't love you? I don't. Quite frankly, I wish he would love you a little less, because the petting and cooing gets old."

I rolled my eyes, which I think was the reaction Dad was looking for because his grin was triumphant.

"I know you think I'm being ridiculous," I said, collecting myself to the best of my ability. "It's just ... if I believe Mrs. Davenport was saying what she truly felt, doesn't it stand to reason that Griffin believed what he said?"

"I think you're comparing two very different things. Carol Davenport never liked you. She blamed you for Angelina's failings. She was an unhappy woman who had nothing but mean bones in her body.

"On the flip side, Griffin loves you to distraction. I guarantee he's going to hate himself when he wakes," Dad continued. "He'll feel bad enough for the both of you. I don't think harboring doubts about his love will do either of you any good."

"I hate it when you're right," I grumbled, crossing my arms over my chest. "I don't want Griffin to feel guilty. This wasn't his fault."

"It wasn't your fault either."

"It feels like my fault. This wouldn't be happening to him if he hadn't hooked up with me. Nothing paranormal ever happened to him before me."

"Do you think he would've been safe from the storms if you weren't around to look out for him?" Dad countered. "Griffin is the type to run headlong into danger. I think it's very likely that he would've gotten himself in trouble helping others without even knowing what was happening."

I exhaled heavily, frustration rolling through me. "Must you always be right?"

"Only when it comes to my children."

"It's annoying."

"So is walking around with a face full of toilet paper because my only daughter needed to shave her legs in a hurry for a date with a football player." Dad's grin was smug. "Ah, you didn't realize I knew about that part of the story. Well, I did. And you have much better taste in men now than you did then."

I didn't want to laugh. It was the exact worst time. I couldn't help myself, though. I giggled and wiped my hands over my face to slap back the tears.

"Thank you, Daddy."

"You're welcome." Dad smiled at me for a long time before shifting his eyes to Griffin. "I believe he's about to wake. Prepare yourself, because I think the next Grimlock family meltdown will be a doozy."

I had a feeling he was right. Still, I plastered a warm smile on my face and hovered over Griffin so he would be looking directly at me when he woke.

It was time for round two.

🪶 16 🪶

SIXTEEN

"Hey."

Griffin's eyes were cloudy when he woke, confusion evident. He smiled when he saw me and stretched. "Hey. Are we taking a nap? I don't remember getting home."

Hope surged. Maybe he wouldn't remember after all. I saw that wasn't the case, though, when he furrowed his brow and ran a hand through his hair. His face twisted as things slowly started coming back to him.

"How are you feeling?" I asked, working overtime to tamp down my worry.

"I ... oh, God. Oh, my ... ." He jerked away when I tried to rest my hand on his arm. "Don't. Don't touch me!"

My heart lodged in my throat as I blinked rapidly in an attempt to fight back tears. "It's okay. It's not your fault."

"No. No. No." Griffin shook his head and pressed his eyes shut. "I can't believe I said that to you. I can't believe I almost ... ."

I cut him off by grabbing his wrist, giving it a hard squeeze to get his attention. "You didn't hurt me. You didn't lay a hand on me."

"I tried to. I would have." Griffin jerked his arm from my hand. "Don't touch me right now. I just ... can't."

"Griffin, please don't let this eat at you." My voice cracked and I was furious at myself for it. Crying wouldn't help anything. "You can't control what happened. It came out of nowhere."

"Stop making excuses for me!" Griffin's eyes fired and his tone was harsh, causing me to jolt. He held up his hands, tears swamping his eyes. "I'm sorry. I don't want to frighten you, but I clearly have. I need a little space. I need to ... I don't know. I need to think."

I didn't like the sound of that one little bit. "No good ever comes from thinking. I should know."

Griffin didn't as much as smile. "Baby, I need a little time away from you right now. It's not you. It's me."

Ah, the breakup excuse the world over. I was having none of that. "No. I won't let you pull away. I ... ."

"Aisling, I think you should go." Dad took me by surprise when he smoothly gripped my arm and pulled me from the bed. "Griffin needs time to decompress. He needs quiet. You're not conducive to rest."

"What a weird way to insult me out of nowhere," I grumbled.

Dad smirked. "I'm not insulting you. I'm trying to help Griffin. Besides, I have a job for you. You need to head out if you expect to get it done for dinner."

I narrowed my eyes, suspicious. "You have a job for me? You have a job for me now? Are you kidding? I'm not going on a job."

"It's not that type of job." Dad remained calm despite my theatrics. "I need you to go with Cillian to the funeral home."

"Why?"

"Because Harry Turner's family is there – I already checked – and they're making plans for his viewing and service. I need you to talk to them about the witch story Griffin told you earlier."

"How do you even know about that? I didn't have time to tell you."

"No, but Redmond did." Dad refused to back down. The look on his face promised mayhem if I pushed too far. "You need to go with Cillian to see if you can find information on that symbol. I'll stick close to Griffin and make sure he's all right."

Warning bells went off in my head though I knew it was ridiculous to even consider the notion Dad was lying to me and had something else planned. "You're not going to kill him while I'm running stupid errands, are you?"

"Kill him?" Dad arched an eyebrow. "Why would I kill him?"

"You just said ten minutes ago that you know how to hide a body. I don't want his body hidden. If he's not here when I get back ... ."

Dad made an exaggerated face. "You're so dramatic. I promise he'll be here when you return. I swear it. I have no intention of hurting him. I do think, however, my presence is preferable right now compared to yours."

"That's a frightening thought," I muttered, darting a gaze to Griffin to see how he felt about the suggestion. He stared at the blanket, his face intense. "Do you want me to leave?"

Griffin swallowed hard and forced his eyes to me. "I don't want to upset you right now. I need to think. It would probably be best if you took a little break."

I hated his flat affect. "You'll be here when I get back? You won't leave, will you?"

Griffin opened his mouth but didn't immediately answer.

"He won't leave," Dad said firmly. "I'll make sure he's here. I'll take care of him. You just need to get out of the house for a bit. Things will be better when you return."

I wasn't sure I believed that. "What if they're not?"

"Then we'll tackle it together."

I wanted to stay. My heart told me leaving was a bad idea. My head, though, recognized Griffin was struggling not to explode and demand I leave. If that happened I'd dig my heels in and push him to the point of no return.

"Fine." I blew out a sigh as I ran my hands over my hips to settle myself. "I'll be back. If you're not here when I get back, Griffin, I will track you down ... and I'll bring my brothers along. If you think I'm a pain, just wait until I force them to do my bidding."

"Be careful while you're out." Griffin's voice was low. "If it storms, run. Stay away from anyone who might be affected. Don't try to help, even though I know that will be your first instinct. Just ... run. Promise me."

"I'll promise if you promise to be here when I get back."

Griffin snagged my gaze and I could see the myriad of hurt feelings and guilt floating through his dark eyes. "I promise to be here. Now you promise to be really careful."

"I promise." I meant it. "I'll be back before you know it."

"DON'T POUT."

Cillian gave me a derisive look as we walked through the funeral parlor door.

"I'm not pouting."

"You're pouting."

"I am not."

"You are, too."

"I am not."

"You are ... you know what? Fine, you're not pouting." Cillian held his hands up and did a wonderful impression of our father trying to control his temper. "You're in a fine frame of mind. Angels want to weep in your presence because your benevolence is so overwhelming."

"Ha, ha." I elbowed his side as I shifted and sighed as I surveyed the room. "I'm sorry. I can't stop worrying about Griffin."

"I know, Ais, but he needs time to come to grips with what happened. I don't know what I would do in his position. I know it wasn't his fault – he probably knows the same deep down – but the idea that he could've hurt you is wrecking him. I know it would wreck me if the same thing happened with Maya."

"But I'm fine."

"Yes, but the idea of hurting you is almost worse than the reality. You need to give him a little breathing room. Dad will talk to him."

That was exactly what I was worried about. "What if Dad is mean to him?"

Cillian rolled his eyes. "Dad is nicer to Griffin than he is to us half the time. Don't worry about it. Dad will be the best thing for Griffin. He won't let him wallow, but he'll give him a bit of space to work through the monstrous guilt chasing him."

The word "monster" triggered something in my head. "I never knew he could look like that. I didn't think he had it in him."

This time when Cillian looked to me there was sympathy in his eyes. "Everyone has the potential to hurt those they love the most, which is why love is a leap of faith. You have to know that Griffin would never purposely hurt you."

"I do know that. I'm still going to be haunted by that look on his face for a long time."

"Nowhere near as haunted as he'll be by the one he saw on your face. No one wants the person he loves to be afraid of him, and that will eat at Griffin now. You have to find a way to get past that."

"That's why I wanted to stay at Grimlock Manor. Griffin needs me."

"Griffin needs oxygen and peace," Cillian countered. "He'll need you eventually, but he needs solitude first."

"Fine. I hate it when you make sense." I dragged a hand through the hair I hadn't bothered to brush after it was blown in a million different directions by the storm. "So ... what are we supposed to do first?"

"I don't know," Cillian admitted, narrowing his eyes as he stared into one of the rooms. Several people – many of them sniffling and crying – sat with a well-tailored man in an expensive suit as they flipped through what looked to be a catalog. "I'm guessing that's them."

Cillian licked his lips as he turned back to me, his expression hard to read. "How about I handle the group in there and you meander around to see if you can find any stragglers to question?"

"Why do you want to be the one to handle the people in there?"

"They're women. You don't often make a good impression on women."

He wasn't wrong. I was insulted all the same. Still, I didn't want to deal with Harry Turner's bereaved loved ones, so if Cillian wanted to do the bulk of the heavy lifting on this one I was happy to let him.

"Go ahead." I flashed a smile that wasn't exactly genuine. "I'll look around for ideas in case I want to bury Braden in the near future."

"That sounds like a plan."

Cillian gave my shoulder a squeeze before heading off to work his charms on Turner's relatives. I watched him for a moment, shaking my head at the way he smoothed his hair and squared his shoulders, and then headed toward the room on the other side of the lobby.

I wasn't sure what to expect. There was always a possibility that one of Turner's loved ones had detached from the crowd for a moment of quiet. If so, it was my job to ask questions and get to the bottom of the witch rumor.

Instead of Turner's relatives, I found someone else. It wasn't who I expected and yet, given the day I was having it felt somehow right.

"Angelina?"

Angelina jerked her shoulders at the sound of my voice and dropped the coffin pillow she was looking at as if it were on fire. She looked almost guilty ... although why was beyond me. "What are you doing here?"

"I was just about to ask you the same question," I said, sauntering into the room and taking a seat on the uncomfortable couch centered between the display cases. "What is it with this little furniture? It's stupid looking."

"It's antique and original," Angelina said with a sigh. "It's worth a lot of money, and only those with taste would bother taking the time to restore it. I'm sure it's better than whatever particle board furniture you've got."

Oddly enough, I was glad she drew first blood in our ongoing verbal war. I wasn't feeling up to being the aggressor. "Yes, but with particle board you can replace it every year without feeling guilty."

"At least you have a reason." Angelina returned the pillow to its proper spot in the display. "Why are you here? Are you trolling for dates?"

"It's a long story."

Angelina arched an eyebrow, surprised. "Wait ... you have a legitimate reason for being here? I can't wait to hear this."

"We're trying to get information about a dead guy." I saw no reason to lie. Angelina was well aware of our family secret. She could easily figure out things on her own. "We need to determine if his mother was a witch, because he might have something to do with the evil storms hitting the area."

Angelina's shoulders jerked as she stared me down. "Evil storms?"

"Don't tell me you haven't noticed the storms."

"There have been a lot of them the past few days," Angelina confirmed. "Is that what you're talking about?"

"Sure. Why not? We'll go with that."

Angelina knit her eyebrows. "You're lying. You're talking about something else."

"It hardly matters." I reclined on the couch. "What are you doing here? Are you looking for a new bed? I think a casket is a great idea if you're looking to entrap a man. If you close the top he probably won't be able to escape. The older you get, the more you'll probably need something like that."

"Oh, your wit astounds me," Angelina sneered. "How have you not gotten a job as a standup comedienne yet?"

"I'm saving that for next year."

"Ha, ha."

She still hadn't answered my first question and I was starting to get uncomfortable with her rather obvious silence. "Did something happen with your mother?"

"Do you care?"

Did I? I wasn't sure. "You know what happened earlier wasn't because I wanted to mess with you, right? It probably seems that way, but ... I honestly was trying to help."

"Because of the evil storms?"

I shrugged. "There's very little point in me explaining. You won't understand. I just ... I wasn't trying to make things worse. I can very rarely say that and mean it, but I mean it now."

Angelina sighed and threw herself on the other end of the couch, rubbing her forehead as she stared into nothing. "I figured that out when you didn't press charges against her. You could have – she hurt you. I've been trying to figure out why you didn't ever since we left the precinct and I had to take her back home so she could rest with the day nurse."

"There was no point in pressing charges. She clearly wasn't in her right mind."

"No, clearly not," Angelina agreed. "Her medication makes her wonky."

"Your buddy Detective Green wanted to charge me even though I was the victim in that particular scenario – wow, there's something I never thought I would say – and he pushed hard. Did you have something to do with that?"

"No. I told him there was no need, but he seems to have a thing for you – and not in a good way. He asked me what I knew about you. At first I thought he was asking if you were a good person – and you know how I would've answered that question – but it was more than that. He's digging hard on you because he believes you're a murderer or something."

I wasn't surprised by the admission, but it didn't sit well. "What did you tell him?"

"Are you asking if I shared your family secret?"

I stared at her.

"Well, I didn't." Angelina rubbed between her eyebrows. I could feel the weariness emanating from her. "He wouldn't believe me if I told him the things I've seen happening around you. Even if he did, I'm pretty sure that I don't want to be involved in any of that."

"You definitely don't. You still haven't told me why you're here. I'm starting to get a complex about your non-answers."

"I'm here because my mother is insistent about planning her funeral. She wants choices ... and catalogs ... and sample material. She doesn't care that it's morbid. She merely cares that she gets to choose."

I was dumbfounded. "Seriously?" That sounded like the worst thing ever. "Do you think that's because she feels as if choices have been stripped from her, so she wants to be in charge of the few things she can control?"

Angelina's mouth dropped open. "Wow. That was almost profound the way you phrased that."

I grinned. "I can be profound."

"Not usually. As for your theory, I guess that's as good a reason for her behavior as any." Angelina groaned as she stood and turned back to the display. "I have to take a catalog home. She wants her funeral planned before ... well, before it's necessary."

"Maybe it won't be necessary for a long time," I suggested hopefully.

"No. I know that's not true. It will be soon."

My stomach flipped. "Soon?"

"Very soon. The doctor says she has weeks at most. It could happen any day now. I could wake up tomorrow, walk into her room and ... well, it will definitely be soon."

"I'm sorry." I found I actually meant it, which was sobering. "I can't imagine what you're going through."

"Your mother died."

"Yeah, well ... ."

"Then she came back to life," Angelina added. "You got a miracle."

"Is that what you want? A miracle, I mean."

"I don't know. But I want something other than this." Angelina shook herself from her reverie and grabbed a catalog from the counter. "I don't think I'm going to get what I want for a long time. Even when the death itself is fast, what's left behind isn't."

She wasn't wrong. "I hope things get better."

"You do?"

I shrugged. "It's no fun to mess with you when you can't insult me back."

"True enough. Maybe one day, huh?"

"Yeah. Maybe one day."

17

SEVENTEEN

I was nervous and intent on seeing Griffin when we returned to Grimlock Manor. Cillian babbled on and on about ... well, something ... for the duration of the ride back to the house. He seemed to think that I was not only interested but listening, which was pretty far from the truth.

"Yeah. It's fascinating." I breezed past him as he opened the front door and headed toward the stairs. "I'm sure everyone else will be thrilled to 'ooh' and 'aah' over that enthralling story."

Cillian made a face. "You weren't even listening, were you?"

"Not even a little."

I was on the first step when a hand grabbed the back of my hoodie and jerked me back, causing me to nearly lose my footing and face plant on the foyer's ceramic tile.

"Hey! You almost killed me. Knock it off."

I wasn't surprised to find Dad staring at me when I struggled to turn. He didn't immediately release my hoodie, which told me I was in for a lecture.

"Where do you think you're going?" Dad asked pointedly.

"Um ... in life or right now?"

"Don't try to be cute."

"But I do it so well."

Dad growled, a sound I recognized well from my teenage years. He was very close to losing it.

"Don't take that tone with me." I adopted a petulant voice. "I'm going to see Griffin and you can't stop me."

"I think you should give him a bit longer."

"No."

"Aisling ... ."

"No," I repeated, firmly shaking my head. "I want to see him. He doesn't know it yet, but he needs to see me. I'm going to fix him."

Dad let loose a weary sigh. "Why is it that women feel the need to fix things that might be incapable of being fixed?"

The words were like a sharp smack across the face, and my smile slipped. "What do you mean? You didn't let him leave, did you? He hasn't disappeared so I'll never be able to find him, has he?"

Dad's expression was hard to read. "May I ask why you think that?"

I shrugged, his somber eyes causing me to squirm. "Because he's a do-gooder. He's one of those people who always does things that are in the best interests of others. I'm worried he's going to think that being away is best for me ... and it's not. And I'm going to kick him if he tries."

"Ah." Dad continued to hold on to my hoodie. "I don't think you have to worry about that. Even if Griffin did believe that in the heat of the moment, the idea would be fleeting. I believe the boy is hopelessly in love with you ... which is both sweet and annoying. It often makes me want to throttle him."

"Well, great." I tried to jerk away from Dad, but managed to move only two inches. "Let me go so I can talk to him. I need to make him feel better."

Braden snickered as he strolled into the foyer, Redmond, Aidan and Jerry on his heels. "Did you just admit to Dad that you're going upstairs to seduce Griffin to make him feel better?"

"No, gutter brain, I did not!"

Dad used his free hand to cuff Braden. "Don't ever say anything remotely like that again."

"Fine." Braden was rueful as he rubbed the back of his head. "I thought you were holding her here so she couldn't go upstairs and be slutty. It was a misunderstanding."

"You're a complete and total idiot," I supplied. "Like I would ever admit to Dad that I'm about to be slutty. That runs counterintuitive to every instinct I have."

"That's my sweet girl," Dad teased, his smile slipping when I tried to escape the hoodie and leave it behind in an effort to flee upstairs. "Don't push me, Aisling."

"What's going on here?" Mom appeared in the open doorway – I couldn't remember if we'd left it open or she simply let herself into the house – and frowned when she saw my struggle with Dad. "Are you being punished?"

"I have four brothers," I reminded her. "My entire life is punishment."

"Yes. Poor you." Mom ruffled my hair as if I were an adorable eight-year-old trying to manipulate my father. She turned to Dad. "Why are you forcing her to stay here?"

"Don't worry about it." Dad's tone was breezy. His relationship with Mom was something of a work in progress. He'd loved her beyond reason when she died. This person who came back wasn't the woman he married, though. I couldn't blame him for being standoffish.

Several of my brothers, on the other hand – Redmond and Braden specifically – couldn't seem to get it through their thick heads that Dad didn't want to pick up right where they'd left off and pretend we were a sitcom family and that bygones were bygones.

"Obviously something is going on," Mom pressed. "I think I have a right to know."

"You don't have a right to anything," Dad countered, his eyes flashing. "You're here because I allow it. You're not owed anything."

"Dad." Braden shifted to put himself between them. "She's worried about Aisling. I think that's allowed."

"I do, too," Mom sniffed, crossing her arms over her chest. "Aisling is my daughter, too. If something is going on ... ."

"Nothing is going on," Dad snapped.

"Something happened this afternoon," Braden volunteered, causing Dad's eyes to widen. Braden explained what happened during the storm, including Redmond's takedown of an out-of-control Griffin. "So, you see, things are a little tense," he finished.

"I do see." Mom's eyes were thoughtful as she glanced among faces. "And you're holding Aisling to keep her away from Griffin so he doesn't hurt her?"

"No." Dad's fury was palpable. I knew Braden was in for a lecture later regarding family business and exactly how much should be shared with Mom. Unfortunately for Braden, he'd sat through the lecture multiple times the past few months, learning nothing each time. "I think Griffin needs time alone. Aisling will simply upset him."

"Why would Griffin be upset?" Mom challenged. "He attacked her."

"He didn't do it on purpose," I snapped, glaring at Mom. "The storm made him do it."

"I'm not sure I believe in evil storms," Mom said.

"I don't really care what you believe in," I shot back. "It's none of your business."

"Aisling, it's going to be fine." Dad kept his voice calm as he focused on me. "Don't let her get to you. What she says doesn't matter."

"Why?" Braden asked. "She's right. Griffin did go after Aisling."

"And Redmond stopped him," Dad said. "As I recall, Jerry went after Aidan. I didn't see you expressing the same attitude toward Jerry."

"That's because Jerry is part of the family."

"So is Griffin."

Dad's simple declaration caused the air to whoosh out of my lungs. I stopped struggling, my muscles going limp as I simply hung from my hoodie in front of Dad. At that moment I knew he had Griffin's best interests at heart. If he truly believed it was a mistake for me to head upstairs, then perhaps he was right.

Dad looked at me, surprised. "Are you done fighting?"

I nodded. "You don't think Griffin wants to see me, do you?"

"I'm pretty sure Griffin is being consumed by guilt right now," Dad replied, choosing his words carefully. "I tried talking to him, but he wouldn't even look at me. I decided to leave him for a bit. I'll try to discuss things with him again later."

"So you think I should just stay away from him? Don't you think that will make him believe I'm afraid of him ... or that I'm somehow angry ... or that I don't want to be around him?"

Dad opened his mouth to answer, but snapped it shut before a sound escaped. He tilted his head to the side as he considered the questions.

"I think you broke Dad," Aidan said after a moment. "He looks confused and he's quiet. No one in this house is ever quiet."

"I'm debating the proper answer," Dad said. "I'm not sure there is a proper response for what's happening here." To my utter disbelief, he released the back of my hoodie. "Go upstairs and talk to him."

"Really?" I was agog at the shift in his demeanor. "I thought you just said that was a bad idea."

"I don't know if it's a good or bad idea," Dad clarified. "I do know that you have certain instincts when it comes to Griffin, and because you know him best those instincts are probably correct. You'll know what to do when you see him."

"I will?" That was news to me. "I just plan to sit on him until he agrees it was a mistake and lets it go."

Dad shrugged. "Go ahead and try that. What could it possibly hurt?"

I hoped he wouldn't end up regretting that question.

GRIFFIN LAY ON MY bed, one of my old stuffed dogs on his chest, staring at the ceiling when I walked into the bedroom. He didn't bother to glance in my direction even though I knew he was aware of my presence.

"Telling your troubles to Mr. Bark, huh?" I climbed on the bed next to Griffin and tried not to take it personally when he inched away so he wouldn't accidentally touch me.

"Mr. Bark?" Griffin arched an eyebrow and shifted his eyes to me. He looked hollowed out and a bit haunted. It caused my stomach to flip.

I gestured toward the dog. "Dad bought him for me when I was five or six. I thought the name was clever at that age."

"I'm sure." Griffin ran his hand down the dog's head. "How did your trip to the funeral parlor go?"

"I don't know. Cillian talked to the family. I ran into Angelina, so I was distracted. Cillian babbled on and on about something on our way back, but I was more interested in seeing you than listening. I'm sure he can catch me up later."

"You ran into Angelina, huh?" I could tell it took a monumental effort for Griffin to engage in the conversation. "You don't look bloody and bruised ... ." He winced as he trailed off.

"Nope. I'm perfectly fine." I kept my voice purposely breezy. "We barely insulted one another, if you want to know the truth. It wasn't even worthy of a spot on our top one-hundred list."

"You have a top one-hundred list?"

"Top one-hundred interactions," I confirmed. "Everyone loves a good countdown list. I'm no exception."

"Good to know." He licked his lips, his eyes uncertain. I could tell he wanted to say something, was gearing up to do it, steeling himself for my reaction, which made me uneasy. "Why was she at the funeral parlor?" Until he found the courage he would engage in mundane conversation.

"Her mother is insisting on hammering out all the details of her funeral before she dies," I replied. "Angelina was there picking up fabric samples and catalogs."

"Huh." Griffin's expression was hard to read. "You look sad about that. If it were someone else, I can see you being sad. This is Angelina. I can't even imagine you feeling sorry for her."

"Yeah, I don't know what to make of it either," I admitted. "When my mother died she completely ruined her funeral."

Griffin furrowed his brow. "What?"

I nodded. "Angelina was with her mother, and I was spoiling for a fight, but all she kept saying was how sorry she was for me. I wanted something to be normal, anything really, and I focused on her. That's when I knew things would never be normal again.

"At the time, I thought she was being smug and all ... well, Angelina," I continued. "I thought she had an angle for acting the way she did. Now I can't help but wonder if she simply felt sorry for me. I think there might've been sympathy there, but I was too stubborn to see it."

"And that's why you feel bad for Angelina now?" Griffin prodded.

I shrugged. "I don't know. I feel bad for her, which makes me angry at myself, but I can't shake it. Her mother is dying. She's completely on her own. She has no one."

"Maybe that's the way she prefers it," Griffin noted. "I think, when it comes to the death of someone we care about, we're all alone."

"I'm not alone. I have Dad ... and my brothers ... and Jerry. I have you." I slid a sidelong look in his direction and found him staring intently at my face. "I do still have you, right?"

Griffin heaved out a sigh as he pressed his eyes shut. "Baby, I love you. That will never change, but ... ."

I held up a hand to cut him off. "If you try to make some stupid move to leave so you can protect me, I'll hunt you down and lock you in the trunk of my car until you change your mind."

Despite the fact that we were mired in a surreal situation, Griffin barked out a laugh. "That right there is why I love you." He leaned forward and rested his forehead against mine. I wanted to curl into him, to let him hold me, but I knew he wasn't ready for that yet. "I'm afraid, Aisling."

He barely whispered the last three words, yet they cut through my heart as if he bellowed them. "Why are you afraid?"

"I can't hurt you. I won't let myself hurt you."

"You didn't hurt me."

"No, but I wanted to." He tucked a strand of hair behind my ear. "It was as if I was inside my head and knew what I was doing was wrong, but I couldn't stop myself from reacting the way I did. There was a fire raging inside my head. No matter what I felt for you – and the love was still there, which I swear almost made it worse – I couldn't make myself stop.

"I thought my heart was going to shred at the look on your face, but I couldn't stop myself even then," he continued. "I was trapped in my own body, and if your brother hadn't stopped me I would've torn you apart."

"Redmond did stop you." I refused to dwell on what-ifs. "You're here. You're safe. We know to be more careful from here on out. Those are the most important things."

"You're the most important thing to me," Griffin countered. "I need you to be safe."

"I am safe. I'm here with you. There's no safer place."

"Oh, you're killing me." Griffin drew me in for a long hug and I buried my face in his shoulder. He shuddered as he gave in to the contact, which caused a few tears to leak from my eyes. "I'm so sorry."

"Don't apologize." My voice cracked. "It wasn't your fault. You need to let it go."

"I don't know that I can."

"You have to. I'll torture you if you don't."

"You'll torture me, huh?"

I nodded when I felt his hand move to my cheek, soft fingers swiping at tears. "I can get through anything but losing you, so you're going to have to pull yourself together. It's going to take the whole team to figure this out ... and you're a big part of the team."

"I am? When did that happen?"

"I think it happened the day I met you, although it took me a lot longer to figure it out. You're the other half of my personal team, and I need you."

"I need you, too." Griffin pulled me completely on his lap as he rocked back and forth. "I'm still sorry."

I opened my mouth to argue, but he shook his head to cut me off.

"You have to let me feel guilt and work through it." Griffin's tone was firm. "That's non-negotiable."

I knew he was right.. "Okay. If you want to feel guilt, you can. You can work it off by giving me a massage later."

Griffin chuckled and the sound echoed in my ear ... and in my heart. "That sounds like a plan." He kissed my forehead before resting his cheek there. "I think we need to stay here until this is over. I don't plan on being caught unaware outside again – especially when you're near – but you're safer when you're close to your father and brothers."

"If that makes you feel better, I can live with it. It will give me a chance to let Dad spoil me."

"Yes, because that's such a rarity."

"Yeah, well, I like to go with my strengths."

We lapsed into a few moments of silence. I, of course, was the first to break it. "Are you ready to brave downstairs? Dinner should be ready in a bit. I'm starving."

"Five more minutes." Griffin exhaled heavily as he tightened his grip on me. "I just need this for five more minutes."

"That sounds like a great idea."

❧ 18 ❧

EIGHTEEN

I could tell Griffin wasn't keen on joining the rest of the family for dinner – and I considered bringing dinner to him so he could remain isolated and comfortable – but ultimately I knew it was important to force him to interact with everyone. He would be better for it in the long run.

Everyone was in the parlor having drinks, so I wordlessly led him there, our fingers linked as he morosely trudged beside me. I directed Griffin toward the empty couch on one side of the room and headed to the drink cart. This situation definitely required alcohol.

"How are you feeling?" Jerry asked Griffin, his face lined with sympathy.

"I'm fine." Griffin flashed a weak smile. "I just needed some time to regroup."

"You look better," Dad noted, reclining in his favorite chair as he looked Griffin up and down. "I wasn't sure sending Aisling to you was a good idea, but it looks as if she got the job done."

Griffin furrowed his brow. "What do you mean?"

Dad's smile was hard to read. He looked sympathetic to Griffin's plight and yet amused at the same time. "She's often hard to control and read, but you already know that. She immediately headed toward the stairs when she got back because she was determined to see you. I wasn't sure that was a good idea, so I tried to stop her."

Griffin quietly thanked me for the drink when I handed it to him and gave me a soft pat on the knee as I sat. He wasn't back to his usual playful self, but he was trying hard and I had to give him points for the effort.

"It was good you let her up," Griffin said after a moment. "We needed some time together."

"You definitely did." Dad smirked. "If you even think of doing that little dance you do when you're right, Aisling, I'll make you eat liver for dinner."

"What is for dinner?" I asked, changing the subject. "I'm starving."

"I thought we could all use some comfort food," Dad replied. "I went with roast beef, mashed potatoes, corn and cake."

I was instantly suspicious. "What kind of cake?"

"Red velvet."

All favorites of Griffin. I should've seen that coming. Griffin did a little dance of his own whenever Dad had red velvet cake and roast beef. I wanted to weep I was so grateful for Dad's effort. Instead I remained nonchalant. "That sounds good. I could use some comfort food."

"I believe we all could," Dad said. "We were just talking about what Cillian learned at the funeral home, something I believe you didn't help with at all, young lady. I didn't send you with your brother simply so you could interfere with Angelina."

"I didn't interfere with her." Sadly, that was true. "Do you know her mother insists on planning her entire funeral and making Angelina grab catalogs and fabric samples?"

Dad raised his eyebrows. "No. That sounds like Carol, though."

Mom, who had remained largely silent as she sat between Redmond and Aidan, made a face. "She always was a piece of work. I'm guessing she wants to go all out and turn her funeral into a worship session or something," she said. "I always hated that woman."

"I still hate her. She's mean and nasty. Angelina looks like death warmed over. I think she's about ready to drop."

"Really?" Dad's lips curved with amusement. "Since when do you care about things like that? I would think that Angelina's misfortune would make you dance rather than succumb to sympathy. It's not like you to fret over Angelina's feelings."

"I'm not fretting," I shot back, leaning closer to Griffin to share some of his warmth. He eyed me for a moment, uncertain, and then slipped his arm around my back. Another step in the right direction, although minor. "I hate that word, by the way. It's a lame word."

"Fine. I don't know what other word to use," Dad said. "I can't understand why you're working yourself up over Angelina. You've always hated her."

"I still hate her." That was true. "It's just ... she's alone. She's doing it all on her own. If something happened to you – which no one wants for a really long time – at least I wouldn't be alone. I'd have my brothers, Jerry and Griffin to help. Angelina has no one."

Dad's expression turned thoughtful. "I think you're saying that you've learned empathy."

"I don't know what I'm feeling. I only know that I could barely spit out one insult before I gave up and it's making me uncomfortable. I prefer being able to tell her she's worse than vomited refried beans without feeling bad about it."

Dad barked out a laugh as he shook his head. "Even when you're maturing you always manage to slide back into your comfort zone, don't you?"

I shrugged. "I don't know. I guess. What did Cillian learn at the funeral home?"

Cillian made a face as he leaned back in his seat. "I told you on the ride home."

"I had other things on my mind."

"Yes, she needed to see her love muffin," Braden sneered, although he looked as relieved as everyone else to see Griffin up and about. "That's all she could think about."

Griffin smiled. "Well, that makes me feel a little better. My face still hurts a bit, but I'm thankful for the pain because it means I didn't hurt her."

I was surprised he addressed the elephant in the room. I thought he might let it go for another twenty-four hours at least, but that wasn't the way he opted to deal with things.

"I'm sorry I had to hit you," Redmond said after a beat, shifting uncomfortably. "It was the only thing I could think to do."

"You did the right thing," Griffin insisted. "If I'd hurt her ... ."

"You didn't hurt her," Dad said hurriedly. "She's fine. She's still here to run her mouth and manipulate all of us to get what she wants. Everything turned out well, so ... let's not dwell on it."

"Now, wait a second," Mom countered. "If Griffin wants to feel bad about what he did, I think that's only fair."

I narrowed my eyes to dangerous slits as I glared at Mom. She would be the one to make things uncomfortable. That used to be my job before she came back from the dead, but she'd taken over the role of chief family annoyer since her return. It was, quite frankly, a relief to cede the title.

"He should feel bad about what happened," Mom continued. "He could've really hurt Aisling, especially since I doubt very much she would've done anything to protect herself. That's not how we raised her, but I see it on her face. She would've let him hurt her rather than hurt him to save herself."

That did it. I knew what Mom was doing and I had no intention of letting her get away with it. "I wouldn't have let him hurt me. It's true I would've done my best to make sure he wasn't injured, but I wouldn't have simply sat there and let him hurt me."

"No, she wouldn't have," Dad agreed, his eyes flashing with impatience as they landed on Mom. "Lily, is there a reason you feel the need to make things worse every single time you wade into a family conversation?"

Mom balked. "I was trying to help."

"Well done." Dad rolled his eyes. "As for Griffin feeling bad, it's not necessary. Aisling is fine. Griffin has shown his willingness to die for her on more than one occasion. We know that he didn't attack of his own volition, so we should put it behind us."

"I agree," I said, making a face at Mom that caused Griffin to crack a legitimate smile.

"I'm not trying to dwell on it," Mom insisted. "I know you think that, but it's not true. I was pointing out a simple fact."

"Really?" I was done playing this game. "Do you feel guilty about the people you eat to sustain yourself? I mean ... I'm not trying to make you feel bad or anything, but it is a simple fact that you're doing something to survive – something you don't want us to know about – and we all have an idea what that something is."

If looks could kill I'd be deader than Harry Turner and his hairy back. I didn't care. I was sick of Mom's attitude when it came to Griffin. I almost preferred when she was upfront about her dislike for him. The passive aggressive game she played was somehow worse.

"Thank you for your input, Aisling," Mom hissed.

"You're welcome." I leaned back in my seat and smiled at Cillian. "You were going to say something about what you learned at the funeral home before the conversation careened off topic."

"You helped it careen," Braden grumbled, his irritation obvious. He always was a mama's boy. "You shouldn't talk to Mom like that. It's not fair."

I ignored the admonishment. "What did you learn at the funeral home, Cillian? Did Harry's relatives admit that he had a witch for a mother?"

"Yes and no," Cillian replied, shifting uncomfortably as he glanced between Mom and me. He clearly didn't like the conversation, but he wasn't about to force an argument. Unlike Braden, if it came to a fight I knew Cillian would be on my side. I had a feeling Braden would be my only sibling to turn on me, and it was a sobering thought. "Turner's sister and niece were doing most of the planning. They brought his ex-wife along for the ride, although I'm still not certain why."

I forced myself to focus on the conversation. If Cillian had to relate the tale to me a third time he would definitely shift his loyalty to Mom. "So the ex-wife stayed close to the family even after the divorce?"

"Apparently so, and if I had to guess I'd say that the ex-wife was closer to the sister than Harry was."

Hmm. "Maybe he was more of a jerk than we realized," I suggested after a beat. "Maybe no one liked him and they all wanted him dead. Maybe whoever is conjuring the storms killed him and managed to hide it. Maybe ... ."

Dad held up his hand to silence me. "Let's not go off the rails, Aisling. Your imagination is a dangerous thing when unrestrained. Let's focus on what we know. What did you find out, Cillian?"

"Well, there was no easy way around it, so I kind of mentioned that I'd heard Harry had ties to a witch from a friend — and I was vague about the 'friend' part — and flat out asked them," Cillian replied. "I pretended to be a paranormal enthusiast. They actually bought it."

"It's the hair," Jerry said sagely. "Everyone knows that paranormal enthusiasts have long hair."

Cillian grinned. "Good to know. Anyway, Miranda — that's the sister — said their mother fancied herself a witch, but the only thing she could do was dose people's drinks and pretend it was magic."

"Huh." I shifted on my seat and rested my head against Griffin's shoulder. He glanced down at me and smiled, slipping his arm around me and tugging me close as we listened. It wasn't just that I was feeling sappy. I wanted him to be comfortable touching me again. In truth, I missed even the simple touches — like when he ran his hands up and down my arms or simply poked my side — and I wasn't a fan of how unsure he seemed. I wanted to help him bounce back as soon as possible.

"The mother wanted to be a witch. She joined several covens," Cillian continued. "Apparently she always left disappointed because none of the covens had real power."

"So the witch rumors were an exaggeration," Griffin mused.

Cillian shook his head. "That's what I thought, too, until the ex-wife let a minor detail slip. I don't know if they were trying to hide it or Miranda simply forgot, but when they mentioned it I realized they clearly didn't understand that Annemarie Turner was in deep with at least one real witch."

"Oh, well, don't leave us in suspense," Redmond said dryly.

"Yeah, you're starting to remind me of Aisling when she tells a story," Braden complained. "She goes on and on and never gets to the point. I hate that."

I shot him a glare. "I'm going to make you cry later, Braden," I warned. "When you're least expecting it, I'm totally going to smack the crap out of you."

"Somehow I think I'll survive until you head home," Braden said dryly.

Griffin cleared his throat. "Actually, until the storms are done and the problem is solved, we're staying here."

"You are?" Dad pursed his lips. "I'm fine with it, for the record, but may I ask why?"

"Because I want Aisling safe and I know you guys will protect her from whatever is doing this," Griffin replied without hesitation. "I also know that you'll kill me to save her if it ever comes to it. I don't think she's capable of doing it, so ... you guys will have to do it for her."

I glared at him as he averted his gaze. "No one is killing anyone."

"I know." Griffin patted my knee. "That's the plan. But if something should happen, I need to know you'll be safe."

"She'll be safe." Dad was calm. "You'll both be safe. I'll make sure of that."

Griffin smiled. "Thank you."

Cillian let loose an exasperated sigh. "Do you guys want to hear the end of my story or not? I mean ... geez. I've started this story three or four times now and never get to finish it. Am I that boring?"

"That's what I was trying to tell you," Braden replied, grinning when Cillian scowled. "Oh, I'm just kidding. Tell us the rest of your story."

"Now I don't know if I want to," Cillian sniffed.

"You obviously want to," I argued. "You're so excited that you're squirming around. Just tell us and get it over with."

"I'm going to tell you despite that remark." Cillian's handsome features flushed with color as he leaned forward. "Apparently Turner's mother had one friend who hung around longer than the others and she believed this woman was a real witch. She told everyone in the family who would listen, although I got the distinct impression they didn't believe her.

"Well, don't leave us in suspense," Aidan prodded. "Who is it?"

I knew the answer before Cillian could supply it. "Genevieve

Toth," I said, shaking my head. The name escaped on a hiss. "It has to be her."

Cillian picked up one of Dad's architectural magazines from the coffee table and lobbed it at me. My reflexes were slow, so it smacked me in the head and bounced off.

"You just stepped on my story, Ais," Cillian groused.

"I didn't mean to." I rubbed the side of my head. "That hurt."

"Let me see." Griffin's fingers were gentle as he probed my scalp. "It didn't break the skin or anything." He kissed the sore spot and gave me a hug. "You're okay."

I leaned into the hug and smiled. After almost a full minute, I realized the rest of my family were staring at us with overt distaste.

"What?" I was immediately on the defensive. "We're not doing anything."

"You're being gross and schmaltzy," Redmond said. "No one wants to see that. You're usually sneakier when you do it. Go back to acting like that."

"They're fine," Dad argued. "Actually, they're fine for tonight," he clarified. "They've had a rough day and can do whatever they want. Tomorrow I want to go back to the sneaky stuff. This is ... playing with all my father buttons. It's not a nice feeling."

I chuckled. "Whatever." I focused on Cillian. "So Harry Turner's mother hung around with Genevieve Toth."

Cillian nodded. "That means all the rumors about Harry's mother being a witch could very well be true."

"So where do we go from here?" Griffin asked, his voice strong. "We need a direction."

"We do," Dad agreed. I didn't miss the way his eyes landed on Mom for an extended turn before they continued bouncing around the room. "I'm not sure where we go from here, but at least we have a name to focus on."

Unfortunately it was a name that kept popping up. I thought about what the shaman said about one person being behind everything. Was it possible Genevieve Toth wasn't really dead? It would explain so much, and yet I couldn't come up with a feasible scenario in which she'd somehow survived.

I had no idea what to make of any of it.

NINETEEN

We slept hard, Griffin especially. I woke to find him wrapped around me from behind and I took a moment to enjoy the feeling.

"I know you're awake." Griffin's voice was low and warm against my ear. "Did you sleep okay?"

I nodded as I rolled to face him. "How about you?" He looked better in the morning light filtering through the window. The worry remained at the edges of his eyes, but his smile was quick. "Did you sleep?"

"I did. I feel better."

"Did you have nightmares?"

"No. I ... ." He paused and changed course. "I had a disturbing dream or two. They weren't as bad as I thought they'd be."

"Do you want to tell me about them?"

He shook his head. "No. You can probably imagine what they were like."

I could indeed. I gave him a quick kiss. "It's okay. We'll figure it out. We always do."

"I know." He gave me a long hug before releasing me. "Why don't you get in the shower first? If I remember correctly, your father mentioned something about having an omelet bar this morning. That's your favorite."

That was a personal favorite. Still, I was leery about leaving Griffin alone. I didn't want to turn myself into a mother hen, but I wasn't keen on being away from him. "We could shower together."

Griffin chuckled. "If we do that we'll be late for breakfast. I might be okay with that, but your father won't be."

I found I didn't care about Dad being upset. "Leave him to me. He's putty in my hands."

"So am I, but I need to call my boss, and you're too much of a distraction if I do it with you in the room."

"Why are you calling work?"

"I'm not going in today."

"You're not?" I couldn't help being surprised. "Why?"

"You know why."

"We can take precautions against the storms. You can carry an umbrella."

"And what happens if there's an incident where I have to drop the umbrella to save someone? I'll tell you what happens in a situation like that, someone will get hurt. I want to make sure that doesn't happen."

"But ... ."

"Just let me handle work." Griffin's tone turned icy and serious. "I don't want to argue with you, but I need to take the day off. I know you don't understand, but that's the way it has to be."

I didn't understand. Griffin was a good cop precisely because he was so dedicated. It wasn't like him to hide or run away. Still, if he wanted to stay here where I knew he would be safe, that didn't sound like the worst idea I'd ever heard. "Okay." I gave him another kiss. "I'm going to hop in the shower. You're going to regret not joining me."

"I already am." Griffin's smile was back and it made me feel warm all over.

I TOOK A LONG shower on the off chance Griffin would change his mind and join me. When he didn't, I tried not to obsess about it. I

AMANDA M. LEE

shrugged into a robe and was about to return to the bedroom when I heard voices on the other side of the door.

Because I'm me and the world's biggest busybody, I decided to eavesdrop instead of making my presence known. It took only a few seconds to realize Dad and Griffin were talking.

"You look better this morning." Dad's voice was easy and calm. "I'm glad. I was worried about you."

"There's no need to worry about me. Worry about Aisling. I wasn't joking last night. I expect you guys to protect her in case ... well, in case it happens again. I would rather die than hurt her."

"Oh, geez." I couldn't see Dad's face but I could picture the expression. I learned my patented eye roll from him, after all. "I don't know if you've always been this dramatic or if Aisling has brought it out, but you need to chill out."

"I don't find threatening to hurt my girlfriend funny."

"It's not funny," Dad said. Your reaction is a little funny right now, but I still get it. Griffin, look at me." I wanted to open the door so I could see them, but I knew that would prematurely end the conversation. "You didn't hurt Aisling. She's fine. What's hurting her now is the fear, and almost all of that fear revolves around you."

"Don't you think I see that?" Griffin challenged. "I see it on her face. I don't want to, but it's always there, right under the surface. I can't shake it. What would've happened if I'd got my hands on her?"

"I trained my boys to know there was a difference between smacking each other around and beating up Aisling," Dad said, changing course. "They still smacked her around, mind you. Children can't help themselves. She can hold her own in a fight if it comes to it."

"I'm a grown man. I could hurt her much worse than her brothers ever did."

"Maybe, but Aisling can take care of herself. She's always been that way. She would've handled the situation even if it had only been you and her. I have faith in that."

"And what then?" Griffin challenged. "What would've happened if I put my hands on her and she managed to fight me off? Do you think we ever would've been the same? Do you think we would've survived that?"

"It's not your fault, son. You didn't do it on purpose. You were taken over."

"That doesn't change the fact that I remember every moment of it. I remember the fury ... and I remember the look on her face. It almost crushed her."

"It didn't, though," Dad persisted, his voice demanding. "Griffin, I'm not one for wallowing. I understand that you were upset yesterday and I don't blame you, but one of the reasons I've grown to accept you as part of this family – and even become rather fond of you, although I'll deny it if you ever tell anyone – is because you're strong.

"You're strong enough to put up with Aisling's temperament, which isn't easy," he continued. "Not only do you put up with her, you don't let her run roughshod over you. You're strong when you need to be and a big marshmallow when she needs you to be."

Griffin chuckled. "Is that how you see me? Aisling's strong marshmallow."

"Son, you're exactly what I wanted for her." Dad sounded serious and his words caused tears to prick at the back of my eyes. "You have no idea how afraid I was that I turned her into a bit of a monster with all the spoiling. You see her for who she is, accept her, and don't put up with any of her crap. You're a freaking godsend, as far as I'm concerned."

"I think that might be the nicest thing you've ever said to me."

"I mean it. You have to snap out of this." I heard an odd noise that sounded roughly like a cuff to the back of the head. "You've been through a lot. What happened yesterday rattled you. I don't know anyone who wouldn't be rattled."

"Actually, that's not true," he corrected. "A bad man wouldn't have been rattled. Someone who doesn't deserve my daughter wouldn't have been rattled. You deserve her, and more than anything she wants you not to be afraid to spend time with her."

"I don't want to hurt her," Griffin pressed. "I'll never forgive myself if I do."

"I know that, but you can't live in fear," Dad pressed. "Aisling is fearless, much to her detriment sometimes. You'll be left behind if you live in fear. You don't want that."

"I don't understand how you can be okay with me right now," Griffin admitted. "Why don't you want to kill me for threatening her?"

"Because you weren't in control and I'm aware that you would kill yourself rather than hurt her if you were in command of all your faculties," Dad replied without hesitation. "You love Aisling. She loves you. You're a part of the family. We help family."

"You make it sound so simple."

"It is for me. We're going to figure this out. I have no doubt about that. But you can't stop living your life while we're searching for answers. That will distract Aisling, and she's unbelievably hard to live with when she's distracted."

I was pretty sure I should be insulted by the statement. Dad was being so good with Griffin that I decided to let it pass.

"I'm still not going to work today," Griffin said. "I told my boss I had a family emergency. I'm too shaky to go back until I settle a bit."

"You just need another day to heal."

"Yeah, because another day will fix everything," Griffin deadpanned. "In another day I'll forget the look on her face when I threatened her."

"You'll probably never forget that." Dad gentled his voice. "You will move past it, though. Some things are meant to last and you and Aisling are one of them."

"I never thought I would hear you say that."

"That makes two of us."

I couldn't hear what was happening in the other room when they stopped talking. There was nothing but a wall of silence to contend with. I'd almost convinced myself they'd left – it was ridiculously quiet – when the bathroom door opened and allowed Dad to pin me with a dark look.

"I was just coming out," I said instinctively, tucking my robe tighter around my frame. "What are you doing here? This is a very pleasant surprise so early in the morning. Of course, I could've been naked when you opened the door, which would've scarred us both, but things worked out okay so I'm willing to overlook the fact that you didn't knock."

Dad rolled his eyes. "Save it. I know you were listening. I'm fine with it."

"Oh, well, good." It was easier when I didn't have to lie or pretend to be innocent when I'm almost never innocent. "That makes things easier. Is the omelet bar set up?"

Dad smirked. "Yes. Get ready for breakfast. I have a job for you this morning."

"Really?" I couldn't help being intrigued. "Is it just for me or do I have to take a brother along for the ride?"

"What do you think?"

I already knew the answer. "Just make sure it's not a brother who irritates me."

"And exactly which one of them fits that bill?"

"No Braden."

"I CAN'T BELIEVE WE got stuck with cemetery duty again," Braden complained as he pocketed his keys in the parking lot of Eternal Sunshine Cemetery – a place that was almost like a second home because we visited so often – and headed toward the walkway that cut through the property. "I hate visiting the cemetery."

There were a lot of things I hated about this day and visiting the cemetery was only one of them. "It had to be done." I was resigned to our task and I merely wanted to get through it. "Once talk of Genevieve Toth surfaced, it was only a matter of time before we had to visit her mausoleum again."

The mausoleum we were visiting wasn't the original. I'd burned that down almost a year ago. At the time, I hoped that would be the end of Genevieve's dark legacy. Apparently I'd been wrong. Very, very wrong.

"I can't believe they rebuilt this stupid thing," I said once we were in front of the structure. It looked almost exactly like the old mausoleum, though this one had a few changes we discovered several months before when searching for a missing reaper girl. "I wish it would've stayed gone."

"Yeah, well, it's here and we have to deal with it." Braden glanced around to make sure we were alone. It was spring in Michigan – and a weekday – so the odds of a lot of people hanging around the cemetery during work hours were slim. Still, given our luck, it was always wise to look. "Let's head inside and get this over with."

When Dad suggested Braden and I visit the mausoleum I thought it was a terrible idea. It wasn't that I thought we wouldn't find answers – we often found answers at the mausoleum, which only increased its creepiness factor – but I wasn't keen to climb into Genevieve's world for what felt like the hundredth time.

Seriously, the woman cast something of a pall over our lives and I was growing to hate the mere mention of her name.

"Yeah, let's get it over with," I echoed as I followed Braden into the structure.

It was dark inside, the only light coming from the windows on either side of the building. A lantern hung from a chain at the front of the room. I knew that from past experience and brought a lighter to save time. After igniting the lantern, I grabbed the chain and carried it to the back of the mausoleum, where all the vault slots were located.

Technically this wasn't the Toth mausoleum. It was the Olivet mausoleum. Genevieve and the Olivets shared ancestors, so it was basically the same. After the fire – which I started to save myself and Aidan – we thought the mausoleum was gone for good. Someone rebuilt it quickly, though, and this time they added a dank basement. The basement was located under the previous mausoleum. It was a freaky room and I wasn't looking forward to searching it.

"Should we go straight to the basement?" Braden asked, glancing around. "This place looks quiet and clean. I don't think anything weird has been going on here."

It went against my better judgment to agree with Braden – like, ever – but I nodded. "Yeah. I don't want to spend all day here. I'd rather be back at Grimlock Manor with Griffin."

Braden sighed as he pressed the hidden button to open the basement door. It took us a lot longer to locate it the first time, but we knew where to look now. "You need to give him room to breathe," he chided. "He's doing a lot better than I would be under similar circumstances."

"That's because I've been suffocating him," I argued, lifting the lantern so I could better see the ancient and crumbling steps as we descended. "If I don't give him room to breathe he has no choice but to get over things to shut me up."

Braden made a face as he grabbed the lantern. "Give me that. I can't see thanks to the way you're swinging around. Besides, I should be the first to go down."

Now it was my turn to offer a disgusted expression. "Is that because you're a man?"

"I know you're trying to start a fight, but yes. Just let me go first."

"Fine." I grunted as he slipped around me on the narrow staircase. "As for Griffin, he's doing much better. I think he's going to be back to his old self by the time we get back."

"And I think you're dreaming," Braden countered. "He's not going to be back to his old self until we figure out how these storms are happening and he can go outside without being terrified that it's going to start to rain out of nowhere."

Braden had a point. I really hate that. "He'll be okay."

"He will be." Braden took pity on me and shook his head. "He loves you. I like to still think of him as Detective Dinglefritz, but it's clear you and he are supposed to be together. Don't work yourself into a tizzy."

"I very rarely work myself into a tizzy."

"You do it at least once a day."

"That's a vulgar lie."

"Yeah, yeah." Braden rolled his neck until it cracked, placing the lantern on a bare altar as he looked around the room. It appeared empty – felt empty – and yet we'd been at this long enough to know that didn't mean our answers weren't close. "How about you take one side and I'll take the other? If anyone finds anything, we call out to the other. How does that sound?"

I shrugged. "It sounds like a normal search."

"Did I say it didn't?"

"No, but you're acting as if you've come up with the best plan ever invented and it's the same plan we always come up with."

"Sometimes I think you argue just because you like to," Braden groused. "Has anyone ever told you that?"

"You just did. Does that make you feel special?"

Braden growled. "Just go over there and search. If you could do it in silence that would be really great."

"Right back at you."

"You always have to have the last word, don't you?"

"I believe you have me confused with you."

"No, it's you."

"It's you."

"You!"

"You!"

I lost track of who had the last word, which I hate. "Just look."

Braden waited until he was sure I was searching to speak again. "I got the last word. Ha!"

I was always offended when people said Braden and I were the most alike. Sadly, I knew it was true.

"Not now you don't," I said. "Now I have the last word."

"This is going to go on all day."

He wasn't wrong.

❧ 20 ❧

TWENTY

The room wasn't large but it looked markedly different from the last time we were there.

"They've cleaned up," I mused as I studied a shelf against the far wall. "All the stuff that was here before, from when they were keeping the Grimleys captive, is gone."

"Yeah. I noticed that, too." Braden was intent as he studied a stack of books on a small table in the corner. "I don't think these were here before either."

I glanced to the stack. "Do they look interesting?"

Braden shrugged. "They're in another language. I think it's Latin, but I can't be sure."

"Take them," I suggested. "Cillian will be able to read them."

Braden arched an eyebrow. "You want me to steal books from a mausoleum?"

"Why not? They might be interesting, and it could throw off whoever is doing this if we take them.."

Braden shrugged. "You have a point. We'll grab them on the way out." He moved to a shelf at the back of the room. "Have you found anything?"

"Not really. I ... ." I broke off when my eyes fell on the wall, tilting my head to the side as I took in the three adornments adding a bit of color to the gloom. "I take that back. I see ... something."

"What?" Braden abandoned his search and joined me, his eyes immediately traveling to what looked to be colored discs embedded on the wall. "What are these? Were they here before?"

I shook my head. "I don't remember seeing them. Look here." I traced the one in the middle. The frame remained, but whatever disc was inside was now gone. "I think this is where Harry Turner got the disc I saw in his house."

Braden pursed his lips. "How can you be sure?"

"It's just a feeling. It's the same size, and look at the others. They're made of the same material. I think it's freaking silver, which seems stupid to leave around because anyone could steal it."

"Do we know what they are?" Braden moved closer, his nose practically pressed to a frame. "They have symbols on them. We could take photos and text them to Cillian."

"Or we could just steal these, too," I suggested, grabbing one of the frames from the wall. "See. They come right off."

Braden made a face. "So now we're stealing books and what could be evil discs? Are you sure that's a good idea? What if touching them makes you go insane or something?"

"Don't be ridiculous. I touched the one in Harry's house and I'm perfectly fine."

"Are you sure? I've always thought you bordered on insane."

"Ha, ha." I grabbed the second frame. "We'll take them to Grimlock Manor and let Dad and Cillian look them over. If they're nothing, we'll bring them back ... or throw them away or something if we're feeling lazy."

Braden snorted. "Cillian will melt down if you throw away ancient books."

"Well, what he doesn't know won't hurt him." I clutched the frames under my arm. "Grab the books while I look around. If I don't see anything else, we'll head straight back to the house and consider this a job well done."

"Fine."

After another ten minutes I was satisfied there was nothing else of interest in the basement, so we closed it up, put the lantern where we found it after extinguishing the flame and walked out into a gloomy day with a sense of purpose. I was feeling good ... until I found Detective Green staring back at us.

"Uh-oh," I muttered, shifting the frames.

"Uh-oh is right," Green intoned. "You're in big trouble."

"Why does he look familiar?" Braden whispered, uncertain.

"This is Detective Green. He's the one who arrested me for murder a few weeks ago."

"Ah. I should've put that together." Braden forced a smile that was almost comical. "It's so nice to see you again, detective. How are you doing this fine and ... wet day?" Braden shifted his eyes to the ground and lifted his shoe. "Did it rain when we were inside?"

The question caught me off guard. Now that he mentioned it, the air did smell a bit musty. "Oh, double crap." I flicked my eyes to Green and found his pallor unnaturally pale. It didn't necessarily mean anything – he could've avoided the rain, after all – but I had a sick feeling in the pit of my stomach. "You weren't out in the storm, were you?"

Green wrinkled his nose. "What does it matter to you?"

"I'm just curious." I took a small step to the side to increase the distance between Green and myself, bumping into Braden in the process. "Move to the left a bit," I whispered. "Try to keep moving. Maybe we can get out of this."

Green was a good twenty feet away yet the look on his face made me believe he heard the order. "Stay right where you are." He didn't draw his service weapon, which was visible on his hip, but his voice held enough authority that I was understandably worried.

"Listen, Detective Green, I think you've got the wrong idea here," Braden offered. "We're simply picking up family artifacts from our mausoleum and taking them home to our father. We deal in antiquities and antiques – which I believe you already know – and he wants to inventory the items in the mausoleum."

That sounded completely plausible, and I wanted to applaud Braden's lying efforts. He was good when he wanted to be. Green didn't look as if he agreed with my assessment, though.

"That's your family mausoleum, eh?" Green gestured toward the building behind us. "The one that says 'Olivet' is yours?"

"It is on our mother's side," I lied. "She was related to the Olivets."

"Why aren't you going into that mausoleum over there?" Green flicked his finger to a small structure down the way. "That one has your last name on it."

Of course he would notice that. He was a detective, after all. "Well ... ."

"It doesn't really matter," Braden offered, cutting me off with a firm headshake. I couldn't understand what he was thinking, but it was clear the gears in his mind were working ... and working fast. "We're not in Royal Oak, detective. We're in Detroit. This isn't your jurisdiction."

Hey, why didn't I think of that? "He's right," I interjected. "It doesn't matter what we're doing because you don't have the authority to arrest us."

"That's not exactly true," Green said, a sneer on his face as he stepped forward. I didn't fail to notice that the mist was heavy enough to leave a dull sheen on my skin. I couldn't help but wonder if that would be enough to trigger Green's internal Hulk. It was something to consider, which made me all the more nervous. "I'm a police officer and I see you guys stealing from a cemetery. It doesn't matter if I have jurisdiction here. If I see you breaking the law, I can take you into custody wherever I am at the time."

"Is that true?" Braden asked me.

"How should I know?"

"You're marrying a cop."

"That doesn't mean I know all the ins and outs of law enforcement," I groused. "My brain is only so big. I can't fit any other facts in it. I'm full up for the day."

"That's such crap."

"Fine. I never asked." My agitation fired. "Does that really matter right now?"

"It would help if we knew he was telling the truth. If he's not, I could fight him."

One look at the grim set of Green's jaw told me that was a bad idea. "No, I don't think we should go that route unless it starts storming again." I lifted my eyes to the sky. "I think the mist is having a muted effect on him. That's all I can come up with."

"It's not much."

"No," I agreed. "If you think you can do better, by all means. Why don't you handle the problem?"

"Fine. I will." Braden squared his shoulders. It was a mistake to put him in charge. I knew that. I did it anyway and now we were going to suffer. "If you could just hold on one minute, I have something I need to do."

To my utter surprise, Braden shifted the books he carried to me and pulled out his phone. "Just one minute." He held up a finger to still a confused Green and typed 911 into the keypad. He waited until someone answered to speak again. "Yes, my name is Braden Grimlock and I'm being harassed in Eternal Sunshine Cemetery. There's a man here who claims to be a Royal Oak police detective and he's displaying some rather aggressive tendencies. I'm worried for my safety and that of my sister, who happens to be with me."

"Hey! What are you doing?" Green realized far too late what Braden intended to do. "Put that phone down."

"Yes, that's him and he's threatening us," Braden said. "I don't know what to do. I was raised to always follow police orders, but there's something very off about this situation. I'm afraid I'm about to be hurt, and if something happens to my sister ... well, let's just say my father will never get over it."

"Put that phone down!" Green roared.

"You do?" Braden swallowed hard as he stared down Green. "That's great. Tell them we're waiting on the pathway at the back end of the cemetery and the sooner they can get here the better." Braden disconnected the call. "They're in the cemetery – apparently they were already here for something else – and heading our way. I think we should let the Detroit police sort this out."

"You're going to regret making that call," Green seethed, his chest heaving as he clenched his fists at his side. "You have no idea what you've done."

"Yes, well, it's done now." Braden was blasé. "You should stay over there so there are no misunderstandings when the other officers arrive. I don't want anyone to accidentally get hurt."

I slid him a sidelong look, both impressed and worried. "Do you think that was a good idea?"

Braden shrugged. "I have no idea, but we didn't have many options."

"Maybe we should call Dad, too."

"I leave that call to you. He'll yell at me."

He would probably yell at me, too. "We'll wait it out and only call if we get arrested."

"Good plan."

I RECOGNIZED ONE OF the responding officers. He was based out of Griffin's unit and once helped me with a vending machine that tried to steal my Diet Coke. Despite that, I didn't know if his presence was a sign of good or bad things to come.

"I'm Inspector Craig," he announced, glancing between faces. "Can someone tell me what's going on here?"

I stared at him for a long moment, debating whether I should drop Griffin's name or keep him out of it before speaking. Finally I decided that – for better or worse – I would not risk Griffin's standing to get myself out of trouble. I'd been in jail several times before. It wasn't the end of the world.

"I think this man is following me," I announced, extending a finger in Green's direction and causing him to widen his eyes to comical proportions. "He came out of nowhere and threatened us. I'm really worried given all the stories I've heard flying around the news lately about violence and whatnot."

I did my best to appear vulnerable as I leaned closer to Braden. "The only reason I think I'm still alive is because my brother is with me and he's been really brave."

Braden caught my gaze and I could see the wonderment there before he recovered and latched onto the story. "This isn't the first time my sister mentioned this man showing up out of nowhere," he said. "It happened at a coffee shop the other day, too. It's starting to get uncomfortable, and I don't think that's fair to my sister. She doesn't deserve to be terrorized for no reason."

"It sounds a little odd," Craig said, stepping forward. "Can you show some identification please, sir?"

Green was incensed. "I'm a police officer, for crying out loud! I'm with the Royal Oak Police Department. I was trying to arrest these two for theft when they called you."

"Why would we call the police if we're thieves?" I countered. "That doesn't make a lot of sense."

"It doesn't," Craig agreed. "I need to see some identification, sir."

"Fine." Green dug in his pocket and came up with his badge. "Are you happy?"

"Keep your hands away from your weapon," the second officer said, tensing when Green's hand brushed against his holster. "We don't want any accidents here."

"There aren't going to be any accidents," Green snapped. "These two are the criminals. I'm trying to arrest them."

Something occurred to me and it didn't sit well. "How did you know where we were?" I asked, changing course. "I spent the night at my father's house in Grosse Pointe. I never went home yesterday."

"Do you live in Royal Oak?" Craig asked. He kept looking at me as if he should recognize me but couldn't quite place my face. On a normal day I would've been insulted – I'm quite lovely and distinctive – but I knew better than to push my luck.

I nodded. "I live there with my boyfriend. But we spent the night at my father's house last night. Both of us, together. Detective Green here would've had to follow me there ... and spend the night ... to know when I was leaving and figure out where I was going."

"And just for the record, you're doing what here?" Craig pressed.

"Gathering family items for my father to add to our inventory list," Braden answered smoothly. "Every few years we need everything photographed and logged. We're in antiquities and antiques – our father is well known in the area – and it's inventory time. It's a pain, but it has to be done."

"And that's what you have there?" Craig gestured toward the stack of items in my arms.

"Yes." I offered him a gander. "They're family antiques that won't mean anything to anyone but us. We're not doing anything wrong."

"Oh, but they weren't in their family mausoleum," Green complained. "They were in the Olivet mausoleum. They're Grimlocks."

"Grimlock?" Craig cocked an eyebrow. "I knew I recognized you. You're Griffin Taylor's fiancée."

I nodded and bit my lower lip. "He's going to be upset about this. He's been worried about Detective Green's interest, too." That wasn't a total lie. Griffin wasn't happy with Green's constant attention, but not due to sexual concerns. I had to play the hand I was dealt. "It's been a very trying couple of weeks."

"You can't possibly be falling for this," Green complained. "She's exaggerating and making stuff up. I haven't been stalking her."

"Who said anything about stalking?" Braden adopted an innocent tone. "I don't believe we used that word, even if it might be the correct word."

"I think he has that word on the brain for very obvious reasons." I leaned closer to Craig and dropped my voice to a conspiratorial whisper. "He tried to pin me for murders that I couldn't possibly have carried out a few weeks ago. I think he's ... disturbed ... because he couldn't solve that crime."

"I remember that." Craig offered up a half smile that told me I'd already won. I managed to keep my hips from swinging, but just barely. Doing my "I won" dance in a cemetery while surrounded by cops would not go over well. "Detective Taylor was very upset because he felt you were being unfairly targeted."

"She had bodies drop at her townhouse and right next to her in downtown Royal Oak," Green countered.

"And yet look at her," Craig said. "She's tiny. How could she possibly carry a body downtown? I mean ... no. That's just stupid."

Braden and I exchanged a quick look. This was going better than we'd envisioned.

"I think, just to be on the safe side, we should take this down to the station and sort it out there," Craig added. "That's probably the safest bet for everybody."

Wait ... what? "Can't we just go home?" I did my best to look pitiable. "I'm shaken from him showing up and threatening me ... again."

"I'm going to threaten to shut that mouth for you if you're not careful," Green warned.

"He's very violent," I whispered.

Craig rested his hand on my shoulder. "I won't let him touch you. Detective Taylor wouldn't like that at all. You can ride with me down to the station if it makes you feel safer. Your brother can follow in your vehicle and we'll get everything sorted there. I doubt it will take more than twenty minutes."

Double crap on toast! This day was going from bad to worse. "I would love to ride with you," I lied, my stomach twisting. I couldn't deny his request unless I wanted to look guilty. I was still playing the innocent victim, so I had absolutely no choice but to capitulate.

Griffin would be absolutely furious when he heard about this.

21

TWENTY-ONE

I knew Braden would call Dad from his vehicle, so I didn't bother messing with my cell during the ride. Inspector Craig put me in the back of his cruiser, but he hadn't cuffed me. He apologized profusely because I was essentially in a cage. I figured he was more worried about Griffin's reaction than my feelings, but this was hardly my first time in a patrol vehicle so I wasn't about to freak out and start crying.

Craig helped me out when we arrived at the station, casting me the occasional glance as we walked through the back door. I could practically see his mind working, but I offered nothing by way of explanation. The game had shifted and it was time to go into damage control mode.

"Are you okay?" Craig asked as he showed me into an interrogation room. "Do you need anything? How about a soda or something?"

"I'll take a bottle of water." They were the first words I'd uttered since leaving the cemetery and the relief that flashed across Craig's face was profound.

"Sure. Have a seat."

I rested the items I removed from the mausoleum on the table and settled in one of the chairs. I had no idea how I was going to get out of this one, but I was sure it would be a story my family bandied about over drinks and laughter for years to come. For now, though, I couldn't find anything funny about the situation.

"Let's talk about what happened," Craig suggested when he returned to the room. His partner was conveniently absent, which probably meant he was talking to the higher-ups. Word would spread fast that Griffin's live-in girlfriend was in the house ... and being questioned. I was sorry for that because Griffin had done nothing wrong.

"What do you want to know?"

"What were you doing at the cemetery?"

"I already told you."

"Tell me again."

I could've done that. I could've repeated the story. I was a gifted liar when it came to situations like this, after all, but I didn't want to risk making an error because I'd told the original story on the fly and didn't get a chance to pin down details and commit them to memory before opening my big mouth. "I would rather contact my lawyer."

The change in my demeanor threw Craig for a loop. "I'm sorry, but ... what did you say?"

"Lawyer," I repeated. "I want one."

"You're not under arrest."

Oh, that's what they always said. I knew better than playing that game. "I still want a lawyer."

"I'm just trying to figure out exactly what happened this afternoon."

"And my lawyer can answer those questions for you." I refused to back down. "You know you can't question me without a lawyer present after I've requested representation. You're breaking the law."

Craig balked. "I am not. I think I know the law better than you do."

I'd been arrested enough times to argue the point with him but calling my record into question would probably be a bad move. "I want a lawyer," I repeated. "I'm not answering another question without a lawyer present."

Craig sucked in a steadying breath. "Ms. Grimlock, I'm not trying to be a hardass here. I need information from you if we both expect to make this go away."

He was good. I was better. "I haven't done anything wrong. My lawyer will explain that to you once I'm allowed to call him. If you don't allow me to call him, I can file a complaint with the city and we'll take it from there. It's up to you."

"Ms. Grimlock ... ."

The door to the interrogation room flew open to allow Griffin entrance. He was dressed down for a day at home, simple jeans and a black T-shirt. He looked a little tired, which was probably good since he'd taken a personal day, but otherwise he seemed okay.

I was thankful for that.

"I believe she asked for a lawyer, Inspector Craig." Griffin's fury was palpable. "In fact, I'm certain she's asked for a lawyer multiple times. Is there a reason you haven't disengaged?"

Craig swallowed hard. "I ... um ... I'm just trying to get answers from her. She's not under arrest."

"Then you shouldn't have transported her to the station for questioning, should you?" Griffin briefly glanced at me before focusing his full attention on Craig. "Why is she even here?"

"She was caught removing items from Eternal Sunshine Cemetery." Craig recovered, although only marginally, and gestured toward the stack of items on the table. "A Royal Oak detective tried to take her into custody and she refused."

"Royal Oak?" Griffin turned back to me. "Green?"

I nodded. "Apparently he's following me."

"Son of a ... !" Griffin viciously swore under his breath. "Inspector Craig, I need a moment with Ms. Grimlock. If you could wait outside, I'd appreciate it."

Craig clearly wasn't happy with the suggestion. "I'm supposed to question her."

"And that's still on the table but I need to talk to her first."

"I ... you ... the captain ... ."

"If you have a problem with it, take it to the captain," Griffin growled. "For now, get out."

Craig abandoned his attempts at argument and scurried from the room, casting a final look over his shoulder before Griffin closed the door. The look on Griffin's face was fierce and I couldn't tell if he was going to hug or shake me.

"Are you okay?" He pulled me in for a quick hug, which was the reaction I was hoping for.

"I'm fine." I tilted my head back so I could stare at his face. "I'm so sorry this happened. We had no idea he was outside the mausoleum. He took us by surprise."

"We don't have a lot of time." Griffin sat next to me and drew my hands into his. "Stick to your story." He kept his voice low. "I'm going to talk to the captain. Hopefully I'll be able to make this go away."

"Don't do that if it will get you in trouble. You didn't do this. I did."

"Yeah, well, we're a unit. Your trouble is my trouble."

That's exactly what I was afraid of. "I know you feel guilty because of what happened and that makes you want to do something – anything, really – to protect me, but you should stay out of this. If they throw me in jail I'll survive."

"You're not spending the night in jail." Griffin was firm. "I'll figure a way out." He pressed a quick kiss to his forehead. "Your father is on his way with a lawyer."

Because my last lawyer turned out to be a homicidal maniac I couldn't help but wonder who Dad was tapping for the job. I pointed Craig toward the corporate office when he asked during the drive, but I didn't have a specific name. I was happy to hear Dad was on the case. "Real quick, we have something to talk about. Green is clearly following me. We weren't home last night. That means he knew I was at Grimlock Manor and followed me from there."

"And you didn't see him?"

I shook my head. "Braden was driving. I wasn't paying attention."

Griffin shifted his eyes to the stacked items on the table. "And that stuff?"

I shrugged. "It might be clues and it might be nothing. We don't know."

"Okay." Griffin squeezed my hands. "Hold tight. I'll see what I can do."

"Okay."

Griffin reluctantly released my hands as he stood. "Is there anything else?"

"Just one thing. When we first saw him, Green was bordering on a rage. It must have stormed when we were in the mausoleum. It passed, although he was furious when Braden called 911. There was this weird mist thing hanging around and I think that was affecting him."

"He didn't touch you, did he?" Griffin's eyes darkened and sent a chill down my spine. "Did he lay a hand on you?"

"No. I'm fine. Braden was there and it was his bright idea to call Detroit cops."

"I think he made the right choice."

I rolled my eyes. "Don't tell him that. I'll never live it down."

Griffin cracked a smile. "We'll figure it out, baby. Just hold on."

"I have nothing better to do."

"I'll be back."

"I'll be waiting."

I SAT ALONE IN THE interrogation room for what felt like forever. In real time it was probably only thirty minutes, but it felt infinitely longer. When Craig finally returned, he wasn't alone and he didn't look happy.

"Ms. Grimlock, we have a few more questions for you."

I glanced in turn at the men standing behind him. They looked older and I recognized one of them from a softball game Griffin made me play with his co-workers the previous summer. He was one of Griffin's bosses, but I was having trouble remembering his name.

"Lawyer." I uttered the one word as I stared at my fingernails.

The man I was certain I recognized sat in the chair directly to my left. "Ms. Grimlock, I'm not sure you remember me, but my name is Adam Teske. I'm Griffin's captain."

"I remember you." I mostly did. I remembered him being something of a jerk. Of course, I wasn't fond of cops in general. Griffin was the lone exception. "What do you want?"

Teske shifted at my tone. "I don't believe I've earned the attitude."

"Really?" I was done playing at being pleasant. "So far today I've been sent out for inventory even though Griffin wasn't feeling well and I wanted to take care of him. My father made me go and I'm still not happy about it. I got ambushed in a cemetery. I got transported in a police car. Now I'm stuck in interrogation, and I just know my father is going to have a meltdown. This isn't my finest hour."

Teske leaned back in his chair. "Your father is in the lobby now. He's a very ... formidable ... man."

"Just wait until you keep disallowing my lawyer to visit me."

Teske balked. "That is not what's happening."

"That's exactly what's happening. I'm not new at this. I know what's going on."

"Yes, I pulled your record when I heard that there seemed to be a disagreement of sorts about your presence in the department." Now Teske was on the offensive. "You have a very colorful history."

I couldn't hide my smirk. "I don't like being ordinary."

"I don't think anyone would ever accuse you of that." Teske made a clucking sound with his tongue. "You've been accused of motor vehicle theft several times."

"Those were all misunderstandings. Er, well, except for when Dad accused me of it. Then I really did steal his car, but he had it coming because he tried to keep me from leaving the house."

"And why did he have that coming?"

"Because he was keeping me locked up simply because I was a girl. He didn't lock up my brothers. Now, if he wanted to punish me for something I'd done wrong I would've been fine with it. Locking me up simply because I have a vagina is not allowed."

The turn in the conversation made Teske uncomfortable if the color flushing his cheeks was to be believed. *Hmm. That was very interesting.* Like most men of a certain age, talk of female body parts made him squirm. I could work with that.

"You've been arrested several times for fighting in public and general rowdiness."

"What can I say?" I held my hands palms out and shrugged. "I have a certain way about me."

"You certainly do," Teske agreed. "That's why we're not buying your story. Why were you in that mausoleum?"

Here we go. "Lawyer."

"Your family mausoleum is located several plots down," Teske persisted. "Why were you in the Olivet mausoleum?"

"Lawyer."

"Detective Green is convinced you're up to something nefarious," Teske said. "He thinks you might be hiding body parts or something."

I snorted. "Hiding body parts at a cemetery? What a novel idea." I rolled my eyes. Then something occurred to me. "Green didn't say that at the cemetery. He must've said that here. That means he followed me ... again."

Teske straightened. "Okay, I'm going to be straight with you. Detective Green is trying to have you transferred to the Royal Oak Police Department. Detective Taylor is adamant that won't happen because Detective Green is stalking you.

"Now, I tend to believe Detective Taylor because he's a good cop who has never given me a lick of trouble," he continued. "He's devoted to you, which means he has a conflict of interest in this situation. That means I can't agree with him because it will look as if I'm playing favorites."

"That sounds terrible for you," I deadpanned. "You must be very upset. Me? I went to work today and got harassed by a creepy guy who keeps showing up wherever I am. Do you understand that I didn't spend the night at home last night? Griffin and I spent the night at my father's house. That means that Detective Green followed us from there, probably camped out on the street in his car all night. You don't find that weird?"

"I find it extremely weird, and Detective Taylor said the same. You have to understand, we can't simply lob accusations at another officer. That's not how it works."

"Yes, the blue wall of silence or whatever you call it," I muttered, shaking my head. "I honestly don't know what to tell you. I've given you my story. I'm not going to change it. You need to either charge me or let me go."

"And what if I can't do either?"

I opted for honesty. "You've been very blunt with me, which I appreciate. It's my turn to be blunt with you." I licked my lips and smiled. "You've met my father. I can guarantee he's still on his best behavior because things haven't had time to completely spiral out of control. That will change quickly.

"He's a very rich man who always gets what he wants," I continued. "The lawyer he's hired is probably topnotch and used to messing with cops. I'm going to guess there's a lawsuit in your future because I've asked to see my lawyer like, fifteen times and been ignored. That's not going to sit well with my father."

Teske visibly blanched. "Then answer the questions and we can get you out of here."

"I've already answered the questions. I'm not doing it again. I'm tired ... and cranky ... and I want to go home. You either need to let my lawyer in or let me out. Those are your only two options."

"So that's your line in the sand?"

"It is."

"Fine." Teske got to his feet. "I don't think you're going to like how this goes."

I snickered. "I can guarantee you're not going to like how this goes. It doesn't matter now. We've both made our choices."

"We certainly have."

"WELL, THAT WASN'T TOO difficult, was it?"

Stan Pine was full of energy as he escorted me out of the interrogation room twenty minutes later. It turned out I wasn't wrong about Dad's choice in lawyers. Stan muscled his way inside not long after Teske and I threw down our gauntlets. I didn't have to say another word because Stan shut Teske down at every turn.

Finally, Teske had no choice but to allow me to leave ... with my pilfered items. The look on his face as I waved while vacating the room was almost comical.

Dad and Griffin both hopped to their feet in the lobby when they saw me exit the back hallway.

"Are you okay?" Griffin had his arms around me within seconds.

I patted his back, amused at the worry flitting across his face. "I'm fine. I've been through worse."

"That doesn't matter," Dad muttered. "I'm suing them for not allowing Stan back with you right away. I'll own this precinct by the time I'm done."

Whenever he gets worked up Dad is full of bravado and threats. I touched his arm to soothe him. "It's fine. There's nothing they can do. Green is causing problems. Where is he, by the way?" I scanned the lobby and came up empty.

"He's in the back," Griffin replied. "He seemed smug when he came in, as if he was certain they would turn you over to him. You were right about him looking sick, by the way. I thought there was a decent chance he would fall over. I haven't seen him since your release."

"What about you?" I couldn't stop myself from asking. "How is this going to affect you?"

"I'll be fine."

I wasn't sure I believed him. "He asked about my record. That means he pulled everything. He knew about the drunken fights with Angelina and the multiple charges of car theft that I managed to wiggle out of. That won't reflect well on you."

"I don't care."

I cared. "Griffin ... ."

Griffin pressed his finger to my lips to quiet me. "You and I decided right from the start to take each other fully. I have no problem with that and I actually find your record funny. If my boss has a problem with that, well, that's his problem. It doesn't change a thing between us."

I couldn't let it go. "But what about if you want to be promoted or something? This could hold you back for good."

"Aisling, the only other job I want right now is to be your husband." Griffin was sincere. "We're going to figure it out. I don't care if everyone here thinks I have the oddest wife in the world and I'm never promoted. I can't worry about those things."

I shifted my eyes to Dad. "Isn't he cute?"

Dad groaned. "If you're going to get sappy let's take it outside. We parked in the garage, so storms shouldn't be an issue. I want to get back to the manor before another round hits. With the materials you found and what Braden told me, we have a few things to discuss."

I should've seen that coming. "Can we have fried chicken and mashed potatoes for dinner?"

"Yes."

"Can we have an ice cream bar, too?"

Dad inhaled deeply through his nose. He was used to being manipulated, but it still grated at times. "Why not? With everyone staying at the house, what harm could possibly come of introducing pounds of sugar to the equation?"

I was pretty sure that was a rhetorical question. "I want sprinkles, too."

"You always do."

TWENTY-TWO

Griffin insisted I ride back to Grimlock Manor with Dad in case a storm sprung up and we somehow ended up helpless by the side of the road. Dad shoved me in his vehicle after five minutes of arguing the point, and we followed Griffin the entire way home, me glowering in the passenger seat while Dad did his best to pretend he didn't notice.

Five minutes from home, Dad decided to give it to me straight.

"If you keep pushing him you're going to drive a wedge between the two of you." Dad's tone was serious. "I know you don't want that."

"That's not what I'm trying to do. He's being ridiculous."

"He's doing what he thinks is right for you," Dad corrected. "He's willing to do anything to keep you safe – which makes me like him more than you right now – and he's struggling to engage with the rest of the family because he's weighed down by guilt.

"Now, I understand that you want him to go back to the way he was and get over it, but he's not quite there yet," he continued. "You can't force him to feel what he doesn't feel. A good girlfriend would give him the space he needs to recover without pushing him."

I narrowed my eyes. "Are you saying I'm not a good girlfriend?"

"I'm saying you're a lot of work – so very much work – and sometimes you need to put his needs before your own if you expect this marriage to work." Dad was deadly serious. "You put him first on the big stuff, but then you slip and put yourself first soon after. Maybe keep him first for more than an hour or so."

I wanted to argue – it was my first instinct, after all – but I couldn't. Dad was right, which I really hated, and I needed to get it together for Griffin's sake. "I'll ... um ... do better."

Dad didn't exactly smirk, but his lips curved so much I knew he was basking in his win. "I think that's a wise choice."

"Yeah, yeah, yeah." I left the pilfered items on the floor of the car for Dad to collect when we parked in the garage and hopped out so I could meet Griffin in front of the house.

"I guess I'll get this stuff," Dad called after me.

I ignored him and met Griffin in the driveway. He was barely out of his truck and wide-eyed when I threw my arms around his neck.

"What's this?" Griffin was confused as he looked to Dad, who clutched the mausoleum items against his chest.

"I had a talk with her during the drive and told her to stop trying to force you to her way of thinking," Dad replied dryly. "I don't think she really heard what I was saying."

Griffin patted my back and snickered. "No, she did." His chuckle turned into a full laugh after a moment. "She just doesn't care. She wants to do things her way." He gave me a hard hug and kissed my cheek. "You're just going to wear me down until you get your way, aren't you?"

"I've decided that's what works best for me," I admitted, licking my lips as I pulled my head back. "I'm going to sit on you until you do what I want."

"Well, that will make for fun dinner antics."

"I just want you to be okay, but now I've made things worse."

Griffin furrowed his brow. "How have you made things worse?"

"You're in trouble at your job and all your co-workers are talking about your car thief girlfriend who likes to publicly brawl while yelling obscenities and dousing people with bottles of Nair."

Griffin wrinkled his nose. "Nair? I don't remember reading anything about Nair."

"Ah, yes, the great hairless homecoming queen snafu of 2006," Dad intoned. "It made several smaller newspapers and is still talked about at PTA meetings. Apparently Aisling's determination to teach Angelina a lesson about rigging votes to get on the homecoming court is something of a cautionary tale."

Griffin laughed so hard he had to bend at the waist. The sight was enough to warm my heart.

"Oh, geez." Griffin swiped at his eyes. "I needed that."

I rested my hand on his shoulder. "I'll reenact it for you later if you think it will put you in a better frame of mind."

"I look forward to that." Griffin straightened when a far-off rumble of thunder interrupted our fun. "We need to go inside." He kept his smile in place, but was firm. "At least I need to go inside."

"We're all going inside." Dad shifted his load so he could hand Griffin the books. "We need to look over what Braden and Aisling found and form a plan."

"That sounds like a good idea." Griffin shoved the books under one arm and wrapped the other around my shoulders. "I also want to hear the full story of what happened with Green. The fact that he showed up at a Detroit cemetery makes me exceedingly nervous."

"That makes two of us," Dad said. "If he's been following Aisling and we haven't noticed ... ."

He left it hanging, but I knew exactly what he was thinking. "What other weird stuff do you think he's seen?"

Dad shrugged. "I have no idea, but I doubt it's good."

He wasn't the only one.

"WHAT IS ALL THIS STUFF?"

Cillian eyed the books with overt suspicion as we dropped them on the coffee table in Dad's office.

"That's a gift for you," I replied, grinning. "Don't say I never gave you anything."

"Great. I've always wanted old books." Cillian grabbed the top one and flipped it open. "It's in Latin."

"Why do you think we brought them here instead of reading them there?" I challenged. "Speaking of that ... where is Braden? I haven't seen him since I got arrested."

"He followed you to the station but then I sent him on a mission," Dad answered. "He should be home relatively quickly."

That was a rather vague response. "What mission?"

"He's breaking into Green's house with Aidan," Cillian replied. "Dad wanted to do it when he knew Green was otherwise occupied. Aidan was the only one available, so he sent Braden as backup."

"You broke into a cop's house?"

"I didn't hear a thing," Griffin announced, throwing himself on the empty couch and rubbing his forehead. "I don't want to know that Braden and Aidan are breaking the law right now."

"I had no choice," Dad supplied. "Green makes me nervous. He knows something about us."

"Yeah, I expected a call from him after the zombie attack," Griffin admitted, continuously rubbing his forehead as if warding off a headache as he leaned back and got comfortable. For him that meant resting his feet on Dad's antique table, which I could tell irritated Dad to no end even though he didn't immediately say anything. "He was at the house when they moved on us. We left him here with Lily. I never checked on him afterward. Maybe that was a mistake."

"How was he that night?" Dad asked, his eyes remaining on Griffin's feet. "How did he take the zombie attack?"

Griffin shrugged. "He just kept saying that he didn't understand and he couldn't really fathom what was happening. I didn't have time to focus on him because we knew we had to get to you."

"And you left him with Lily?"

"Yes. She told us to run and warn you guys. She was adamant. We didn't have many options, so that's exactly what we did."

Dad heaved out a sigh and circled the table, ultimately knocking Griffin's legs from their perch before sitting in a chair. "I don't know what to think."

Griffin shot him a look. "What was that for?"

"That table is an antique, not an ottoman."

"Oh, look," I teased, sitting next to Griffin. "You're back to getting in trouble. All is right in the world."

"Ha, ha." He poked my side. "As for Green, I'm worried. If he followed Aisling to the cemetery, that means he probably followed her before. He could've seen something."

"What?" Cillian challenged. "If he saw her collecting a soul that means he saw her with a dead body. Why wouldn't he take her into custody then?"

"Maybe he saw me coming out of Harry Turner's house," I suggested, something occurring to me. "Maybe that's what kicked his obsession into overdrive. He already knew something weird was going on with me because of the zombies. Even if he refuses to believe that's what he saw – which is the general theory I'm operating under – he probably thinks I'm up to no good."

"Anyone who has ever met you thinks you're up to no good," Dad pointed out. "But you're correct. The fact you were on a job with his boss a few days ago might have sent him over the edge."

"The next day I ran into him at the coffee shop," I noted. "I was surprised but thought it was a coincidence. I was much more inter-ested in messing with Angelina than paying attention to him. Angelina told me at the funeral home that he was asking questions about us."

"What were you doing at the funeral home?" Mom asked, strolling into the room.

Dad lobbed a dark glare in her direction. "Do you knock?"

"This is still my house," Mom reminded him, blasé. "I don't have to knock."

"Except you do." Dad refused to back down. "We've come a long way since your return, Lily, but manners dictate that you knock when entering this house. It's not your home."

Mom stared at him for a long beat. "Fine. If it will make you feel better, I'll knock. Satisfied?"

"Hardly but it will do for now," Dad grumbled, turning back to me. "What did Angelina tell you exactly?"

"Just that Green asked her questions about me," I replied, watching as Griffin snagged my hand and turned it over so he could trace his fingers across the palm. "He asked her out on a date but he seemed more interested in talking about me. He thought she would be a good ally because she clearly hates me."

"How much can she possibly know?" Mom asked as she settled next to Cillian. "What are you looking at?"

"A book," Cillian replied absently, his main focus on one of the dusty tomes we stole from the mausoleum.

"Angelina knows more than you might be comfortable with," I said. "She certainly knows more than I'm comfortable with."

"How?" Mom knit her eyebrows. "It's not as if she hangs out with anyone in this family."

"She did date Cillian for a time," I pointed out. "She's also snuck in to spy once or twice, and there have been a few instances when wraiths interrupted my fights with her and she saw me dispatch them."

Mom was aghast. "Cillian dated Angelina?"

"Thanks, Aisling," Cillian said dryly, never looking up. "I can't think of a better time to bring that up."

"You're the one who dated her."

"Yeah, what were you thinking with that?" Griffin asked, amusement lighting his eyes. I was so glad to see mirth there instead of guilt that I was willing to milk the Angelina thread for as long as possible to elicit a laugh or two.

"I was thinking that maybe there was something there that there wasn't," Cillian replied. "I thought she couldn't possibly be as bad as she pretended to be and that I just needed to give her a chance."

"Yeah, how did that work out for you?" I challenged.

"Not well."

"She cheated on you." My righteous anger from the incident in question returned. "She cheated on you and was a total asshat."

Mom's eyes fired. "She cheated on you? You deigned to date her and she cheated on you? No wonder you picked the pretty nurse with the heart of gold after extricating yourself from that ridiculous relationship. After Angelina, you knew it was best to play it safe."

Something about the way Mom phrased the statement set my teeth on edge. "Maya is fun and exciting," I argued. "She's not safe."

Griffin cocked an eyebrow. "Was that an insult I missed or something?"

Was it? I couldn't be sure. It felt like an insult. "I ... um ... ."

"It wasn't an insult," Mom supplied. "I meant it as a compliment.

Maya is an extremely pleasant woman who puts up with a lot when dealing with this family. She never argues with anyone or complains. That makes her safe. I hardly think that's an insult."

I wasn't so sure. "Do you think Griffin is safe?"

Mom immediately started shaking her head. "No. He fights with you all the time. He just tried to kill you."

I was moving to leap off the couch and launch myself at Mom as Griffin caught me around the waist and held me tight at his side. "Aisling, don't. She's right."

"She's wrong." Dad was firm. "You were under the influence of a storm."

"Is that like being under the influence of whiskey?" Griffin grappled with me. "Knock it off."

"Besides that, you do disagree with Aisling and I think that's good for her." Dad wasn't about to get in a huge fight with Mom when we had so much else going on, but he also wasn't one to back down. "We've had this discussion already. Your willingness to call Aisling on her crap is why you'll survive. Lily is only trying to stir up trouble. Ignore her."

"I am not trying to stir up trouble." Mom made a face. "Why would you say that?"

"Because it's obvious that's exactly what you're doing, and we don't have time for it. We need to find out who is in charge of these storms and why they're being unleashed in this specific area."

"This specific area?" I stopped fighting Griffin's efforts to corral me. "Huh. I didn't even think about that. You checked to see if other areas were reporting the same problems with storms?"

"Of course I did." Dad extended his long legs in front of him, looking relaxed even though I knew Mom's presence made him edgy. "It would've been reckless not to check. The only area reporting this problem is here. That means it's localized. It doesn't go north of Flint. Whoever is doing this is based in this area."

"And how do you expect to find out who that is?" Mom challenged. "There are millions of people living in southeastern Michigan. We need to narrow it to one person."

"And we already have a jump on that. Aisling saw the disc in Harry

Turner's house. She found these other discs in the Olivet mausoleum basement. There's obviously one missing. That disc had to originate from this set."

"That's kind of leap, don't you think?"

Dad shook his head. "No. Half of everything that's happened to us in the last year has originated in the Olivet mausoleum. Perhaps more than half."

"So you think this circles back to the Olivets?" Mom furrowed her brow, confused. "I don't see how."

"Not the Olivets," Dad clarified. "Genevieve Toth. She's the central figure in all of this."

"Genevieve?" Mom didn't bother to hide her shock. "Genevieve is dead. How could she be causing this to happen?"

"She might only be related tangentially," Dad replied. "According to the whispers, Harry Turner's mother had ties to Genevieve. He had the disc. Perhaps it's someone in that family pulling the strings this time."

Mom was mollified. "I guess that makes sense. I can't remember if you told me before, but what was this Turner's mother's name?"

"Annemarie," Cillian answered. "Annemarie Turner. She was obsessed with witches and power, although we can't be sure if she had power of her own. She seemed to want to surround herself with others who had legitimate magical ties, which suggests to me that she wasn't in possession of her own magic."

"And the books?" Mom gestured to the huge book Cillian flipped through. "What do they have to do with this?"

"They're from the mausoleum, too," Dad answered. "Aisling decided to take them because she couldn't read them. She thought Cillian would have better luck. It was a good plan until Detective Green caught her leaving with them."

"Detective Green? What was he doing in Detroit?"

"That's the question we need answered." Dad dragged a restless hand through his hair. "Green is the wildcard here. We have no idea what he knows and what he's trying to accomplish. We have to find out ... and I have no idea how to do that."

TWENTY-THREE

Mom stayed for dinner, of course. She got her kicks by irritating Dad, and her mere presence was often enough to send him over the edge. He held it together, for the most part, and we spent the meal hashing things out.

"So this Annemarie Turner woman wanted to be a witch, but we're not sure she was?" Jerry loved a good horror story as much as the next person. He was affected by the storms, so he was doubly invested in figuring out who was causing them. "Is she dead?"

"She is," Cillian confirmed. He brought one of the books to dinner and read as he ate. "Her family said she was something of a nut and raised Harry off the grid much of the time."

"What do you mean by that?" Griffin asked. "Did she go all prepper or something?"

"Prepper?" Mom was back to being confused as she sipped her wine. She doled portions of food onto her plate, but didn't eat much, instead opting to push it around and pretend she was eating.

"Preppers plan for the end of the world," Braden supplied. "They're survivalists. They think there could be a nuclear attack or something that they plan to survive."

"Like the zombie apocalypse," I offered. "I've already survived that, so I'm good."

Griffin chuckled as he speared a chicken breast from the platter. "You rocked the zombie apocalypse. You didn't just survive it. You kicked the crap out of it and looked good doing it."

"Oh, you really do get me." I beamed as I rested my head against his shoulder. Watching Griffin interact this way made me realize he was well on the way to recovery. That was the thing I cared about most, after all. "I did rock that zombie apocalypse."

Mom sighed. "There's more wine, right?"

"There is," Dad confirmed. "I'm not sure you need any, though."

"Oh, I need some."

"Go back to Annemarie Turner," Dad instructed Cillian, doing a terrible job of ignoring the way Mom poured half a bottle of wine into her glass. "You said she was off the grid. I need more information on that."

"I don't know what I can tell you." Cillian dragged his eyes away from the book. "I only know what I heard from the sister. Annemarie was weird. She was described that way by everyone who had ever met her. Apparently she wanted to stand out, but she was no great beauty so that was difficult. This is all coming from the sister, mind you, so she put her own spin on it."

"Let me guess: The sister was the beauty in the family and Annemarie was jealous," Mom drawled.

Cillian nodded. "That's exactly what she said. Anyway, Annemarie met Harry's father, who was a day laborer – which was somehow important to the story, although I never figured out how – and she got pregnant before they were married. That was apparently quite the scandal in those days."

"It would've been considered improper for the time, there's no getting around that," Dad said. "She obviously married Harry's father. That would've dampened the scandal."

"I think it put an end to scandal as far as everyone but the sister was concerned," Cillian clarified. "She seemed the type to lord it over Annemarie for a very long time."

"That sounds lovely," I muttered. "For once I'm glad I have brothers instead of a mean girl sister."

"Oh, don't kid yourself," Braden said. "If you came home pregnant you would've been in a heck of a lot of trouble. If Dad didn't kill you, we would have."

"I would've killed Griffin if she came home pregnant before the wedding," Dad clarified. "Aisling merely would've been locked in the basement."

"Oh, now, that's not much of a punishment," I teased. "There are snakes in the basement, but if I came up pregnant it obviously would've been because of my addiction to trouser snakes. How do you think locking me in the basement would've fixed that?"

Dad extended a warning finger in my direction. "Don't push me."

I smiled into my mashed potatoes as Griffin shook his head.

"Please don't push him," Griffin said. "The last thing I need is your father threatening to kill me because you're playing a game."

"It might be fun," I countered. "But we don't have time for games now. We'll have to make time for that one later."

"Yes, we're all looking forward to that," Braden drawled. "We should build a bonfire out back and let Dad chase Aisling around it for old time's sake."

"Why would you chase her around a bonfire?" Griffin asked, legitimately confused.

"Because I didn't wear a bra under my tube top and he was very upset about my reaction to the cooler night temperatures," I answered without hesitation.

Dad's cheeks flushed with color. "I can't believe you brought that up again."

"Hey, at least she's wearing a bra," Redmond offered. "We should be thankful for small favors."

Dad poured more bourbon. "I hate it when we spend too much time together like this. The conversations always turn crude ... and you know I don't like crudity."

"Which explains how you got stuck with all of us," I deadpanned, causing everyone but Dad to snicker. "Oh, come on. You know you like crude talk a little. You simply like it when you're alone with the boys. When I'm involved, you're uncomfortable with it."

"I definitely am," Dad agreed. "Let's go back to talking about Annemarie. She's a much more entertaining subject."

"I don't know how entertaining the story is," Cillian hedged. "She sounds like a nut. She married Harry's father about four months before giving birth. The scandal was swept under the rug and the family moved to a small house in Ferndale.

"They lived there together for two years, and I don't think they were a happy two years," he continued. "The sister kept going on and on about how Annemarie was never happy with her lot in life and that's why she kept looking for more."

"That must be how the witch search came up," Aidan mused, breaking a breadstick in half so he could share with Jerry. My best friend was a carbohydrates Nazi and claimed the calories didn't count as long as the original item came from Aidan's plate. Aidan was trained in how things worked in Jerry's world relatively quickly when it came to food and knew better than to contest the issue. Sometimes it was easier just to shut up and split your breadstick. "It sounds like Annemarie wanted to stand out, and if she couldn't do it with her looks she wanted to do it with her standing in society. Getting knocked up by a day laborer with limited potential was probably a blow to her ego."

"Probably," Cillian agreed. "Harry's father died in a car accident when Harry was five, but they'd already been separated for several years, although it was on the down low. Family lore says Annemarie cast a spell to make it happen because she was unhappy and wanted all of his money. I have no idea if that's true. It could easily be something that people made up.

"After that, Annemarie sold the house and moved Harry to St. Clair County for a bit," he continued. "She joined up with a religious movement called The Seekers. I made a note of it on my phone at the time so I could look it up. I did that this afternoon before getting the call about Aisling being arrested ... again."

"I wasn't technically arrested," I countered, waving my fork for emphasis. "I was transported for questioning. I was never arrested. I was never read my rights. That doesn't count."

"Only in Aisling's world does that not count," Braden snickered.

"She wasn't taken in for something she did," Dad pointed out. "Green followed her. You could've been taken in just as easily as Aisling. In fact, I'm not exactly happy that you let the cops separate the two of you and put Aisling in the car."

Braden balked. "Hey! I wasn't expecting any of it. I was the one who thought fast enough to call the Detroit police. How much worse do you think things would've been if they hadn't showed up?"

Dad opened his mouth to respond, what I'm sure was a hot retort on the tip of his tongue. Instead he changed course. "You're right." He turned to Griffin. "Do you think he would've tried to put Aisling in his car and leave Braden behind? He could've hurt her under those circumstances."

"He could have," Griffin agreed, clenching his fork so tightly his knuckles whitened. "I've thought about that a few times myself. I can't figure out his end game. He knew Braden was with her because he was watching."

"Maybe he intended to separate them," Aidan suggested.

"Or maybe he intended to take Braden out of the picture." Dad's expression was dark. "He couldn't have taken Aisling without anyone knowing unless he did something to silence Braden. Braden acted out quickly and then Green's plan was shot to hell because the police showed up right away."

"See. I was the hero today." Braden speared some asparagus and bit into the fleshy end. "I deserve a prize."

Dad stared at him for a long moment. "What exactly do you want?"

"I think a waffle bar tomorrow morning should do it."

"Consider it done." Dad shook his head and poured more bourbon. "I think it's weird that all my children can be bought off with food. I don't know what to make of it."

Mom's smile was benign. "I think it's kind of cute."

"You would," Dad muttered. "You started bribing them early with candy if they behaved in public. I wanted to spank them and be done with it, but you thought a risk-and-reward system would be better."

"And I was proven right."

"I think the jury is still out." Dad sipped his drink. "I believe you were in the middle of a story, Cillian. I don't know why we keep getting off track when you're trying to tell us something. Please continue."

Cillian rolled his eyes. "I should get a special something for you guys interrupting me all the time."

Dad sighed. "What do you want?"

"I would like a drafting table for the upstairs library."

The request was so offbeat Dad was understandably caught off guard. "A drafting table?"

Cillian nodded. "I do a lot of research up there and Restoration Hardware has a table that would fit with the décor."

"I have no problem buying you a drafting table." Dad pursed his lips. "If you wanted something like that, you should've asked. You do all the research, so it's only fair you have the furniture you need to be comfortable."

"Oh, well, thanks." Cillian's cheeks reddened as I stared at him. We snagged gazes and I could tell he recognized the unsaid thought passing through my brain. If he was going to ask Maya to marry him and move out, why did he need a drafting table?

Ultimately I knew it didn't matter because Dad loved buying furniture. Still, it was a weird request.

"Annemarie," I said, drawing everyone back to the conversation. "She'd just joined a cult when you left off in your story."

Cillian's eyes widened. "How did you know it was a cult?"

"They called themselves 'The Seekers.' What else could it be?"

"Good point." Cillian knocked back some whiskey before continuing. "Annemarie married the guy in charge of the cult. They seemed to be survivalists planning for the end of the world. They were anti-government and wanted to be left to themselves.

"That ended about five years later when a bunch of the guys in charge – including Harry's stepfather – were arrested for sexual misconduct," he continued. "I found the records online. They were tossed in jail for having sex with the teenage girls. The cult disbanded and Annemarie took Harry back to Royal Oak. Once there, she focused on witches, and that seemed to be her obsession until her death about fifteen years ago."

"How old was she when she died?" I asked.

Cillian shrugged. "I don't know. I didn't check. I would guess she was in her seventies."

"So what do we know from that story?" Redmond asked. "I mean ... what does knowing Annemarie's background do for us?"

"I have no idea." Dad answered honestly. "This whole thing is a mess, and I don't know what to make of it. I think we're on the right track, but I have no idea where to go from here."

"I'll help Cillian go through the books after dinner," Mom offered. "I can read Latin. Maybe together we can work faster to find something."

"That's a start, but I don't know if it's enough." Dad cast me a side-long look. "We need to put an end to these storms. The longer they continue, the more danger they pose. Something really awful could happen – like a mass shooting – and then we'll all be haunted forever."

That hadn't occurred to me. "So we'll work together on research. It's all we have right now."

"Let's hope that changes ... and soon."

GRIFFIN FOUND ME IN the kitchen about an hour after dinner. Everyone was upstairs conducting research – some people were chasing answers on Green while others researched Annemarie, and still others toiled with the Latin tomes. I needed a breather, so I came to the kitchen for some water.

"What are you thinking?" Griffin asked, causing me to jerk my eyes from the window. He held up his hands when he saw how edgy I was. "I'm sorry. I didn't mean to frighten you."

"I'm not frightened of you," I stressed, grabbing his hand. "Stop thinking I'm frightened of you. I know you would never hurt me."

"I can't help myself." Griffin wrapped his arms around me from behind and watched as a bolt of lightning split the sky on the other side of the glass. "Another storm." He tensed but didn't release me. "I guess it's good I'm safe in here, huh?"

I nodded without hesitation. "I plan to keep you that way."

"Good idea." Griffin nuzzled my neck before resting his chin on my shoulder. "You seem lost in thought. Do you want to tell me what's bothering you?"

That was a loaded question. "My mother."

"Is this about what she said earlier? I'm not offended. She was right. I could've really hurt you."

"You didn't, and we won't let it happen again. You would never have considered hurting me in the first place if it wasn't for the storm. She knows that. She just likes to dig at you, and I can't figure out why."

"Maybe she doesn't think I'm good enough for you."

"The woman eats people to survive," I pointed out. "She did a good job of masking what she was doing tonight, but she only took two bites of her food and dumped the rest. Why do you think that is? I'll tell you why; it's because she's eating people. She sucking their souls and discarding the human husks as if they were garbage."

Griffin's lips curved against my neck. "I thought I was the only one who noticed that. The food thing, I mean. I wasn't talking about the human husks, because I never really thought about it."

"No. I noticed. I'm sick of her poking you. I don't like it."

"And how would jumping her in the middle of a serious conversation have helped that situation?"

"It would've made me feel better. I can't fight with Angelina right now because there's no way for me to come out looking good, so I have to fight with Mom. There's no other option."

"Well, as long as you've given it a reasonable amount of thought."

We rocked back and forth, enjoying the quiet moment. We'd spent time together the past few days, but it was hardly intimate time. I was just about to suggest that we separate from the group and head to my room when a hint of motion in the yard caught my eye. I leaned forward and peered through the window, waiting for another flash of lightning to help me identify what I was searching for.

"What are you looking at?" Griffin asked, alert.

"There's something out there."

"What? A wraith?"

"Smaller than a wraith. I ... don't get worked up." I patted his hand.

"It's probably a raccoon or something. This neighborhood has the best garbage in the city."

"Probably." Griffin didn't sound convinced. "Where did you last see it?"

"Right over there." I pointed, my eyebrows flying up when the lightning flashed again and I recognized the shape skulking around the backyard. "It's Bub!"

"The gargoyle?" Griffin's distaste grew. "What is he doing out there? We haven't seen him in weeks."

I considered the creature one of my mother's minions. He hadn't been around ever since things started thawing between Mom and the rest of us. "Maybe he's here for her."

"I don't think so." Griffin pointed when the lightning flashed again. "He's sneaking out through the back gate. He's here for another reason."

I was certain he was right, which is why I broke from his grip and strode toward the door.

"Where are you going?" Griffin barked.

"I'm going after him. He's clearly up to something."

Griffin grabbed my wrist to stop me, desperation practically rolling off him. "Don't. He could lead you to trouble and I can't go with you. It's storming. I can't go outside."

I read the distress on his face, but I had a limited window to operate within. "Go upstairs and pull Aidan and Redmond from the group. Don't let Mom and Braden know what's going on. Send them after me. They'll be okay."

"What if they can't find you?"

"They will. Have faith." I grabbed a hoodie from a hook by the back door. It belonged to one of my brothers, but I didn't have time to make a different choice for fashion or size sake. "Get Redmond and Aidan. I'll be fine. I swear it."

Griffin didn't look convinced, but there was nothing I could do for him. I darted out the back door and headed toward the fence. Bub spying could never be misconstrued as a good thing.

What exactly was he up to?

❊ 24 ❊

TWENTY-FOUR

I could have waited for my brothers. Back-up is always a good idea. But I didn't. Bub's appearance in the backyard lit a fire under me and I was determined to track him down.

I zipped the hoodie as I hit the spongy ground, ignoring the pounding rain as I ran toward the back gate. It was open – almost as if it were a trap to entice me, something I recognized (and then discarded) as a possibility – so I sprinted through it and gazed back and forth in the alley.

It wasn't a city alley. It was more of an easement to keep the sprawling houses from sitting on top of one another. There was nothing to the right, but I saw the hint of a shadow, something that could've been wings or maybe that weird tail thing Bub swished about when agitated, to the left. That's the direction I headed.

The lightning was frequent, the thunder bone-jarring when it rumbled every forty seconds or so. The storm was clearly close, maybe right on top of us, and I didn't think Bub's appearance in the thick of things was a coincidence. He wanted to show me something.

Of course, that could've been wishful thinking. I was so desperate for answers I thought the friendly neighborhood gargoyle was going to give them to me. I needed an explanation, and I was certain Bub was trying to fill in some holes.

The cross street I landed on at the end of the alley was flooded. That happened often in my father's neighborhood because the sewer system was older. He had backup sump pumps for his backup sump pumps, yet never bothered to spend the money or time to update the basement because flooding seemed inevitable. When I was a kid I hoped the water would drown the snakes my brothers told me lived there. So far I'd been disappointed.

Bub showed himself under a lightning flash a few seconds later. He was across the street, making sure never to look over his shoulder in case he might meet my gaze, but his pace was slow and unhurried. That seemed odd given the raging storm.

The flooded road was empty, so I darted across, grimacing when the water hit mid-calf and completely soaked my Converse. If I thought Bub had money I'd make him pay for them. Bub continued leading the way, ignoring the houses and storm as he plodded. He could fly, yet he walked, which I found suspicious. He didn't want to get away. He wanted me to see where he was going. And where he was going was ... crap! When he finally veered from the sidewalk and picked a destination it was the creepy abandoned church on the corner I always avoided. Of course he was going there. Good luck didn't exist in my world this evening.

"You son of a ... ." I grumbled under my breath, but followed him up the walkway, increasing my pace when he used his tail to open the door before sliding inside. He knew I was following. He knew I was close. Yet when I opened the door and stepped inside he'd vanished.

I jerked my head in every direction, annoying myself with the way my damp hair smacked against my face. I even dropped to my hands and knees – which took monumental effort because the floor was dirty and I was convinced this was where every bug in the neighborhood went to die over winter – but he wasn't around.

I made a face. "What game are you playing, Bub?" I spoke louder than I meant to. It didn't matter, of course. The building was abandoned. It was supposed to be demolished in the fall but the city planners put it off until spring. No one hung out in the building, so I didn't expect a response. Despite that, I felt as if Bub remained close enough to hear my whining. "What do you want me to see?"

He didn't speak but I heard a rustle of wings and when I flicked my eyes to the front of the church I registered what I didn't notice upon initial entry. Someone had lit two candles that sat on what used to be the altar. And something else rested there ... something that looked suspiciously like a book.

"Really?" The only reason I kept talking was because I was too nervous to embrace eerie silence. "You brought me here for a book?" I took a timid step forward, jolting when the door flew open behind me to offer Redmond and Aidan entrance.

"What were you thinking?" Redmond barked, striding to my side. "You don't run off in the middle of a magical storm to chase a gargoyle. Do you have any idea how upset Griffin is?"

I imagined he was plenty upset, but I held up a finger to silence Redmond and he immediately shifted to his attack stance.

"What?"

"He was here," I whispered. "He walked in right ahead of me, but I can't find him. He's gone."

"Did you ever think that might be a trap?" Aidan complained, taking his spot on the other side of me and looking around. "Ugh. This place is filthy. No wonder they're tearing it down. I probably have bugs crawling through my hair this place is so gross." As if to emphasize his point he quickly shook his head and shivered. "You know I don't like bugs."

"I crawled on the ground looking for signs of Bub and came up empty," I complained. "I managed to survive. Suck it up."

"Why did he lead you here?" Redmond asked. He had a knife in his hand that I hadn't noticed on first glance. "I mean ... why would he want you to come here?"

"There's a book on the altar," I noted. "It looks a lot like the books we found in the mausoleum."

"It does," Aidan agreed, moving closer to the altar. "Do you think this is what he wanted you to see?"

I shrugged. "What else?"

"I guess that means we should take it, huh?"

"I guess." I relaxed my shoulders as Aidan grabbed the book, dragging a hand through my tangled hair as I tried to make sense of Bub's motivations. "He waited until he knew I was in the kitchen to tempt me outside. He wanted to give me this, but ... he didn't want anyone to know he was giving it to me. Why do you think that is?"

"He's a gargoyle, Ais," Redmond replied. "Why does he do any of the things he does?"

That was a fair question. "I think he did it this way because he didn't want Mom to know what he was doing." The words surprised me, bubbling up out of nowhere, yet when I thought about them I knew I was onto something. "Bub doesn't want Mom to know about this."

"Why would that be true?" Redmond asked. "I mean ... Mom is on our side."

"Is she?"

"Of course she is." He looked to Aidan for support. "Right? Mom is on our side. She fought with us. She saved Aisling. She's on our side."

Aidan held his hands palms up and shrugged. "I want to believe she is, but maybe Aisling has a point. Why would Bub go through all this trouble to deliver a book when Mom was already in the house?"

"Maybe Bub is working against Mom."

"Or maybe something else is going on." I gave the church a final scan before shaking my head. "It really doesn't matter now. We need to get back to the house. Griffin is probably melting down."

"Yeah, I think that thing he's been doing where he walks on eggshells and doesn't yell at you because he's wracked with guilt is pretty much over," Aidan noted. "He's livid."

Under different circumstances I might've been upset by that news. Oddly enough, I was happy at the prospect. "Good. If we fight we can make up. I'm in the mood to make up."

Redmond rolled his eyes. "You're such a pig."

"If I were a boy you wouldn't say that."

"No, you'd still be a pig. You'd just be one I could congratulate, because ... you know ... you'd be a dude. You're not a dude."

"Now you're the pig."

"At least we're keeping it in the family."

MOM WAS GONE BY the time we returned to the house. I was thankful for that, especially when I found out Griffin managed to pull my father away and tell him what was going on without tipping her off. Dad smoothly navigated her out of the house as soon as he found out, and the manor was in a righteous tizzy when we walked through the door.

"You're grounded!" Dad barked when he caught sight of me.

I rolled my eyes as I shifted out of the hoodie. "We've been over this before. I'm an adult. You can't ground me."

"As long as you're under this roof, I can ground you," Dad shot back. "It's supposed to storm all night, so that means you can't leave because I know you won't risk Griffin being out in inclement weather. So, do you know what that means, my dear? Oh, yes – you're grounded!"

"Whatever." I exhaled heavily as I kicked off my sodden shoes. "I'm wet and need to change into something comfortable. Aidan has another book for Cillian."

Dad shifted his eyes to the item in question. "It looks like it's from the same set as the others."

"I don't think that's a coincidence. Bub clearly wanted me to find it. I simply can't decide if he's doing it on Mom's behalf or if he's working against her."

"Mom's not involved in this," Braden snapped, his eyes flashing. "Mom is on our side."

Part of me wanted to believe that, if only for Braden's sake, but I was far too suspicious to simply accept his words without proof. "I guess we'll have to wait to see."

"No, we already know the truth." Braden refused to budge. "Mom is part of the team."

"We'll focus on the book for now and deal with your mother's part in this particular tale later," Dad said. "Everyone get up and get changed – I don't want anyone getting sick – and then we'll meet in the library to go over the book. Absolutely no one is to leave this house without permission. Do you understand?"

"We've got it, Dad," Aidan said wearily. "No one wants to leave."

"I was talking to your sister. She's grounded, after all. I want to make sure she understands the rules."

"All I heard was 'blah, blah, blah,'" I muttered as I moved toward the stairs. "I still maintain you can't ground me."

"Don't test me, Aisling. You'll find you're very wrong on that assumption."

BY THE TIME I DONNED fuzzy pajama pants and an oversized sweatshirt and returned to the library I was feeling markedly better. The change of clothes helped to ward off the cold, but the chilly look on Griffin's face made me realize things were hardly settled.

"Don't look at me like that," I complained as I flopped on the couch next to him. "I had no choice. I know you're upset, but ... what else did you expect me to do?"

"I expected you to wait for backup." Griffin folded his arms over his chest and stared forward. "I expected you not to give me a heart attack and run into a storm when I couldn't follow."

"Well, that wasn't really an option for me." I rested my hand on his knee and bit back a smirk when he shifted to dislodge it. "Bub clearly wanted me to follow – that's why he made sure I was the one in the kitchen – so I did what I had to do."

"You should have waited."

"I'm fine." I moved my hand back to his knee, this time letting a full grin wash over my face. "Don't be upset, baby. What do you want me to do to make it up to you? Would flowers and candy help?"

Griffin arched an eyebrow. "You're feeling awfully playful for someone who could've gotten seriously hurt."

"Bub had no intention of hurting me," I argued. "He wanted to make sure I got the book."

"But why?" Cillian questioned, flipping through the pages of the new offering. "It looks the same as the others."

"It's in Latin?" Dad prodded.

Cillian nodded. "It's a different color and the text is different, but it's clearly part of the same set."

"Can you load it through that program you have?" Aidan asked. "Will that cut down on the work you have to do?"

"Yeah, and I plan to scan it in before bed and then let the program run overnight. We probably won't have answers until morning."

"We can't expect more than that." Dad sipped some bourbon and eyed me contemplatively. "You did a stupid thing. You know better than running out of the house in the middle of a magic storm to chase a gargoyle."

"I bet that's a sentence you never thought you'd say," I teased.

"It's not funny, Aisling!"

I threw my hands up, defeated. "It's not funny," I agreed. "It's not funny at all. I reacted on instinct. I don't know what else to tell you. I knew he wanted to show me something. Otherwise he wouldn't have let me see him.

"I knew when I was following him down the flooded street – totally gross, by the way – that he was purposely going slow enough for me to follow," I continued. "I knew he could've been leading me into a trap. Heck, that book could be part of a trap. I knew all of that and I still did it. Flog me now."

Dad pinched the bridge of his nose, a position he took when trying to calm himself and refrain from exploding. "You knew all of this and yet you put yourself at risk. Why?"

"Because we're not the ones being hurt this time," I answered without hesitation. "Griffin is being hurt. Jerry was hurt. We're fine for a change. I don't like it. It makes me feel helpless. I can't spend the rest of my life planning a way around storms so Griffin stays safe. I want this over.

"It's not just Griffin and Jerry, though," I added. "It's not just Maya either. What about all the other innocent people who are being affected? If this doesn't end soon we could lose a lot of people. Those who don't die might never be the same. I can't live with that."

"Basically she's saying she's Detroit's newest superhero," Braden supplied. "She's here to save the downtrodden and sacrifice herself in the process." He gave a slow clap. "You truly are a marvel. We should all endeavor to be like you."

I narrowed my eyes. "I know you're upset because I suspect Mom in this, but there's no reason to take it to an uncomfortable level. I don't fancy myself a superhero. I'm only saying that this can't go on.

"The walls are closing in on us here, Braden," I continued. "We have weird storms and warnings from a shaman that one person has been behind all of this. We considered that he was talking about Genevieve. We considered that he was talking about someone we've yet to meet. We also considered he was talking about Mom. We would've been idiots to rule her out."

"It's not Mom!" Braden was ready to explode.

"This is not the time for a fight." Dad inserted himself between Braden and me, worry evident. "We're doing all we can do. We'll let Cillian's program work through the night and pick this back up in the morning. Until then, I think it would be best for everyone if we separated into different corners for the night."

"I agree." Griffin got to his feet and extended his hand to me. "Come on. I think you and I are going to the same corner."

I accepted his hand and graced Braden with a final sneer as we passed in front of him. "Does that mean I'm not in trouble any longer?" I asked, turning serious.

"Oh, you're in trouble." Griffin's lips curved into a slow smile. "I'm going to punish you severely for what you did."

"Oh, that sounds fun." I meant it. "Can we start with a bath? You could turn the water really hot and massage me to start the punishment."

"I heard that, Aisling," Dad called as we sauntered out of the library. "You're double grounded. If you push things too far, I'll make you sleep in separate rooms."

Now that sounded like legitimate punishment.

"I was just trying to make Griffin feel better, Dad," I shot back. "I didn't really mean it. We're going to sleep in footed pajamas and on separate sides of the bed tonight. You have my word."

Dad obviously didn't believe me, but he smiled all the same. "That's my girl. There's a reason you're so often my favorite."

"Yeah, because she's a total liar," Braden complained.

"There's also a reason you're rarely my favorite, Braden," Dad groused. "Go find something to do ... and make it as far away from your sister as possible."

"Finally something I want to do," Braden muttered. "The day is looking up."

TWENTY-FIVE

Griffin was awake before me, his phone in his hand.

"I remember when we used to wake up and stare at each other," I lamented, grinning when he shifted his eyes to me. "It was all longing looks and playful silent suggestions for what we could do before getting out of bed. It seems I've been replaced by technology."

"I'm checking the weather."

"Ah, so I've really been replaced by your weather app. Apparently the thrill is gone, huh?"

Griffin's grin was lazy as he rested the phone on the nightstand. "You think the thrill is gone?"

"Obviously you find the phone more interesting than me."

"We'll just see about that." Griffin dove on me, his hands finding my waist and digging in to tickle.

I laughed hard as I tried to escape, my cheeks burning as I gasped for oxygen. "You're hurting me."

Griffin immediately pulled back. "I'm sorry."

What a sucker. He always fell for that. "It's okay." I tried to look pathetic and sad. "It didn't hurt much."

"Good. It's going to hurt a lot worse this time." Griffin resumed his tickling as I squirmed.

"Hey! You're not supposed to keep doing that when I pretend to be hurt."

"You're not supposed to pretend to be hurt."

He had a point. "Okay, but if I can't fake being hurt I'll have to go on the offensive."

"Bring it on."

I put everything I had into the tickle war, and by the time I was done Griffin's face was as red as mine. My hair was a snarled mess, the covers were twisted and hanging off the side of the bed, and my chest was heaving.

That's when I noticed Dad standing in the open doorway, his arms folded across his chest.

"We weren't doing anything," I said instinctively, shoving my hair away from my face as I adopted an innocent expression. "This isn't what it looks like."

"It looks like you were engaging in a tickle war," Dad noted.

"Oh, so it's exactly what it looks like. I wasn't sure."

Dad made a face. "You're a lot of work, kid. Sometimes I think you're more work than the other four combined."

"That's only because they're boys and you don't care who they have their tickle wars with."

"Good point." Dad moved into the room and sat in the chair next to the bed. He looked serious, which made me uncomfortable and served to suck the fun right out of the room.

"Oh, don't start lecturing." I pressed my hand to my forehead. "I have a headache. You'll make it worse if you start lecturing."

"Since when do you have a headache?" Dad asked.

"Since you came in here with that look on your face."

"Yes, well, I'm not going to lecture you." Dad crossed his feet at the ankles. "I am, however, going to beg a favor."

My antenna went up. I knew my father well enough to recognize that he wouldn't have risked coming in here before breakfast if he didn't want something big. "I'm not sure that's a good idea," I hedged. "I think I might be too tired to do you a favor."

"You don't even know what it is," Dad pointed out.

"Am I missing something?" Griffin interjected. "What's going on here?"

"Dad is about to drop the hammer on me and frame it as a favor," I supplied. "He's going to make me do something I don't want to do and then act as if I'll break his heart if I don't do this special favor for him. It's a little game we like to play."

"I don't like playing it," Dad stressed. "It's a necessary evil. And, yes, I'm going to ask you to do something you don't want to do."

"I hate it when this happens." I covered my eyes with my hand and wished I could go back to the tickle war.

"What do you want?" Griffin asked, propping himself on his elbow. "If this is about her running out into the storm last night, we talked and she's sorry."

That's not quite how I remembered things. We talked and I was sorry he was upset. I wasn't sorry I chased Bub. In fact, the more I thought about it, the more I had to wonder exactly what Bub had up his sleeve. Actually, since he was a strange looking owl-dog, he didn't wear sleeves. He was definitely up to something, though.

"Please." Dad offered an imperial wave of his hand. "We both know you gave in because you didn't feel like fighting. You're not quite ready to take her on after what happened and I understand that. That's why I'm here to take her on."

I didn't like the sound of that one bit. "I didn't do anything."

"You always do something. As for what you did last night ... it was hardly the dumbest thing you've done this week."

That was definitely an insult. "What's the dumbest thing I did this week?"

"I believe that happened when you got out of the car to help Carol Davenport."

I frowned. "She's old ... and dying. She needed help, and I was the only one close to give it."

"And how did that work out for you?"

"That doesn't mean I'm sorry I helped." I could be stubborn when the situation called for it. "I would do it again."

"Yes. That's why you're the bane of my existence." Dad drummed his fingers on the armchair as he regarded me. "We need to talk about something serious. You're not going to like it, but it's how it has to be ... at least for breakfast."

I had no idea what he was getting at, but he was clearly worried. "Just tell me what it is."

"I want you to promise first."

"No."

"I'll lift your grounding if you promise."

"You can't ground me." My eyes fired. "I'm an adult."

"You're barely an adult." Dad stared me down. "Promise."

"No."

"I'll make sure you have another ice cream bar at dinner tonight if you promise."

Oh, now he was hitting below the belt. "I can't be bought."

"I'll make them stock up on those Halloween sprinkles you like even though it's off season and I have to pay triple for them."

Well, I liked to think I couldn't be bought. In truth, it was the exact opposite. "Fine. I promise."

Griffin's eyebrows flew up his forehead. "He just bought you off with sprinkles."

"Halloween sprinkles," I corrected. "They have little ghosts and mummies. They're seasonal ... and awesome."

"I'm going to stock up on those stupid sprinkles and hold them over your head for the rest of our lives."

"That's fine. I know your secret tickle spot. We're even."

"Oh, how did I become the father who sits back and watches his daughter in bed with her boyfriend and listens while they talk about secret tickle spots?" Dad groused, shifting on his chair. "At some point I took a wrong turn and never recovered. I simply can't figure out when."

I grinned, enjoying his discomfort. "What is this big favor you want to ask me?"

Dad's fake grimace slipped and was replaced with a real one. "I need you to stop spouting theories about your mother while Braden is around. He can't take it right now."

I stiffened as I leaned forward. "You want me to lie even though I know in my gut she has something to do with this?"

AMANDA M. LEE

"I don't want you to lie," Dad replied. "I want you to spare your brother's feelings. He's struggling right now and he's going to crumble if we don't protect him."

I opened my mouth to argue but abandoned the effort, instead shifting my eyes to the window. The sun was bright through the curtains and it looked like a lovely day. That was something to look forward to given our current predicament.

"I know it's hard for you." Dad was somber as he leaned forward. "I know you believe your mother has a hand in this. Truth be told, I'm starting to think that, too. That doesn't change the fact that Braden doesn't believe that."

"He won't believe that," I corrected. "He refuses to even entertain the possibility."

"Because he can't. It's not that he won't. It's that he can't. Why don't you see that?"

I did see it. That was part of the problem. "He'll have to face it eventually. There's a very good chance she's been our enemy all along."

"Not *all* along," Dad argued. "Only since she came back. The mother you grew up with was a good and kind woman. She would never have done these things."

"No, you're right. What I said wasn't fair." I meant it. "Whatever came back isn't the same person. I know we've had this discussion a hundred times, but that shaman was very firm when he said we've been fighting the same enemy all along. What if that enemy is Mom?"

"Then that will likely kill your brother." Dad looked sad. "I'm doing the best I can for all my children. I'm asking you to hold it together and not cast aspersions on your mother until I can ease Braden into this. Do you think you can do that for me?"

I pressed my lips together and nodded. His worried expression forced me to acquiesce even though I wanted to shake Braden until he accepted reality. "I won't mention Mom being evil in front of Braden ... at least for now. He'll have to get on the team eventually, though. You know that, right?"

Dad swallowed hard as he got to his feet. "I do. But I'm terrified that he'll pick the other team."

That possibility hadn't even occurred to me. "He wouldn't. He

226

knows better."

"Oh, Aisling, he does know better," Dad agreed. "That's his mother, though. He can't see past that. You manage to see the truth despite your feelings. He can't seem to make that happen, which will be the death of him if I can't find a way out of this."

"He won't die. I won't let him." I was deathly serious. "We'll make him see the truth."

"Braden is a lot like you," Dad reminded me. "You can't make him see what he doesn't want to see. He's my son. I want him protected, just as I want you protected. I need your help keeping him on the straight and narrow right now.

"I've already talked to Redmond, Aidan and Cillian," he continued. "They're on board. I need you to be, too."

I nodded without hesitation. "I won't say anything."

"Thank you." Dad leaned over and gave me a kiss on the forehead. "You have ten minutes to finish your tickle war. Don't forget, we're having a waffle bar for breakfast."

I smirked at his back. "Close the door. We might want to tickle each other naked."

Dad left the door open. "I know what you're trying to do and it won't work," he sang out. "I can't hear you."

"I'll change that at breakfast."

"I'm sure you will."

BY THE TIME WE HIT the dining room for breakfast, we had showered and were prepared to pretend nothing was wrong. Cillian was in the middle of going through his research, so it seemed a perfect time for us to join the party.

"Sorry we're late," I offered lamely when Dad lobbed a dirty look in my direction. "We slept in."

"Oh, is that why I heard you giggling when I passed your room?" Aidan challenged, his eyes filled with mirth. "I believe there was some squealing, too. I had no idea you squealed in your sleep."

"I'm gifted." I added three large waffles to my plate and doused them with blueberries, syrup and whipped cream before moving toward the table. "Don't let me interrupt the fun. What were you guys talking about?"

"You interrupted the fun when you were born," Braden supplied, sneering when I glared. "Things were much better before we had you to deal with."

Sensing trouble, Griffin rested his hand on my shoulder as he sat next to me. "I think the world turned into a brighter place when you were born, baby. Don't listen to him. I've decided all the Grimlocks are crabby first thing in the morning. It must be genetic."

Dad offered Griffin a grateful smile. "I agree. No fighting over waffles. That's a new family rule."

"Fine." Braden focused on his food. "Go back to what you were saying about the spell, Cillian. That sounded interesting."

"I found several things in the translations," Cillian explained, sipping his coffee. "This book has a lot more information than the others."

"Which seems to indicate the other books were left behind on purpose," I mused. "I'm guessing whoever left them wanted to distract us so he or she could finish out whatever play they've got cooking."

"Probably," Dad agreed. "The thing is, I don't understand what Harry Turner has to do with all of this. The only reason we even know what's going on is because Aisling broke the rules and went through Harry's stuff. She knows he had the disc, which is probably knowledge we shouldn't have. I'm kind of curious if that means he cast the spell."

"I'm curious about that myself," I admitted. "We have a problem if we want to sneak into Harry's house, though, and that problem goes by the name of Mark Green."

"Yes." Dad nodded. "There's every indication he's still following you. I think authorizing you to break into Turner's house is a bad idea."

"Wait, you're authorizing them to break into homes now?" Griffin held up a hand in confusion. "I'm not sure I can listen to this. I'm a cop, after all."

"You're also part of the family." Dad's tone was dismissive. "Something tells me you're going to put our needs ahead of your duty ... especially when we're trying to save lives."

Griffin muttered something under his breath that I couldn't quite make out. It sounded a lot like "know it all," but I couldn't be certain.

"We need to figure out where Green is," I said, trying to change the subject. "Maybe he's parked on the front street and that's how he knows when I'm leaving. It wouldn't be the first time he's tried that."

Dad agreed. "But I looked when I got the newspaper this morning. There are no vehicles on the street. That means he's hiding somewhere else. I had the home office send a sweeper team this morning to figure out where he is and what he can see."

"What good will that do?" Jerry asked, slathering his waffles in whipped cream and strawberries.

"If we know where he is we can distract him and get Aisling out for the afternoon without him following," Dad explained. "We can also get her out through the alley if it comes to that. To my knowledge, he didn't follow you to the church last night. Your brothers would've seen him if he were on the street."

That hadn't even occurred to me. "I doubt Bub would've made himself visible if he knew Green was watching. That's probably why he was in the backyard."

"Which I would guess means that Green can only see the front of the house," Dad said. "That's to our advantage, but we'll wait for the sweeper team's report before doing anything. I have jobs for everyone today, and our regular charges have been shifted to another team. This is our main focus."

That was interesting. The main office had to be worried to do anything of the sort. "So, what are we doing?"

"For starters, Aidan and Braden will go to Turner's house," Dad replied. "I want them to toss it. You gave it a cursory look when you were there, but not with a trained eye. You were just biding time so you didn't get your hair wet."

"You make me sound so shallow," I complained.

"As for the rest, Cillian will be here working with his translations," Dad said. "I have two people coming from the main office who read Latin to help him. We need to get through the books faster, and that means we need more bodies."

"What about ... ?" I was about to ask about Mom when I quickly corrected my course. "What about Turner's family? Shouldn't someone dig further and watch them?"

"That's what you, Redmond and Griffin will do today," Dad answered. "I'm hopeful you'll be able to find something to work with."

Griffin balked. "I can't go out with Aisling. What happens if it rains?"

"You're going." Dad's tone was no-nonsense. "You need to get over your fear. Redmond will have a truck. You'll take umbrellas. You can wear a rain poncho if you like. You need to help the team, and that means you're going."

Griffin looked as if he was going to argue, but remained silent. "Fine. But I want Redmond armed in case something happens."

"No way!" I moved to hop to my feet. "I am not letting Redmond shoot Griffin! If you think that's going to happen ... ."

Dad held up a hand to calm me. "I'm going to arm everyone – and that includes you and Redmond – with tranquilizer darts and guns. That's the best way I know to protect all of you and the people you come in contact with."

Hmm. Not only did that sound like a good idea, it also sounded fun. I raised my hand and waited for Dad to call on me.

Dad sighed, exasperation evident. "Before you even ask the question, Aisling, you will be punished severely if you tranquilize any of your brothers. Do you understand?"

I nodded. "What about Angelina? If I see her, can I tranquilize her?"

Dad tilted his head to the side, considering. "I don't see why not. You have my permission to tranquilize Angelina."

"Yay." I clapped my hands as I smiled at Griffin. "It's like Christmas all over again."

"I'm glad you're pleased."

"I am pleased. We're going to talk about that whole 'arming Redmond' thing during our ride, too, so that's something to look forward to."

Griffin sighed. "This is going to turn into a thing, isn't it?"

"You have no idea."

❧ 26 ☙

TWENTY-SIX

We didn't really chase down Harry Turner's relatives. That was a lie.

Dad sent our group to find Mom and spy on her, with the caveat that Braden not find out. He threatened dire consequences and liver and onions for dinner if we screwed up, so I knew he meant business.

I sat in the backseat of Redmond's truck as he navigated toward Detroit. The only lead we had on Mom's current home was a building she'd used for business a time or two months ago. That's the only place we had to start, so that's where we headed.

"This seems like a waste of time because we don't really know she's there," Griffin noted from the passenger seat. He had an umbrella clutched in his hand and a rain poncho bunched at his feet as he nervously stared out the window. Thankfully the weather remained sunny and bright. If it was overcast I had no doubt we would never get him out of the truck again. He would opt to live there rather than risk hurting someone.

"We have to start somewhere," I argued. "This is the only place we've got, so ... I don't know what to tell you."

"Does anyone else find it odd that we have no idea where our mother is?" Redmond asked, keeping his eyes on the road as he merged with heavy traffic. "I mean ... how many other people can say they have no idea where their mother lives?"

"Or who she eats," I grumbled.

Redmond caught my eye in the rearview mirror. "You shouldn't say things like that."

"Oh, please." I shook my head. "You can't tell me you haven't thought about it. We know she's absorbing souls to stay alive. She pretty much said so. Haven't you wondered where she's getting these souls?"

"I guess I don't want to think about it," Redmond conceded. "But I'm not the issue. Braden is the issue."

"Yes, and Braden is being a freaking pain in the behind. He needs to get over it. That woman may look like our mother, but she's a monster."

"She is, though." Redmond gentled his voice. "She remembers things about when we were kids. She mentioned a conversation I had with her not long before she died. It was something only she and I knew about."

I stared at him for a long beat, my stomach roiling at the hitch in his voice.

"She remembered what I was upset about and told me I'd done a good job in her absence and there was no reason to keep worrying about it," he continued. "She said it to me at a time when I really was worried I was a failure. She made me feel better ... just like she used to when we were kids."

My curiosity piqued, I pursed my lips. "And what did she say?"

"She told me that I did the right thing when I punched Griffin to keep you safe," Redmond replied without hesitation. "She knew I felt guilty because you were so upset and she kind of talked me down. She hadn't done that since I was a kid and I punched Alex Butterfield in the mouth after he grabbed your boob."

My mouth inadvertently dropped open. "You punched Alex Butterfield in the mouth? Is that why he never called again?"

"You let some kid with the name 'Butterfield' grab your boob?" Griffin was aghast. "Were you drunk at the time?"

"Probably," I conceded. "His last name was a shame because he was very cute. He had these great eyes with long lashes ... and this smile that made me go weak in the knees." I tilted my head to the side, considering. "Huh. He kind of looked like you."

Redmond chuckled, genuinely amused. "You do sort of have a type. I think all the guys you dated in high school looked like Griffin now that I think about it."

"I only dated like, four guys in high school because you guys always chased off my dates," I reminded him. "It's not as if I dated half the school."

Redmond made a sound like an angry cat. "I forgot how testy you were when we chased off your boyfriends. That's why it was so fun."

"I'm done talking to you for the day." I crossed my arms over my chest. "I can't believe you punched Alex Butterfield. I wanted him to ask me to prom. He never called me again. I should've known he didn't trip over his own feet and plant his face against a door handle like he said."

Griffin snorted. "Sometimes I wish I would've known you guys when you were in high school. I'm guessing you were a lot of fun."

"And other times?" Redmond prodded.

"Other times I'm thankful that I didn't meet Aisling until I was an adult and could stand up for myself. If I'd met her when I was a teenager I would've run the other way because you guys would've terrified me to the point where I had no choice but to flee."

"That's what they were good at," I groused. "That was their freaking claim to fame during my high school years."

"Once I was an adult, I knew she was worth putting up with all your crap," Griffin added, grinning as he glanced at me. "I didn't get to miss out on anything the way things worked out, so I can't get worked up about that."

The words were touching and schmaltzy. "Yeah. I'm glad we met when we did, too."

Griffin's grin widened as I turned to Redmond.

"I'm going to punch you in the face for chasing Alex Butterfield out of my life as soon as I get a chance," I warned. "You totally ruined my week when you did that."

"He grabbed your boob," Redmond complained.

"I told him to do it."

Redmond stilled. "You did? Why would you possibly do that?"

I shrugged. "I wanted to know what it was like to be felt up. Just for the record, it didn't happen again for another year, which means you must've scared Alex to the point he told everyone to stay away from me."

Redmond puffed out his chest. "So I really did my job."

"If your job is annoying your sister, you definitely did it."

"I'm the best big brother ever," Redmond smiled at Griffin before sobering. "As for hitting you ... I can't be sorry. I mean I am sorry I hurt you, but I'm not sorry I reacted the way I did."

"I'm not sorry you did either." Griffin turned serious. "You saved her."

"I just reacted."

"You saved her, which means you ultimately saved me."

"Oh, geez." I didn't bother to hide my eye roll. "Have either of you boneheads considered the fact that I might've been able to save myself? Maybe I didn't need Redmond to step in and flex his muscles. Maybe I could've handled things better on my own."

Redmond arched an amused eyebrow. "Really? How would that have worked out for you? What would you have done to save yourself?"

"Talk to him." I'd gone over the altercation a hundred times in my mind and knew exactly how I would've reacted. "I would've talked to him in a reasonable tone and he would've backed down."

Griffin immediately started shaking his head. "No, Aisling. I already told you that I was aware of what I was doing and couldn't seem to stop myself."

"You didn't try to stop yourself," I corrected. "Had you been forced into a decision between hurting me or stopping, I believe you would've stopped yourself."

"I think you're wrong."

"I'm never wrong."

Griffin and Redmond exchanged a weighted look that wasn't lost on me.

"Now I know why your father wants us to be a threesome all day,"

Griffin said after a beat. "He knows his only daughter is borderline delusional and wants her to have backup."

Redmond chuckled. "Aisling's always been the one to convince herself something was true even when the rest of us thought otherwise. It's something we hoped she'd outgrow, but she didn't. Braden is the same way."

The dig struck hard. "I am not like Braden."

"You are." Redmond was firm. "The difference in this particular situation is that Braden seems to think that he knows Mom better than anybody else in the family. You're pragmatic where Mom is concerned. I don't think you're pragmatic in the least where Griffin is concerned."

"They're entirely different situations."

"Are they?" Redmond refused to back down, which was frustrating. "Griffin has told you that he wasn't in control of himself because of the storm, yet you think you know his brain better than he does. When you compare that to Braden, who can't see the obvious evidence piling up against Mom, they seem the same to me."

That was definitely insulting. "The real difference is that I'm right and Braden is wrong."

"If you say so." Redmond didn't look convinced. "We're close to the building. We need to find a place to park so she won't see us. I don't think she'll recognize my vehicle, but we have to hide all the same."

He was trying to placate me, but I wasn't in the mood to play that game. "I'm right," I repeated. "Braden is wrong and I'm right."

"We're not going to find out," Griffin interjected. "You're not going to be alone with me if somehow we're stuck outside and a storm hits. You're going to run."

That didn't sound anything like me.

"You are." Griffin turned so he could stare into my eyes. "I want you to promise me you'll run. I won't get out of the truck otherwise."

Yeah, I should've seen that coming. "Fine." I exhaled heavily and rolled my eyes. "I promise."

"You didn't put a lot of effort behind it."

"I wouldn't push me too far on this," I shot back.

"She sounds like Dad when she says that, doesn't she?" Redmond was back to grinning. "Now, come on." He clapped his hands to jolt everyone to attention. "We need to focus on Mom. I would be lying if I said I didn't want our investigation to rule her out. For now, all we can do is wait."

"Fine." I leaned back in my seat. "I want Starbucks if we're going to be stuck in here all day."

"No." Redmond shook his head. "If you have Starbucks you'll have to pee, and I'm not spending the entire day helping you find convenient bathrooms. You have a bladder like an infant when it comes to Starbucks."

That was a blatant lie. "I have a bladder like an iron balloon."

"You do not."

"I do, too."

"You do not."

"I do, too."

"Ugh." Griffin slapped his hand against his forehead. "I almost wish I was out in a storm right now. That's how long this day already feels."

"Well, suck it up." Redmond clapped him hard on the shoulder. "It's only going to get longer. We're stuck in a truck with Aisling all day. This is like the Grimlock version of hell. Prepare yourself, because ... well ... she's the worst when she's bored."

"I heard that," I complained.

"I wasn't whispering."

"It really is going to be a long day." Griffin sounded defeated. "I should've brought headphones."

"Live and learn."

WE LUCKED OUT AND caught a glimpse of Mom leaving the building only an hour after we began casing the joint. From our vantage point, it was easy to see her on the front sidewalk. What surprised us were the individuals she was talking with.

"Those don't look like wraiths." Griffin scooted forward as far as he could and stared in Mom's direction. "Those are ... regular people."

"They look to be," Redmond agreed, squinting. "We really should've brought binoculars. I didn't even think of it."

"Let me look." I lifted my phone and hit the camera app and pointed it in Mom's direction. I zoomed in on her and the main guy she chatted with – he looked to be in his forties and wore a beaten-up leather jacket – and the conversation appeared intense given the way they gestured at one another. I snapped three photos in rapid succession and then slid back, knocking my empty Starbucks cup to the floor as I studied the images.

"Do you recognize him?" Griffin asked after a few moments.

I shook my head and handed the phone to Redmond. "No. I'm willing to guess exactly what he is, though."

Redmond was grim as he glared at the screen. "Rogue reapers."

I nodded. "They're dressed exactly like Duke Fontaine and they've just got that look." Duke Fontaine was a rogue reaper who'd spent decades working against my family. He died when the Olivet mausoleum burned down – essentially because I set the fire – and he'd been nothing but a bad memory ever since. The new development caused me to rethink everything I remembered about that day. "You know, Zake Zezo told us that we were dealing with one person pulling the strings. What if he was talking about a rogue reaper?"

Redmond arched an eyebrow as he handed back the phone. "He made it sound like a woman. That's a man."

"Yes, but we don't know if that guy is in charge."

"So now you're arguing for Mom being innocent." Redmond was understandably confused. "What made you change your mind so fast?"

"Oh, I don't believe Mom is innocent," I clarified. "I think she's involved in all of this. But what if she's not in charge?"

"Okay, let's say I'm willing to get on board with your theory – which I might be because there's a chance that Mom isn't outright evil in it – but who else could be in charge?" Redmond challenged. "Genevieve is dead. I know we considered that maybe she faked her death, but I can't believe that. We were all there. We saw her. Dad killed the crap out of her."

He was right. There was no doubt Genevieve died in the battle. We had to get rid of her body. She was definitely dead. "So maybe someone else is involved entirely," I said. "It's not out of the realm of possibility. Maybe Genevieve had a lot of ties we never considered.

"I mean, we didn't know about her relationship with Annemarie Turner," I continued. "She could've had a million wannabe witches and acolytes ready to do her bidding. Maybe one of them was working with her from the start and stepped in to fill the vacuum when Genevieve died."

"So, under your hypothesis, your mother is working with whoever is organizing this," Griffin said. "You think whoever it is has a band of rogue reapers to command and your mother has to work with them to do this woman's bidding."

"It's not impossible."

"No, it's not," Griffin agreed. "Do you have any idea who we could be dealing with? Also, what does any of this have to do with the storms?"

"Someone cast a spell for the storms. They used the disc I saw in Harry's house. That's the best possible answer. The storms started right after Harry died. Maybe his death was part of the ritual."

"Now that right there is something to think about." Redmond twisted in his seat. "The first storm started while you were still in Harry's house. His death could very well have been a sacrifice."

"So how do we stop the storms?" Griffin asked. "You're making it sound as if they could go on forever."

"I think they could," I admitted. "We have to find the person who cast the spell – whether that's Mom or whoever she's working with – and force that individual to break it. That's our only shot."

"So how do we do that?"

That was the question of the day. "I don't know, but it looks like Mom is on the move." I inclined my chin in her direction. "She's getting in that dude's truck."

"So we need to follow them, right?" Redmond questioned, firing up his engine. "That's our entire purpose for the day."

"Yeah. Follow them."

"Where do you think they're going?" Griffin asked.

I shrugged. "I hope wherever it is has a public bathroom, though." I cast an accusatory look in Redmond's direction. "Why did you buy me the big latte? You know I can't hold my coffee."

"Oh, I just knew it," Redmond growled. "This is the absolute last stakeout we go on together. I'm putting my foot down."

"Yeah, yeah, yeah." I'd heard it all before. "Try to avoid the potholes if you don't want my bladder to explode in your backseat."

"I just ... you're my least favorite sister sometimes. You know that, right?"

"Somehow I think you'll survive."

"You'd better hope we all survive," Redmond muttered. "This is getting dirtier and dirtier by the minute. How much worse could this get?"

The question plagued me, too. "I don't know. Let's hope we're heading toward the end, because I'm afraid what this is going to do to our family."

"Me, too." Redmond slid into traffic. "This could kill Braden."

That's exactly what worried me most. "Whatever you do, don't lose them. We need to know even if the answer isn't what we want."

"I'm on it."

27

TWENTY-SEVEN

Mom and the reaper meandered around town, which wasn't good for my bladder control or Redmond's temper.

"If you whine about having to go to the bathroom one more time ... ."

Griffin took a more sympathetic approach. "Try not to think about it. Think about something else."

I appreciated the effort, but my irritation level was through the roof. "Like what?"

"I don't know. Let's talk about the wedding. Tell me about the dress you picked out."

I rolled my eyes as I wrapped my arms around my waist and bent over. "I can't tell you. It's against the rules. You're not supposed to see my dress before the wedding."

Griffin arched an eyebrow. "You're not showing it to me. You're describing it."

"And since when are you so superstitious?" Redmond added. "I'd think you'd be the last one to believe hokum like that."

"I didn't say I believed it. It's just ... it's tradition."

Griffin's eyes softened. "Fair enough. I think it's cute that you're superstitious."

"I'm not superstitious." My precarious bladder predicament and the teasing were making for some major discomfort. "I'm going to need a bathroom ... and soon ... or you're going to need to get the inside of your truck detailed."

"Don't even think about going to the bathroom back there," Redmond barked. "Griffin is right. Think about something else."

"I can't think about anything else."

"Let's talk about the honeymoon," Griffin suggested, getting into the spirit of the game. "I was thinking we should go to a tropical location so you can wear as few clothes as possible."

"Sure. Fine."

"That's all the input you have on the subject?"

"Griffin, I'm not joking." I was close to crying and couldn't stop the tears from pooling. "I have to go to the bathroom ... now!"

"Go in the cup," Redmond suggested. "I'll make sure to keep my eyes up here."

That sounded like the worst idea I'd ever heard, and my brothers once talked me into believing I could jump off the roof and fly. Luckily my father caught me by the back of my coat before I took flight. If I remembered correctly, my brothers were grounded for a month after that and I was able to eat my weight in ice cream. Hmm. Maybe that wasn't such a bad memory after all.

"I'm not going in the cup," I barked, regaining my senses. "I'm not a dude. I can't manage it without peeing all over my clothes."

"Well, we're supposed to be following Mom," Redmond reminded me. "If we lose her now, we're done."

"I ... ." I gritted my teeth and pressed my eyes shut, not opening them again until Redmond slowed the truck and pulled to the side of the road. I was so relieved I almost kissed his cheek as I fumbled with the door handle. "Thank you."

"Don't thank me. Thank Mom."

"What?" I furrowed my brow, frowning when I realized Mom and her partner had pulled in front of a nondescript house and were heading toward the front door. "What are they doing here?"

"I have no idea, but you'd better go quickly," Redmond replied. "There are some bushes over there. Try not to get caught peeing in some random dude's landscaping, by the way. If you get arrested I might never stop laughing."

"Ha, ha, ha." I bolted out of the truck and raced toward the bushes in question. They weren't tall, but I was desperate. I did my business as quickly as possible, ignoring the fact that I had no toilet paper options and Griffin and Redmond knew exactly what I was doing. When I straightened to return to the truck, I realized Mom and her friend were back in front of the house. I could do nothing but duck back into the bushes and hope they didn't see me.

"Well, that was a waste of time," the man said, his disdain evident.

"Really, Rogan, must you be such a ray of sunshine?" Mom drawled, matching his tone. "We had to ask and you know it."

"I could've told you what she'd say," the man called Rogan snapped. "She had no idea what we were talking about, and now she thinks we're morons."

"I'm sure you're used to that." Mom's eyes flashed with mirth when Rogan clenched his hands into fists at his sides. "Careful now. We both know what's going to happen if you follow through on that inclination."

"It might be worth it to shut your mouth."

Mom's tone was haughty. "You wouldn't finish taking the swing. You'd be gone long before it landed. Remember who you're dealing with."

"I'm not likely to forget." Rogan sneered, showing off a set of ugly, jagged teeth. "So what now? If she doesn't know what happened to the disc, we're out of options. We have nowhere else to look."

"We have somewhere else to look," Mom corrected. "I doubt it's there, but we'll give it a shot all the same."

"And if we don't find it?"

Mom shrugged. "I have no idea. I would suggest that getting out of town might be the superior option. I guess we'll have to wait and see."

"It's always a joy to hang around with you," Rogan complained, stomping toward his truck. "I don't know how I got so lucky."

Mom's smile faded. "I believe karma got us both here."

I remained crouching in the bushes until the truck took off down the street, and then I raced to Redmond's truck and launched myself in the back. "Go!"

Redmond didn't need to be told twice. He gunned the engine and slipped into traffic behind the truck carrying Rogan and Mom. He waited for me to fasten my seatbelt and catch my breath before asking the obvious question.

"What did you hear?"

I recited the conversation from memory.

"Disc?" Griffin scratched at the back of his neck. "Do you think they're talking about the disc you saw in Harry's house?"

"That would be my guess."

"While you were handling your business, we ran the address," Redmond supplied. "Guess who it belongs to."

I hadn't given it much thought, but now the answer was relatively easy to come by. "Harry Turner's aunt?"

"You're smarter than you look, which is a probably a good thing." Redmond grinned as he allowed a car to pass him, making sure to keep Rogan's vehicle in sight but working overtime not to crowd Mom and her cohort. "It can't be a coincidence. They're looking for that disc."

"Which means it's not at Harry's house," I mused. "I need to call Aidan."

Griffin cast me a curious look as he watched me dig for my phone. "Why are you calling Aidan?"

"Because they went to Harry's house to look around and I need to know what they found." I pulled Aidan's name up on my contact list and waited for him to answer. He sounded breathless when he did, but I didn't wait for him to launch into his story. "Did you find anything at Harry's house?"

"Well, hello to you, too." I could practically see his grimace. "Now is not a great time."

I flicked my eyes to the road to make sure Redmond hadn't lost Mom before continuing. "It's not a great time for us either. I need to ask you a question."

"Yeah, I think it should wait until later."

"It can't wait."

"It's going to have to. I'm busy hiding in an alley behind Harry

Turner's house because Detective Green showed up out of nowhere and we had to run," Aidan said. "He could be out here any second looking for us. I really can't talk."

"Who is that?" Braden barked. "If that's Aisling, hang up. We don't have time for her."

I wanted to reach through the phone and strangle Braden, but that wasn't an option so I filed it away for later. "I just have a quick question."

"Fine. What?"

"Did you find the disc in Harry's house?"

"No, and the place has been tossed. I think Green believes we did it, which is going to be an issue because he's going to arrest us if he finds us."

"Did he see you?"

"I can't be sure, but my guess is yes."

That wasn't good. "Oh, well, I guess you should probably hang up then."

"Thanks for the tip," Aidan said dryly. "Wait, before you hang up, did you learn anything from Harry's aunt?"

That was a tricky question given who he was hiding with. Still, if something happened, it was best for him to know. "Mom was with another rogue reaper outside the house. Don't tell Braden!" I rushed the last three words out of my mouth so quickly they ran together. Aidan got the gist, though, and I was thankful.

"I see. Where are you now?"

"Following her and the reaper. His name is Rogan. I've never seen him before. They were talking about a disc."

"The disc that was in Harry Turner's house but isn't there any longer?"

"That would be the one. At least that's my guess. They say they have one place left to look, but after that ... ."

"So someone took the disc," Aidan said. "The bad guys don't have it. The cops don't have it. Everyone is looking for it."

"Pretty much."

"And you were the last one seen with it," Aidan mused.

I stilled. "What is that supposed to mean?"

"It simply means that you were the last one to see it," Aidan replied, refusing to back down. "You have a habit of sticking things in your pockets."

"Are you calling me a thief?"

"No, but you are forgetful. I don't suppose you accidentally took the disc?"

"Of course not." I scoffed at the notion ... and then I actually thought about it. "Well, maybe," I hedged. "The storm was loud and he was yelling at me. I had the disc in my hand and then he said something. There might be a chance I stuck it in my pocket."

"I knew it!" Aidan practically exploded. "Where would the disc be now if you stuck it in your pocket?"

I wasn't sure I liked his tone. "If I accidentally took it – and that's a big if – it would be in the pocket of the jeans I wore that day."

"And where are those now?"

"On the bedroom floor in the townhouse. We haven't been back there in days because we've been staying at Grimlock Manor. No one has been around to do the laundry."

"Which means it's probably still there."

Holy crap! The key to this entire mess, the disc we'd been trying to research for days, was in my jeans back at the townhouse. What were the odds? Wait, don't answer that. Somehow I'm sure the limits of my intelligence will come into that discussion and no one wants that.

"Try to get out of there, and call Dad when you do," I instructed. "I have to go."

"Who are you calling?"

"Who do you think? We're tailing Mom and you're hiding from the cops. That leaves Cillian and Dad to get the disc."

"He's going to be angry."

No, he was going to be furious. "That can't be helped. I'll be in touch." I disconnected the call and ran my tongue over my teeth as I debated the best way to approach Dad.

"Just do it," Redmond ordered, frowning as we approached the familiar gates of Eternal Sunshine Cemetery. Mom and Rogan pulled directly into the parking lot, but Redmond continued down for a block before parking. "Well, this is just ... all kinds of suck."

He wasn't wrong. I heaved out a breath as I hit Dad's number, watching as Griffin gripped the umbrella and stared at the sky. The weather remained clear – which was good – but I could feel the anxiety rolling off him.

"It's going to be okay." I reached forward and squeezed his hand. "I promise. You'll be okay."

Griffin mustered a smile for my benefit, but it was weak. "Call your Dad."

"And then duck and cover when you do," Redmond added. "When he finds out you had the key to solving all of this in your pants he's going to melt down and you really will end up grounded."

I had no doubt.

DAD'S DIATRIBE WAS one for the record books. I wished I could record it and play it back for him when he was drunk one night so everyone could get a good laugh. I didn't have the option ... or time.

Once he cooled down – or at least stopped screaming about how he couldn't possibly be my father because no child of his could be as ridiculous as me – he announced he was going to get the disc and then head for the cemetery unless we called to warn him away. I think he wanted to see Mom in action for himself, but I didn't press him on the issue.

We were behind Mom and Rogan when we reached the cemetery's front gates, but it hardly mattered. We knew where they were going ... and why. We'd been to the Olivet mausoleum so many times we could've made our way there in our sleep.

I plodded along the sidewalk, Redmond and Griffin on either side, and pondered what the new revelation would mean for us. I wasn't surprised Mom turned out to be evil. I always believed it was not only possible but probable. Still, there was a dull ache in my heart I couldn't quite identify. I was upset that my suspicions had been proven true. It wasn't something I could easily swallow.

I slipped my hand into Griffin's as we walked, thankful for his comforting presence. He slid me a sidelong look before squeezing my fingers and lowering his voice.

"We're not a hundred percent sure yet."

I knew he was trying to make me feel better, but it was a wasted effort. "It's the only thing that makes sense. She's working with someone else – I definitely believe that – but they're the ones who conjured the storm. She was part of it from the beginning. I see no other explanation."

"She might've infiltrated the group to get information," Griffin offered. "Maybe she was working as a spy."

I shook my head. "I know you're trying to make things better for me, but it's really not necessary. I expected this. It's Braden who will be hurt."

"I think you're all going to hurt," Griffin argued. "It's okay to be hurt. She's your mother. No matter what you said – or how many times you've said it – I always believed that part of you hoped she would turn back into the woman you remembered."

"That was never going to happen. It was wishful thinking. I'm not an idiot, and yet part of me believed."

"Is this the same part that believes I can withstand the power of the storm simply because I love you?"

"No. That's a different part. By the way, I still believe that. I haven't been proven wrong on that."

"We're never going to put ourselves in the position to find out."

"Probably not, but I still have faith."

"You're always good for faith."

"Really? When I was a kid my brothers thought I was a pessimist."

"That's because you like pretending you're a pessimist. It takes time to realize you're an optimist. Sure, you're the snarkiest optimist I've ever met, but you're an optimist all the same."

I leaned over and pressed a kiss against his cheek. "That's either very sweet or really insulting. I'm going to have to get back to you on my verdict after this is all over. I'll either reward or punish you then."

Griffin grinned. "I'm looking forward to it. In fact ... ." He broke off when a furtive shadow barreled through the bushes and stopped on the pathway in front of us.

Mom, her silvery hair flying, fixed each of us with a dark look in turn. "What are you doing here?"

I saw no reason to lie. "We're following you."

"Me?" Mom's eyebrows flew up her forehead. "Why would you be following me?"

"Because we know you're looking for the disc."

"Disc?" Mom slapped her hand to her brow. "I just knew you guys were going to screw this up."

"We love you, too," I drawled. "Now spill the dirt. Exactly who are you working for?"

"Myself."

That was disheartening and expected at the same time. "I guess I should've known."

"I guess you should have," Mom agreed. "Now get out of here. If Rogan sees you, he'll kill you."

"I'm not afraid of Rogan."

"You should be."

"And why is that?"

Mom's eyes flashed. "Because he's not alone and ... well ... a storm is coming."

"A storm?" I lifted my eyes to the sky and frowned when I realized things had gone almost completely dark. "Uh-oh." I swiveled in Griffin's direction and found him backing away from me, his hands raised as he tried to open the umbrella and increase the distance between us at the same time. "Where are you going?"

"Stay away from me!" Griffin was anguished. "I'm going. Don't you dare follow me."

He took off running just as the sky opened up and thunder rocked the ground and caused my heart to shudder.

This was definitely not good.

❧ 28 ❧

TWENTY-EIGHT

I moved to chase Griffin, but Redmond instinctively grabbed the back of my shirt to keep me in place.

"What is it with people doing this to me?" I complained, lashing out with my hand in the hope he would release me. "I'm going to start walking around naked so you people can't trap me with my own clothes. Just you wait!"

"You can't follow him, Aisling. It's not safe. I ... stop it!" Redmond barked out the admonishment so loudly I had no choice but to give up the fight and stare at him. "I know you're upset. I know he's upset. But you can't go after him. Not only is it not safe, but he wouldn't want it. He made me promise that I would put you first."

I balked. "When?"

"When you were going to the bathroom in some random dude's bushes – very classy, by the way – and we had a few minutes alone. He was firm and serious, and he made me promise that I would keep you away from him should the worst happen."

I wanted to cry. No, seriously, I wanted to curl into a ball and cry. I wanted to call for my daddy to fix things and shut out the world. I could do none of those things, because I was an adult and I needed to handle my own problems.

"Fine." I stopped fighting and hung limply in front of Redmond. "I won't go after him."

Redmond didn't look convinced. "Do you promise?"

I nodded. "He'll never get over hurting me if it comes to that. We won't survive it. I'll stay away, even though I'm terrified he'll hurt someone else."

"Maybe we'll get lucky and he'll simply stumble over Mom's new boyfriend," Redmond said pointedly, shifting his attention to Mom as he eased his grip on me. I could've escaped. I could've run and found Griffin. But I understood the best thing for Griffin was to leave him be, and I was determined to do right by him.

I had no idea when it happened, but suddenly I felt like an adult. I didn't like it and I wanted to go back to being the immature baby of the family. For now, though, I had other things to deal with.

"How long have you been working against us?" I asked, my tone low and threatening.

Instead of reacting with mortification or denials, Mom merely shrugged. "There are different ways of solving a problem, Aisling. You should know that better than anyone."

I turned to Redmond for confirmation. "Was that an answer?"

He shook his head, grim. "No. It was avoidance."

"You say that like it's a bad thing." Mom didn't act like a woman about to plead for the forgiveness of the children she'd betrayed. "If you expect me to say I didn't want to avoid this situation, then you're not the bright and engaged children I raised."

Her tone and attitude set my teeth on edge. "Did you hear that, Redmond?" I challenged. "She thinks we're idiots."

"I heard."

"I said nothing of the sort." Mom sighed and glanced over her shoulder. When the area behind her remained silent and still, she turned back. "You need to get out of here. I don't have much time, and if Rogan finds you … ."

"We're not particularly worried about Rogan," Redmond fired back. "We've handled rogue reapers before."

"Yes, but he is especially bloodthirsty. He will kill you if he gets the chance."

"I heard him when you were outside Harry Turner's aunt's house," I supplied. "He sounded as if he wanted to kill you, too. He must be an absolute delight to work with when you're betraying your family."

The look Mom shot me was one of overt irritation. "That is not what's happening here."

I waited for her to expound, but she remained silent. "Oh, well, if you say it with such feeling and emotion we must surely have to believe it," I drawled. "I guess that means we're done here." I smacked my hands together in an annoying gesture that I knew would get under Mom's skin. "We're all finished. Everything is good and right with the world again."

Mom gripped my wrist, her fingernails digging in as she lowered her voice and hissed. "Stop making so much noise."

"Why?" I refused to back down. I was in a mood, after all, and I never back down when I'm in a mood. I don't care if I'm right or wrong. I will have my say and make those around me wish I was right just to shut me up. That's how I roll. "We've already told you that we're not afraid of your friend Rogan. All we want from you is answers."

"This is an inconvenient time," Mom said. "I don't have answers to give."

"Oh, well, she doesn't have answers to give." I flicked my gaze to Redmond. "Don't you feel all warm and gooey inside when she says things like that?"

Instead of joining in my "irritate Mom" session, Redmond remained calm as he pinned her with an unreadable gaze. "I wanted to trust you. I convinced myself all the red flags we were seeing and hypothesizing about couldn't possibly be true. I feel a bit stupid for that now."

Mom's expression softened. "Redmond, not everything here is as it appears. I can't explain it all now. I don't have time, and this is certainly not the place."

"It doesn't matter." Redmond rested his hand on my shoulder. "You're not our priority. Ending the storms is our priority. Is that what you're doing in the Olivet mausoleum? You're looking for the discs we took from the basement the other day, right?"

Mom was at her limit. "I know about those discs. I saw them. We're looking for the other disc."

"The one at Harry Turner's house," I supplied. "That's the one you need to turn off the storms, right?"

Mom's expression reflected curiosity and confusion. "How do you know about that?"

"I'm smarter than I look."

"Which we're all thankful for," Redmond added. "Of course, Little Miss Genius didn't listen when I warned her about Starbucks running right through her, but that's beside the point."

I elbowed him – hard – in the stomach. "Now is not the time for this discussion. I made a mistake on the Starbucks. You need to back off and focus on the issue at hand. We need to focus on Mom and her evil boyfriend."

"He's not my boyfriend," Mom protested. "He's not even a co-worker. He's a necessary evil right now. We have to find that disc."

I thought about Dad. He was probably steaming as he barreled toward my townhouse. He would let himself inside with the spare key, curse my very existence under his breath as he was forced to search the pants I was too lazy to pick up from the floor, and then bring the disc to us. I was comforted by that knowledge. There was no way I would share the information with Mom, though.

"Why did you do this?" The longer I faced off with Mom the angrier I got. "Did you think it would be funny? Was it simply a way to get your jollies? Were you hoping to get someone specific with the spell?"

Mom's eyebrows flew up her forehead. "I didn't cast the spell."

I didn't believe her. She was lying. Who else could've cast the spell?

"If you didn't cast it, who did?" Redmond challenged. "Why would you possibly want to come here and clean up someone else's mess?"

"It's ... complicated." Mom held her hands out in front of her in a placating manner. "I swear I will explain all of it later. For now, you have to get out of here. It's the only safe play we have."

"No." I immediately started shaking my head, wiping the water from my forehead as I glared at her. "Even if we could leave, we wouldn't. We have our own play. It's a family play, and you're not invited."

Mom narrowed her eyes. "And what play do you have?"

"Don't you worry about it." I wagged a finger. If I wasn't so worried about Griffin – where he was and what he was doing – I would've enjoyed the fire in Mom's eyes a little more. She thought she could control us and was only now realizing how wrong she was. "I think it would be best if you and your friend left so we can handle this situation."

Redmond leaned closer and lowered his voice. "I know you like to talk big, but do you really think that's a good idea?"

I matched his tone. "Why wouldn't it be?"

"Because we don't know anything about the spell to end this thing, but clearly Mom does."

Crap. He had a point. I hated when that happened. "Fine." I squared my shoulders. "We've discussed it. You can stay. We have a few conditions, though."

Mom rolled her eyes and snorted. "Would those conditions include the fact that you need me to turn off the curse?"

"Is that what this is?" I shifted tactics and turned serious. "Is this a curse?"

"It's the discs," Mom corrected. "The discs were long thought lost, but someone found them and that someone called a storm that he didn't know how to control."

He? Hmm. "And why would someone want to cast a storm spell?"

"I think you'll get a chance to ask him yourself," Rogan said, sliding out of the bushes to our left and fixing us with an intrigued look. "Well, well, well. What do we have here? Mama Bear, you told me the cubs were out of the loop on this one." He made a tsking sound with his tongue. "I think you've been lying to me."

Mom didn't as much as flinch. She remained preternaturally calm as she shot Rogan a withering look. "They think they know more than they really do. They're not a threat to the operation."

"They look like a threat," Rogan pressed.

"Well, they're not." Mom was firm. "Did you find anything of use inside?"

Rogan shook his head. "The basement has been stripped clean. The books and discs that we didn't need are now gone, too. That's on top of the disc we need to stop the storm, and the book that vanished right before all this started. That's a little too coincidental if you ask me."

"Yes, well, if you have a way to find those things I'm all ears." Mom didn't react at mention of the discs or books. She didn't volunteer what she knew. She didn't even offer the possibility that we had any of the items in question. I had no idea what to make of the situation. "Last time I checked, you were as clueless as me as to what happened to those things."

"I still don't know," Rogan snapped. "The fact that your offspring showed up at the exact moment we're searching for stolen items makes me think they know."

"They're here looking for me," Mom lied smoothly. "Aisling is getting married and I'm supposed to go flower shopping with her."

Of all the lies I'd ever heard, that was possibly the worst. Still, there was something about the worry lining her eyes that made me wonder for the first time if perhaps I had read something wrong in the scenario. "Yes, we're having a tremendous fight about dandelions versus lilies," I drawled. "She seems to think we should go with the lilies for obvious reasons, but I'm a big fan of yellow so it's really difficult."

"Lilies?" Rogan furrowed his brow. "Oh, lilies because your name is Lily. I get it."

I arched my eyebrows and did my best to keep to myself the myriad dumb jokes that floated through my mind at Rogan's slow reaction.

"Wait a second." Rogan was back to being suspicious when he looked at me. "Aren't dandelions weeds?"

"That's like arguing that tomatoes are fruit so you can't use veggie dip on them," I shot back.

"I ... what?" Rogan was easy to distract. I liked that in an enemy.

"Never mind." I waved off his confusion. "As you seem to be done here for the day, it's probably best if you head off on your own. I need to keep Mom around to talk me out of my wild dandelion bouquet desire, but we're no longer in need of your services."

"Is that so?"

I nodded.

"Well, I don't think that's going to work." Rogan took a menacing step in my direction, but Redmond cut off his avenue of attack and put a hand out to keep me behind him as he glared at the rogue. "Are you going to take me on, sparky?"

"I guess we'll have to see," Redmond replied calmly. "Whatever happens, you're not laying a finger on my sister."

"Your sister is a mouthy slut."

"Hey!" I extended a warning finger. "I am not a slut. I'm engaged, for crying out loud."

"I like that you didn't bother arguing with the mouthy part," Rogan said. "You're fine with that, huh?"

"The sad thing for you is that I haven't even gotten going yet," I shot back. "I mean ... I haven't even found the time to make fun of your outfit yet. You should probably be thankful that I'm too distracted to deal with that."

Rogan glanced down at his leather coat and jeans. "What's wrong with my outfit? This is a classic."

"Oh, there are so many ways I could answer that question," I muttered, shaking my head. "I guess I'll just go with this." I lifted my hands in front of me and extended both thumbs. "Aye!" I swung my hips as I exaggerated the single syllable.

For his part, Rogan merely stood there with a blank expression on his face. "I don't know what that means."

My smile slipped. "He's old enough to remember the Fonz, right? I mean ... if I know who the Fonz is, he should know."

"You only know from *Nick at Nite* reruns," Redmond argued. "It's not as if you watched that show during its original run."

"Your father loved that show," Mom noted, taking me by surprise with her unnecessary participation. "He used to watch it in his office. When you were up late – which was often because you knew he would spoil you if you were the last one standing. You would go into his office and he would tuck you on his lap and you would watch *Happy Days* together."

I had a vague memory of that. "He had a thing for Mrs. Cunningham."

"I think it was the apron." Mom smiled. "He liked the brood of youngsters running around together, too, even though they weren't all related. There were a lot of boys and one girl."

I didn't remember that, but it sounded right. "He used to keep licorice in his drawer and let me eat it while watching."

"He thought I didn't know about that, but I always knew."

I dragged a hand through my sopping hair. The storm was increasing in intensity, which wasn't a good thing for Griffin ... wherever he was. I scrubbed at the side of my face as I tried to put things into perspective. "Can you end the storm if we find the disc?"

"Do you know where the disc is?" Rogan's voice took on an edge.

"We might," Redmond hedged. "I believe I warned you about stepping too close to my sister, by the way. Back up."

Rogan rolled his eyes. "You're not the boss of me."

"I'll beat you bloody if you don't back up," Redmond warned. "I've already fought for her honor once this week and that was against a guy I genuinely like. I have no problem taking you down."

Something occurred to me and I focused on Rogan. "Speaking of that ... why isn't he affected by the storm?"

"I'm a reaper," Rogan answered. "That means, just like you guys, I'm not affected."

Hmm. "You're a rogue reaper," I pressed. "Does it work the same for you?"

"I was born a reaper but left the business for years before returning," Rogan replied. "The money is better on the freelance side, so that's what I did."

"So you are clear." I rubbed my cheek. "Who cast the spell?"

"Never you mind about that," Rogan snapped. "Just give us the discs and we'll handle things."

"Just tell us who cast the spell and we'll handle things," I countered.

"No. Do it our way."

"That's not going to happen." I folded my arms over my chest. "It's my way or the highway."

Rogan refused to back down. "Then I guess we're at an impasse."

"I guess so."

We glared at each other for what felt like a really long time before another person joined the fray. The face that stepped onto the pathway with us was one I recognized, although it was the last one I expected to see.

"I think we need to talk about a few things," Detective Green said between clenched teeth. "This situation is simply unacceptable. I need answers."

He wasn't the only one.

TWENTY-NINE

"Why is he here?" I took an immediate step away from Green, panic licking at my insides. "Why are you here?"

The look Green shot me was pitying ... and a little triumphant. It made me nervous. "Why do you think I'm here?"

"I'd say you were following us, but that's impossible because we snuck out of the house," I replied without hesitation. "We know you've been watching Grimlock Manor, by the way. You showed your hand when you followed us here the other day."

"And yet I've been watching you for weeks and you just figured it out." Green made a clucking sound. "You're not very bright, are you?"

I considered throwing down – I didn't like him, so it wouldn't be much of a hardship – but Redmond kept his arm in front of me, offering a quelling look before speaking. "It seems you're quite interested in my sister. I don't suppose you want to tell me why? Green cocked a mocking eyebrow. "Your sister? What makes you think I'm interested in your sister?"

"She's the one you've been following."

"Perhaps, but that's only because she lives in Royal Oak and I had to keep up appearances at work if I expected to use the department's resources," Green supplied. "I followed the brother that lives next door to her just as often as I followed her."

If that was supposed to make me feel better ... well, it didn't. "You've been watching us for weeks?"

"Of course I have." Green was haughty. "Did you really think I would simply let things slide after what happened?"

"What happened?" I risked a brief glance at Redmond to see if he was following the conversation better than me. He clearly wasn't. "Are you talking about the zombies?"

"Don't say that word." Green turned serious, and mildly threatening. "Zombies are not real. You did something to cover up your culpability in those murders. Zombies aren't a thing."

I almost felt sorry for him. "I didn't murder those people. Technically none of them were murdered. Er, well, I guess some of them could've been murdered. It's not as if I did a lot of research on them or anything. We didn't murder them. They were dead long before they were resurrected to come after us."

"Knock it off!" Green looked deranged as he gestured with his finger and glared. "Zombies aren't real, and I've had just about enough of your mouth."

"Welcome to my world," Mom lamented, earning a slit-eyed glare from me. She sobered quickly, shaking off whatever she'd been thinking about. "Detective Green, I believe we talked on the phone and you agreed it was time to end this little ... experiment. That was the agreement."

Experiment? People were dead. Others were maimed. Even more were traumatized. What kind of experiment was worth doing all that? "Experiment?" I swiveled so I faced him. "You did this as an experiment?"

Green shrugged, unbothered by my tone. "Something had to be done."

"But ... why?"

"Because you're abominations. You don't belong in this world."

If I was confused before, my uncertainty doubled within mere seconds. "You did this to make us pay?"

"Why wouldn't I? You got away with killing people, and I wanted to teach you a lesson." Green was certainly full of himself, his face contorting with rage as the rain streaked down his cheeks. Something occurred to me and it took everything I had to refrain from jolting.

"You were the ones who were supposed to pay."

"You did all of this because of us?" Redmond was dumbfounded. "You were trying to make us pay? But ... how?"

"He wasn't alone when he cast the spell." Mom kept her voice low and even as she locked gazes with me. It was almost as if she was trying to convey something to me, some warning perhaps, that I couldn't quite make out. Unfortunately for her, I had other things on my mind.

"What is that supposed to mean?" Redmond challenged. "Who was with him?"

"Harry Turner," I answered for Green, a few things clicking into place even as more questions cropped up. "He did it with Turner."

"Clever girl." Green beamed. "You're getting smarter."

"That's not being smart. That's simply not being stupid. He's the only person who makes sense. He was the one who died right before the storms started. He had the other disc in his house."

"A disc that has conveniently gone missing," Rogan grumbled. "We can't end the curse without that disc. We must find it."

"We'll find it." Green sounded awfully sure of himself. "It has to be in Harry's house. I'll find a way to get inside – I was interrupted this afternoon by somebody – and give it a thorough search this afternoon."

"We need to end the spell sooner than that," Mom prodded. "This can't go on any longer. You agreed."

Green's smile turned into a sneer. "I only agreed because the spell didn't work the way I thought it would. When I approached Turner about doing this he said he was open to it because he hated paranormals, too. He said he had the perfect thing. The spell was his idea."

"And it backfired on you," I surmised. "You wanted to aim it at us, but didn't know enough about magic to realize that it couldn't be aimed at us because we're naturally immune."

"Why do you think I call you abominations?" Green's droll tone was irritating. "You should've gone down quickly. You're always out and about and dealing with dead things. It should've been easy to eradicate you.

"Heck, I figured the storm would force you out into the open more than usual," he continued. "More fighting means more death, which means you guys will be out in the open and vulnerable. You're reapers, right? It took me awhile to figure it out. Harry knew what you were, though, and he initially told me to back off."

I was surprised. "He did? Why?"

"He knew quite a bit about paranormals. I was nervous about approaching him. The only reason I risked it was because of the stories about his mother. I always ignored them, chalked them up to workplace gossip. But I knew there was something completely wrong about all of you, so I approached him."

"And he knew what we were?"

"He knew the moment your father showed up at the police station after I dragged you in for questioning," Green replied. "Harry heard him on the phone. He said reapers weren't good or evil. They just were and provided an important function. He told me that going after you was a mistake.

"I didn't like his response, but I played along because I was at a disadvantage when it came to knowledge," he continued. "I didn't know enough about you at the time to fight. I pretended to go along with Harry and came up with the weather spell to draw you out. I told him I was only interested in you, Aisling, because you were clearly evil. He ultimately agreed even though he initially fought against me and we put our plan in motion."

"So he cast the spell with his mother's stuff?" I asked, desperately trying to put the rest of the story together. "Why did it only activate with his death?"

"Because Harry didn't understand the true nature of the spell," Mom answered. "He didn't realize that the blood sacrifice mentioned in the book was more than a drop. Whoever added their blood to the mix would die once the spell was brought to fruition."

"Which is why I was called to his house right after and the storms started that day," I mused, rubbing my chin. "That's also why he was so worked up about me touching the stuff on his shelf. I thought it was weird for a police chief to have so much metaphysical stuff, but it makes sense given who his mother was."

"I was supposed to sneak in and get the disc before his body was found, but you were already there when I arrived," Green said. "I saw you through the window. I thought you were talking to yourself until I realized you were talking to Harry's spirit.

"At first I was worried that he would admit what was happening," he continued. "He didn't expect to die – although I knew he would because I took the spell to some witch in Ferndale for clarification on a few things and she told me it was a death curse – and I thought he might be bitter."

"He didn't tell me. He seemed agitated, but I wasn't paying attention. I had other things on my mind."

"Yes, well, I figured that out eventually," Green said. "I was too afraid to go in the house after you left, and that turned out to be a good move because once Harry didn't show up for work his administrative assistant stopped at his house to check on him. After that, cops and paramedics were everywhere."

"So you couldn't get inside to look for the disc until later," I deduced. "But it was already gone."

"Clearly someone took it during all the activity surrounding his death, but I have no idea who," Green admitted. "At first I wasn't bothered by that. I thought it would show up. Then I realized you were immune to the spell and that you'd figured things out much quicker than I gave you credit for."

"That's when you realized you needed help." My eyes landed on Mom, but her face remained impassive. "You went to Mom because you thought she'd help you end the spell and maybe even work to end us."

"It was a hope. I knew she was the outsider in your little group. I also knew she had a death certificate on file. The witch pointed me in her direction, called in a favor and put me in contact with Rogan. We've been working together ever since."

"How cozy for all of you," I drawled, shaking my head. "You knew and you didn't tell us, Mom. How could you think that was a good idea?"

"I thought I could end things without you knowing," Mom replied with a shrug. "It seemed easier than dragging you into it."

"We were already in it. Jerry and Griffin were already in it."

"Don't take that tone with me," Mom chastised. "I didn't cast the spell. I was merely trying to clean up the mess this idiot created and protect you in the process. I wasn't part of the original plan, so don't get snotty with me. I don't deserve it."

What she did or did not deserve wasn't up for debate. We had bigger problems, and one of them had been niggling at the back of my brain for the better part of five minutes. "How is it that you're not affected, Detective Green?"

Redmond shifted a bit at the question. It obviously hadn't occurred to him to ask. "Crap! I didn't even put that together."

"That's because I'm the smart one in the family." I offered him a wan smile. "I'm going to remind you of that later, by the way. As for you, Detective Green, how is it that you're out in the storm and not trying to kill anyone?"

"Maybe I'm immune, too," Green suggested. "Have you ever considered that?"

I remembered his face during the misting event, the way he looked sick and struggled, and shook my head. "No. You were at a crossroads the other day. Something else is going on today."

"He has a protective talisman," Mom supplied. "It shields him from the storm, but only for short bits of time, which is why it was stupid for him to come out in this." She gestured toward the steady rain. "This isn't ending soon and you're at risk, Detective Green. You need to get out of the storm."

"And leave you to handle this situation on your own? I don't think so." Green puffed out his chest. "I believe I'm the one who has to take this matter in hand and put the plan back in action."

I didn't like the sound of that. "And how are you going to do that?"

Green grinned. "By ending you and your brother, of course. How else do you expect me to do it?"

My blood ran cold as Redmond tensed. We were outnumbered. I could probably take Mom if it came to it – she looked frail a lot of the time, after all – but she was magically pumped up and looks could be deceiving. There was no way Redmond could take both Green and Rogan, and everyone knew it.

"So that's your new plan?" I challenged, glancing around in the desperate hope Dad and the rest of the cavalry had showed up during the talk. "Now you're just going to murder us because your storm plan didn't work?"

"I don't see another option ... and I won't live in a world with the likes of you. You don't belong here. You never did. It's time to take you out of the equation and let humans handle their own affairs."

I opened my mouth, a hot retort on the tip of my tongue, but I knew it was fruitless. Luckily for me Mom decided to make her move during the pause in conversation.

"If anyone doesn't belong here, it's you," Mom said, taking me by surprise when she reached around Green's neck and yanked at a necklace. "It's time you learned a bit about what magic can really do."

Green's face went ashen when he realized Mom had removed his talisman. The fury fueling him was fast and fierce. "You bitch!" He launched himself at Mom so quickly I didn't have a chance to react.

Redmond didn't waste a second as he turned to face Rogan, his hands bunched into fists at his sides. "Run, Aisling! This is your only shot to get out of here." He didn't turn to see if I obeyed, instead flaring his nostrils like a bull and charging Rogan. They collided in a loud and vicious ball of swinging arms and snarls, so much so I had no idea who was winning.

It was then that I remembered the tranquilizer gun in the back of my pants. I grabbed it with shaky hands and moved to point it in their direction, intent on helping Redmond, and then I realized Green had moved away from Mom – who was prone on the ground – and was facing me.

I shifted the gun and pulled the trigger, but he slapped the weapon out of my hand, causing it to skitter across the ground out of my reach.

"I should've killed you the first time I laid eyes on you," Green growled. "The world would've been a better place."

I flicked my eyes to Mom to see if she would get up but she was completely still. She was either dead or knocked out. Ultimately it didn't matter which because she could offer no help to me. I would have to handle Green on my own.

"I could say the same about you," I shot back, turning on my heel and booking toward a hill that led away from the mausoleum. Redmond would have to fight Rogan on his own. I needed a change of scenery if I expected to hold off Green. "You're the evil one in this equation, not us."

Green didn't expect me to run, so his reflexes were delayed by a few precious seconds. I managed to get ahead of him, but I knew I wouldn't be able to sustain my lead because his legs were longer and I wasn't known for my athletic prowess. If I could get over the hill, though, I would have the high ground, and maybe that would help if I turned the tables and fought.

That idea lasted exactly five seconds, until I crested the hill and came face to face with Griffin. He was completely soaked, the umbrella discarded somewhere. His eyes were wild and his shoulders squared. And the look on his face when he saw me was enough to destroy my heart.

"Oh, no!" I feigned moving to my left, but it was too late. Griffin grabbed my arms and hauled me up in front of him, his eyes lighting with interest when he saw my face. I could feel his heart pounding against mine as he pressed me against him, and I had no doubt things were about to fall completely apart. "Griffin ... ."

"I've been looking for you," he gritted out. "I have some things to say, to do."

"Crap! No, no, no!"

"Yes, yes, yes," Green taunted from behind me. "Now you're finally going to get what's coming to you. This is what I've been waiting for. Rip her apart, boy!"

Griffin looked as if he wanted to do just that. I had no options. I couldn't even fight because of the way he had me pinned against him. All I had was my mouth ... which was often my best weapon. I decided to use it now.

"No matter what happens, I love you." Tears mingled with rain as water cascaded down my cheeks. "If something happens, if I don't get back up, don't blame yourself. I know you didn't mean for this to happen and ... I'm okay."

Griffin stared hard into my eyes.

"I want you to be happy," I continued. "Well, not too happy. Like ...

if you kept a shrine to me in the townhouse that would be good. I don't want you to be alone, so you can find someone else, but make sure you love me better ... and make her look at the shrine a lot, because that will make me feel better."

Something shifted in Griffin's eyes, and I couldn't hold back a sniffle.

"I love you," I repeated. "Just remember that."

"She loves you," Green sneered. "She thinks love – even though I don't believe she can feel it – can overcome this spell. That's not what's going to happen, though, is it? Finish it, Griffin. You can finally be saved if you finish it."

Griffin continued to stare into my eyes for a long moment, and then he viciously tossed me to the side. I hit the ground hard, forcing myself to roll away from his frantic feet because I was certain he would pounce. Griffin was gone, and the wall of fury I was certain had been building in his chest was no longer directed at me. It was pointed at Green, and the detective was too full of himself to realize it until Griffin was on top of him.

Fury met fury and rage toppled rage. I forced myself to look away as the fight turned brutal ... and ultimately deadly. I could hear the sounds of death as they filled the afternoon air, but I didn't look – couldn't really – until the screams ceased, the sounds died down, and I felt a presence move in at my left.

Griffin, his fists bruised and bloody, dropped to his knees next to me.

"Griffin?"

"Don't touch me, baby," he rasped. "I'm afraid if you touch me I'll lose control. I ... I'm barely hanging on here."

"It's okay." I turned and wrapped my arms around his neck, pulling him close even as he fought. "I have faith."

"Don't, Aisling. I ... can't."

"You can. You already proved that."

Griffin exhaled heavily as he rested his head against my chest. "Listen to my heart," I instructed, exhaling heavily as the clouds above us began to clear. "Just listen to it and focus. It's almost over."

"I'm sorry." He choked on his tears. "I'm so sorry."

"For what? You saved me."

"I hurt you."

I snorted. "Please. I scraped my knee. Things could've been much worse."

"I still hurt you."

He was a stubborn pain in the butt sometimes, but I was grateful for him. "You can pay me back with a massage and ice cream later. That will be your punishment."

"Aisling, I'm afraid. I can still feel it inside of me."

"There's more than that inside of you. Trust me. It's almost over. I can already feel the sun."

That wasn't a lie. I could feel the storm passing, and with it the tempest inside him. We'd won again ... although there was still work to be done.

᪥ 30 ᪥

THIRTY

Dad's face was etched with concern when he climbed the hill twenty minutes later. He stopped next to Green long enough to look him over and then closed the distance. Griffin's head remained pressed against my chest even though the rain had dissipated.

"Are you all right?"

I nodded as I ran my fingers through Griffin's hair. "He didn't attack me."

"I heard." Dad smiled. "Redmond finished off the rogue and was racing to help you when he saw Griffin drop. It was clear you weren't in immediate danger, so he figured privacy was in order."

"He's okay. He fought the storm."

"I heard. That must've been some terrific willpower he utilized."

Griffin shook his head, finally stirring. His eyes were red rimmed and full of weariness when he lifted his chin. "It was the thing she said about building a shrine for her should I kill her."

"What?" Dad tilted his head to the side. "I don't understand."

"She talked to me," Griffin explained. "She said she loved me and that she didn't want me to blame myself should she not get back up. That got into my head, but it wouldn't have stopped me. It was what she said after that allowed me to take charge, the part about wanting me to be happy but not too happy, about finding love but making sure I still loved her more."

Dad pressed his lips together. "I see." I'm not sure he did. "She wanted her memory to hang over your life forever."

"Pretty much." Griffin stroked his hand down the back of my head. "That's what jolted me out of it. I knew there could never be anyone else ... and it was the way she said it, as if it was the most normal thing in the world."

"Yes, well, she does have a way about her." Dad heaved out a sigh as he sat next to us. He looked as tired as I felt. "So, we're going to burn down the mausoleum."

The announcement threw me for a loop. "I'm sorry ... what? You can't just burn down a mausoleum in the middle of the afternoon."

"The home office is on it." Dad's tone was pragmatic. "They're sending a team down to clean things up. That's them coming right now." Dad pointed toward the pathway where twenty men strode in our direction. "We're going to burn the mausoleum, pay off the cemetery workers and toss in everything that has anything to do with this storm.

"I found your disc, by the way," he continued, holding up the offending item as he shifted to make himself more comfortable. "I don't want to yell at you for having it the entire time – especially because you've had a rough day – but seriously, how could you forget you stole the disc?"

"I didn't steal it," I clarified. "I got distracted and slipped it in my pocket. To steal, you need intent. I had no intent."

"This isn't like when you slipped the lipstick in your pocket at Sephora when you were a teenager," Dad argued. "I'm not angry. I'm just ... flummoxed."

"Good word," Griffin noted, resting his chin on my shoulder as he rubbed his hands over my back. "I'm flummoxed, too."

"You look like you're about to get handsy," Dad countered. "I don't like it when you get handsy."

"That won't happen until tonight." Griffin managed a watery smile for Dad's benefit. "By the way, we're staying at Grimlock Manor again tonight, just so I can be sure this storm thing is over."

"You fought the storm," Dad pointed out. "You beat it. You don't have to worry now."

"It was the hardest thing I've ever done. But I'm not risking Aisling. We'll stay at the manor another night."

"I'm fine with that. Although, to be fair, I'm not thrilled knowing you're planning to get handsy in my house."

"You'll live."

"I will," Dad agreed, rubbing his palms against the knees of his jeans. "So, I heard the story from Redmond. It sounds as if Green was off his rocker."

"He's dead, isn't he?" I glanced at the body. Green hadn't moved since Griffin dropped him. I wanted to be sad about it, felt I should be at least mildly remorseful, and yet I couldn't make myself feel it.

"He is," Dad confirmed. "His body will be part of the cleanup efforts, along with the rogue, who is also dead."

"I should've checked on Redmond after ... well, after. I didn't. I'm sorry."

"You had other things on your mind. Redmond took care of himself, although I had to remind him he had a tranquilizer gun in his pocket. He never used it. He claims he forgot."

He wasn't the only one. "Yeah." I leaned into Griffin as he kissed my cheek. He couldn't seem to stop from touching me, perhaps to anchor himself to reality. I was fine with it. I wanted to be close to him, too. "What are you going to do about Mom?"

"She claims she was trying to handle the situation without putting us in harm's way."

"Do you believe her?"

Dad shrugged. "She gave you the opening to take out the rogue and Green. She was hurt badly in the process. She's pretty beaten up."

"I barely saw what happened." I felt guilty about that, too. "I guess I'm kind of sorry I suspected her. If she didn't act so odd all the time it wouldn't be so easy to accuse her in times of crisis."

"I pointed that out to her." Dad patted my hand. "She's not angry.

She thought she was helping. I don't know what else we can expect from her."

"So ... you believe her?"

"Don't you?"

I searched my heart. "I guess," I replied after a beat. "She did seem frustrated that we were here, and for once I think it was because she was trying to protect us. She ripped the talisman off Green's neck, which gave us the distraction we needed. She also tipped the scales in our favor when it came to the fight."

"She fought to protect you."

"So ... that's it? You're ready to forgive her?"

"I didn't say that. Your mother and I can never go back. But she still is your mother."

"Does this have anything to do with your desperate need to keep Braden on an even keel?" It was an honest question and I didn't miss the way Dad squirmed under my scrutiny. "Braden seems weak at times, but he's strong. If you don't want to allow her in, he can deal with it."

"He doesn't have to deal with it now," Dad said. "For now, your mother is part of the family and she helped save the day. Redmond and Griffin helped, too. I think that deserves a prime rib feast. Maybe some lobster and scallops, too."

"Now we're talking." Griffin brightened. "Can we have cake for dessert?"

Dad's smile was heartfelt. "Whatever kind of cake you want. You are a hero, after all."

I balked. "Hey! What about me? I was a hero, too."

"You can have whatever cake Griffin selects." Dad flicked my ear to let me know he was teasing. "I think we can work something out."

"Does that something include time off?"

"I believe you're getting two weeks off for your honeymoon in a few weeks – I'm going to be paying for that, by the way, and I have a surprise for you – you also get the week of the wedding off," Dad answered. "Do you think you deserve more time off?"

I thought Griffin deserved it, but I didn't want to say that out loud. "Maybe an extended weekend," I hedged.

As if reading my mind, Dad nodded. "You can have the next few days off. I think it will be good for you to take a breather."

"Yay!" I clapped my hands before something occurred to me. "Wait, that was way too easy. You're up to something."

"I'm not up to anything," Dad corrected. "I am, however, a bit relieved. Our list for tomorrow already came through and there's a familiar name on it. I didn't want to give it to you, so this makes it easier to cut you out of the loop without having to come up with an excuse."

"Familiar name?" I furrowed my brow. Then realization dawned on me. "Carol Davenport."

"She's passing tomorrow," Dad confirmed. "I think it would be best if you weren't the one to collect the soul."

I thought the exact opposite. "I'll do it. I'll come in for the one job. It won't take long and ... I'll do it."

Dad cocked an eyebrow. "Will you tell me why?"

"Because I should be the one." I thought back to my many fights with Angelina, and that day at my mother's funeral so long ago. "It will be okay. Trust me."

Dad didn't look convinced, but he shrugged as he stood. "If you want it, you've got it."

"I want it."

"Then it's settled." Dad dusted off the seat of his pants. "They're about to start the fire. I need to supervise. Why don't you head back to Grimlock Manor and get cleaned up? We'll meet you there."

I remained confused. "How are you going to get away with burning a mausoleum and bodies in the middle of the day?"

"I know what I'm doing. Leave it to me."

Because I was tired I did just that.

It took Griffin and me almost five minutes to ready ourselves to depart. We both walked on wobbly legs as we descended the hill, Griffin gripping my hand tightly and refusing to look at Green as Dad's workers cleared the body. We stopped at the bottom of the hill long enough for me to wave at Redmond, silently acknowledging that we were both okay and would talk later, and then I stared at the fire for a few minutes.

"It will be over soon," Griffin noted as Dad threw the disc into the flames, Cillian following suit seconds later with the other discs. They both turned their backs and focused on the workers as Mom approached the fire, her eyes blank as she stared into the abyss. "We'll be able to put this behind us."

I squeezed his hand. "We'll definitely be able to put this behind us." I was about to turn away – actually, I was about to turn toward him because I was ready to move forward – when something about Mom's demeanor caught me off guard.

She dug in her pocket, her eyes never moving from the flames, and then tossed what looked like a fourth disc into the fire. She didn't glance around to see if anyone was watching. She didn't look in my direction. She merely tossed in the disc – and where did that come from anyway? – and turned to join Braden and watch the rest of the takedown.

I opened my mouth to call to her, to ask what she tossed away, but ultimately I remained silent. Was it something to worry about? Had I somehow miscounted? Did it ultimately matter?

In the end I couldn't decide, so I decided to shutter it for a bit and focus on the good this life had to offer. I could think about the disc and what it meant later.

"So what kind of cake are you going to request?" I asked, falling into step with Griffin as we walked away from the cemetery and toward our future. "I think chocolate would be good with prime rib."

"You know I like red velvet best."

"Yes, but we're about to get married. I think we should compromise."

"How is you getting chocolate cake compromising?"

"I'll share my kisses of gratitude with you after I'm done stuffing my face."

"Hmm." Griffin was smiling. "I think that sounds like the perfect way to spend an evening."

"We can agree on that."

"Yup. We definitely can." He swung our joined hands. "By the way, what you said about moving on? It was never going to happen."

"I know. I wanted to look magnanimous in what could've been my final moments. I didn't want to be the person who told you it was wrong to let me go."

"So it was all about you?"

"Yup."

Griffin chuckled. "Never change, baby."

"That's the plan."

CPSIA information can be obtained
at www.ICGtesting.com
Printed in the USA
LVHW110045011020
667596LV00004B/1190